Darius and the Dragon's Stone

A Novel By
D. L. Torrent

Darius and the Dragon's Stone: D. L. Torrent © 2016
2nd Edition

FantasyQuill Books

ALL RIGHTS RESERVED

No part of this book may be reproduced or transmitted in any form or by any means, electronic or mechanical, including photocopying, recording, or by any information storage and retrieval system, without permission in writing from the author, except in the case of brief quotations embodied in reviews.

Written by D. L. Torrent

Cover design by George Patsouras
and Sharon Cramer

Publisher's Note:

This is a work of fiction. All names, characters, places, and events are the work of the author's imagination. Any resemblance to real persons, places, or events is entirely coincidental.

Author's Note:

For you, my reader…wake up and dream. It is my hope that this story will draw you away from reality and sink you deeply into a wonderful world of fantasy, allowing you to create a place in your mind and heart that only you can own.

For Sarah

My constant inspiration
…and occasional distraction

Prologue

The cold wind bit at her face, and the falling snow clouded her view. Frozen tears stung her cheeks, and she stumbled on a branch hidden in the blanket of snow beneath her feet. She whimpered and began to cry, adding to the ice sculptures that were already clinging to her eyelashes. She bowed her head, thinking of what she had left behind, but it was too painful.

Blinking hard to break the crystal curtains around her eyes, she saw a flicker of light in the distance. She plodded forward, gathering what strength she could, and headed for the only glimmer of hope she had left.

When she reached the small inn, she entered quietly. The warmth around her caused her face to sting, but she welcomed the pain to the coldness of outside. The soft bundle she carried squirmed in her arms as she placed a golden wedding band upon the counter. Tears filled her swollen eyes as she smiled yearningly at the innkeeper.

"It's all I have," the woman said softly.

Chapter One

The Search

Klavon sat amidst the destruction, fire burning in his heart as vivid as the fires that blazed around him. He stared at the dead body, a pool of blood the blanket for his enemy. But he could not revel in his victory...she was gone.

Fourteen years later, Klavon stood and stared at the exact spot where Thyre had lay dead at his feet. Every year he returned. He had searched, expanding the distance from these ruins, but he had yet to find her. What had he missed?

Perhaps he was being too careful. Up to now, his pursuit had been done in the shadows, not daring to divulge his presence lest she were to find out and run away, yet again.

But weariness had chipped away at him for too many years, and he stared coldly at the patch of ground beneath his feet. It was time for more drastic measures.

"Norinar," he whispered with a grin. Klavon raised his staff, and an amber cloud swirled in front of him.

"Show me!" he commanded, and the cloud inched its way to the outer edges of its expanse, revealing a window.

Inside, a strong wizard sat, surrounded by beautiful woods. He looked as though he was meditating, his eyes closed and peace written across his face.

"Foolish wizard!" exclaimed Klavon, and with a swish of his staff, he vanished and reappeared, standing directly behind Norinar.

Klavon knew well the strength of this wizard, and he was already prepared. An unseen force clasped Norinar firmly around his neck and raised him into the air. Norinar's eyes flew open and then glazed over, and as he slipped into nothingness, he, along with his sword and staff, fell to the ground.

Klavon walked next to the motionless wizard and smiled. His prisoner's weapons vanished, and a thin red rope appeared and slid around the neck of the unconscious man.

When Norinar awoke, Klavon stood over him. The captured wizard struggled to remove the rope, but the more he tried, the more it tightened.

"I wouldn't do that, if I were you. You see, I have no desire to kill you, but I do need information," Klavon stated. "And should you be forthcoming, I will let you live."

"I know who you are, and I know what you want," said Norinar. "It took you long enough. But I guess fourteen years for you to figure it out is pretty much normal, isn't it? Or am I being too generous?"

Klavon's face distorted, and he seethed. He would

have killed Norinar right then had it not been for his usefulness...at least at that moment. "Oh, old friend, I've known where you are for many years, despite your pathetic effort to move your village in hopes of escaping me. But timing is everything, don't you agree?"

Norinar glared at Klavon and looked around the small clearing.

"They aren't here," said Klavon. "Your sword and staff are...far away, beyond your ability to summon."

Norinar frowned but said nothing, and Klavon laughed.

"You see, I have been searching all these years. Did you really think I wouldn't watch your village to see if she were there?"

"Miora was no fool. Even if she had survived the storm, she would never have come to me. She would rather die...and likely did."

"Hmmm, you see, there is a slight problem. You being Thrye's closest friend, she would surely have sought your help. So now," Klavon said, tightening the rope around Norinar's neck with only a squint of his eyes, "I believe she did come to you, and I believe you helped her find a safe and hidden haven."

"She didn't. Now let me go!" demanded Norinar.

"Why would I do that? You have yet to tell me what I want to know. Besides, you have unwisely gone against me...guilty of hiding her location from me."

"The only thing I am guilty of is allowing myself to be caught off guard by a pathetic sorcerer like—"

"Careful. You are trying my patience," said Klavon.

He stared at Norinar struggling for air, and the thin rope loosened just enough to allow Norinar a breath. "You see. I can be accommodating, so why don't you return the favor?" Klavon's voice became suddenly more serious. "Where is she?" he asked slowly, fire in his eyes and venom in his voice.

"Even if I knew," replied Norinar, equally as slow, "I wouldn't tell you. You are a fool if you believe she survived."

Klavon's anger grew. "I am not a fool! You are! You are willing to die to keep her from me? She belongs with me!"

"She belonged with Thyre. Always did, and you can do nothing to—"

"I am done with you!" shrieked Klavon, and the rope tightened around Norinar's neck.

"Still willing to murder for something that never belonged to you," gasped Norinar.

Klavon moved to within inches of Norinar's face and said, "Willing to serve justice to those who would defy my commands."

"You are not worthy that any would follow your rule," Norinar spat, barely able to release the words before the rope constricted and a last breath escaped his lips.

Klavon stood for several moments, staring down at the dead wizard. "You know nothing of rule, sitting there, vulnerable as you were. Power is rule," he said, and with a swish of his staff, the thin red rope disappeared and Klavon healed the wounds that burned into Norinar's neck. "And deception."

Klavon whispered a few unintelligible words, and Norinar's staff and sword reappeared on the ground next to him. Then a bolt of lightning shot from the end of Klavon's staff, and a large tree broke loose and fell atop Norinar, concealing Klavon's murder in a horrible accident.

His mouth twisted in a frustrated growl, and with a swirl, he vanished and reappeared in the dark courtyard outside his castle. Fraenir was circling above and landed with a hard thud.

Klavon's growl turned to a sinister smile—he couldn't help it. Fraenir was magnificent, a dragon in most eyes, but Klavon knew differently—Fraenir was no dragon for dragons were...weak. And for these fourteen years, Fraenir aided in his search for Miora.

"Have you found anything? Any sign?" asked Klavon, expecting the same answer he'd heard so many times before.

Fraenir's gazed down with a triumphant stare and said, "I have." His raspy voice thundered in his chest.

"She is found?" Klavon asked, hardly believing the words he had just heard.

For a brief moment, he laughed, finding humor in Norinar's misfortune. Had Klavon been aware of Freanir's find, he would have had no need to visit Norinar. *Oh well. I never did care for him.*

"Yes, and all this time she has been only hours beyond the mire. In Brandor."

"What? How? That is nowhere near the village...or what is left of it." Klavon smirked as he thought of the havoc, the complete annihilation he had brought to Thyre's village—a memory that had sustained his search all these long years.

"I know. But your search tactics have paid off, if not as soon as you would have liked," replied Fraenir.

"It was only reasonable to assume she could not go too far...and with that...monstrosity." Klavon spat on the ground, thinking of the child that should have been, but was not, his. "She is stronger than we thought, but of course she is. I would expect no different. She is, after all, destined to stand at my side."

Fraenir nodded. "So what are your plans?"

Klavon stared at the tree-line, the direction of the mire. "The boy is a problem. Bring him to me so that I may end the line of Thyre, the last living person who could possibly come between her and me."

"That will be difficult," Fraenir said.

No one ever questioned Klavon, not without regret. Fraenir, however, was different. Klavon admired the beast's strength, and Fraenir was the only living thing, human or creature, who could speak so openly to him.

"You do not believe I am capable?" asked Klavon.

Fraenir threw his head back and laughed, fire shooting out of his mouth, singing the branches of a nearby tree. "I have no doubt of your capabilities. I have seen them first hand." Fraenir glanced at a pile of human bones at the side of the courtyard. "No, they have a barrier around the entire village. Strong and impenetrable."

"A barrier. Why?"

"I saw no wizard. I can only guess he has left the barrier as a protection in his stead. It is quite powerful preventing me from flying near, but I have keen eyes. I was able to see a book in the wizard's tower where you would expect to see the wizard."

"A book? Now that is peculiar," said Klavon, nodding his head as he tried to recall the significance of such an object.

"I watched from a distance for many days. Still no wizard. Just the book."

"No wizard?" mused Klavon. "Yes, this is quite peculiar."

"And that's not all. The boy...the one you would kill..." Fraenir seemed to relish his words, speaking them in a soft, slow hiss. "I have seen him in the tower, watching the book."

"That is curious," said Klavon. "What of Prydon? Did you see him?"

"I saw nothing of that...vile creature," hissed Fraenir. He glanced down at the scars on his chest and legs. "If I had, I would have killed him."

Klavon laughed, a throaty sound that echoed from his castle grounds. "Fraenir, you are modest. You and I both know that you most likely killed him years ago."

"While I would not want to underestimate him, I do believe that his absence over the past fourteen years would imply that he is indeed dead."

"Good. Now to business," said Klavon. "Brandor's wizard is a fool. I will study this magic, and I will discover its purpose."

Fraenir bowed and returned to the air. Klavon watched and then turned and entered his fortress, making his way to the lab where he would determine his next move. It had to be planned perfectly...for she had been found.

Days later, Klavon stood again in his courtyard. "Are you ready?" he asked.

Fraenir shrieked, and his body shrank and changed into a ball of fire, wings spread as he hovered above Klavon. He was no longer the dragon but a fiery beast, flames for feathers and red hot spikes for talons.

"The curse must be for the boy," said Klavon. "That will ensure he comes to me."

Fraenir bowed, and Klavon closed his eyes and walked into the fire. Not a single flame singed him as he spoke ancient words. When he finished, he opened his eyes and backed out, away from the flaming creature.

"You know what to do," Klavon said. "You will have only moments before the barrier will heal, so you must act quickly."

"I am ready," replied Fraenir, and he shot off into the sky...toward the boy.

Chapter Two

The Book

Darius stood at the wooden doorway, watching his mother hang wet clothes outside their modest home. She snapped a wet towel in the warm breeze before fastening it to the line with some wooden clothespins. The day before, a severed line had left her with soiled laundry and an empty purse. Darius repaired the clothesline, but his mother had lost precious time. She moved quickly, with two baskets of laundry beckoning at her feet. Darius smiled, although his heart was saddened by the hard work she put in, day after day, without complaint.

It hadn't been easy. In fact, it had been barely tolerable. Being outsiders, Darius and his mother, Miora, were hardly accepted by the people of this small village, reflected in the unattractive shack they had been given as lodging—a shack that just happened to lie on the outmost edge of town, hidden from view by a small slope in the valley where the village peacefully carried on its own business.

Over the years, Darius's mother had done her best, taking whatever jobs she could to sustain them, but for fourteen years they had lived an unnoticeably poor life. He watched his mother brush a bead of sweat from her forehead and shook his head, biting his lower lip. Darius wanted nothing more than to change their status with these self-absorbed villagers, but he knew that even if he was able to procure a decent paying job in this forsaken town, his mother would not allow it.

Darius forced a smile as he exited the small house. "I'm off, Mother," he said, throwing a soft leather bag over his shoulder. He stood almost a foot above her and bent down to give his mother a fond hug and kiss.

Her soft blue eyes, full of love, stared up at him, and her gentle hand brushed the wavy brown hair from his face. "Mr. Athus have much for you to do today?"

"Just the usual," he grinned as he bounced off. He called back as he jumped over a small creek, "Cleaning! What fun!"

"Stay out of trouble!" He heard the words float up from behind and smiled back as he waved to her.

His mother was protective of him, and he guessed he understood. As he grew up in this obscure village, he had made few friends. It wasn't that he hadn't tried, but it was almost as if the villagers were afraid of him. He never knew why, and his mother reluctantly and evasively answered when he would question her. "We're not from here, and that scares them. It's easy to be afraid of something you don't understand," she would say.

"What's not to understand?" he would reply. "So we're not from here. We have to be from somewhere, right?"

To this, his mother would simply smile, unwilling

to say anything about their past. "We are where we are safe."

He recalled the familiar conversation and chuckled. *So we're safe. Nothing exciting, but we're safe.* Resigned to his fate, he climbed the slope to the lazy village.

Brandor was a quiet town. Small shops with wares hanging in plate glass windows and houses with inviting porches lined both sides of a well-worn road made barren by wagons and travelers on foot. Large trees shaded the entire valley, and the stream that trickled by Darius's house continued its bubbling journey through town. As he crossed a wooden bridge, he noticed two small fish wrestling to get the last bits of a dead bug, and he paused to watch the sunlight reflect silvery images across the top of the rippling surface.

"Morning, Darius," came a gruff voice.

Darius's tan face wrinkled tightly and his green eyes shot closed. How he wished he was a bug atop the water. He would gladly take his chances with the fish. Perhaps, if he were lucky, he could float along the stream and ride the currents far away from these insufferable people.

"Darius? Do you hear me, boy?"

The words cut into him like a dull knife through a piece of stale bread, and he sighed as he composed his face. Turning around, Darius faced the woman, plump and content, rocking on her front porch and knitting yet another shawl. He wondered what she did with all of them.

"Morning, Mrs. Keedle."

"And I suppose your mother is almost done with the

clothes?"

The woman reminded Darius of a bullfrog, croaking as it sits upon its lily pad. The green frock did nothing to deter the image that filled his mind.

"Yes, ma'am." Darius resisted the strong urge to glare at her and sneer in bitterness.

The old woman did not like him and thought his mother nothing more than a rat to be shooed away...that was, until she was needed to do the dirty work for these ungrateful folks!

He bit his lip. "They are drying as we speak."

"Good. I certainly hope she's not late...again!"

Darius acknowledged her with a simple nod and turned up the path, heading toward the great tower where Mr. Athus would be waiting. He did not look back.

"Because she often is, you know!" The cackle stung at his back as the woman belched out the words, but Darius continued on his way.

As much as he disliked most of the people in this town, Darius had received favor in the eyes of the Keeper of the Book. Mr. Athus boasted complete charge over the Great Book of Brandor, and many had questioned his taking Darius under his wing, but that didn't seem to bother Mr. Athus. No, he seemed to enjoy the bristle he caused in more than one villager's spine, and Darius couldn't help but smile as he thought of Mrs. Keedle the first time she learned Darius was "helping to guard the book."

Darius laughed out loud. If only she had known—his true purpose at the tower was only that of a common cleaning boy. But since Mr. Athus had, on more than one occasion, proclaimed Darius as being his apprentice, Darius hoped his cleaning days were numbered. Until then, he faithfully returned day after day and only dreamed of the day when he might be honored with guarding the book himself. *Then the townspeople will respect me. Then they will wash our clothes.*

Darius reached the circular tower and opened the door to a small storage shed attached to the left of the tall stone structure. A cobweb stretched in front of him and ripped with the tension. A spider scurried up and into a weathered crack in the jam of the door, and after brushing away the remnants of the torn threads, Darius picked up a broom, mop, and bucket.

He leaned the broom and mop against a wall of ivy that wound its way up the side of the building and walked to the well only a few feet away. Attaching the old wooden bucket to a hook at the end of a rope, Darius lowered the vessel. He watched as the darkness swallowed it. When he heard a splash, he waited only a moment before cranking the well-worn handle and pulling up a full bucket of clear water. After taking a drink, Darius grabbed the bucket and returned to the shed. He reached inside and scooped a small pile of white dust from a lopsided sack and dropped it into the bucket. Stirring the water with his hands, lathery foam bubbled up on its surface. Darius closed the door to the shed, retrieved the mop and broom, and, carrying the bucket, entered the building.

"Good morning, Mr. Athus."

Mr. Athus was perched atop a tall, wooden stool. He was writing in a large journal, sitting on an even taller desk that curved around and stood solid to the floor. As Darius entered Mr. Athus's round face beamed, and he set his spectacles down on the desktop.

"Hello, Darius. I have something special for you." Mr. Athus reached underneath the desk and pulled out a small book.

"What is it?" asked Darius as he set down his bucket and reached for the book.

"Dragons," he replied mysteriously. "I bought it off of a peddler, passing through the other day."

"Dragons?" Darius thumbed through the pages. "Are they real?"

Mr. Athus laughed heartily. "Of course, my boy. But I'd never want to meet one! Oh, and here's your pay for last week," he added, tossing Darius a silver coin.

Darius placed the coin in his shirt pocket, checking twice to make sure the button was secure. As thanks for Darius's years of service, he received only a pauper's wage, but it was all Mr. Athus could offer, and Darius dare not lose it.

Of more value, however, Mr. Athus taught him everything he knew. Denied traditional schooling, Darius knew more of this land than most, and the book on dragons was only one of many Mr. Athus had provided.

Darius rubbed his finger along the spine of the book, tracing each letter. "Are they as interesting as wizards?"

Mr. Athus's eyes lit up. "Oh! I should say so!" He nodded and picked up his glasses, placing them squarely in front of his eyes and peering over the rim. "And I'll teach you more about them after you've read the book."

Darius placed the dragon book into his bag. "Thank you, sir."

Mr. Athus smiled and went back to his writing, and Darius set to his chores. He placed the sudsy pail next to the wall at the base of a closed stairway that circled along the inside rim of the tower. Grabbing his broom, Darius climbed the stairs. He circled the tower almost three times before stopping on a landing one level below its pinnacle. He faced a wooden door whose only ornament was a thick metal ring held by the teeth of a dragon. This was where Brandor's wizard had lived and was now Mr. Athus's quarters. Darius paused at the door and gently touched the handle, with no intention of going in. *This is where the wizard stayed*, and he closed his eyes, imagining the wizard exiting his room dressed in wizardly robes to keep watch over Brandor.

One of his favorite lessons was that of the wizards. He had been taught that all villages were granted the presence of a wizard to watch over them. If the wizard was good, the village would flourish. If the wizard was instead a dark sorcerer, the village would be stagnant, barely alive at all, with fear alone the only motive for their existence and loyalty.

Brandor had fortunately been blessed with the kindest of wizards. For years he had exited this very room to watch over the people, caring for them like a father would care for his children. One day, shortly before Darius and his mother entered that inn fourteen years before, the wizard mysteriously vanished leaving nothing behind but the Great Book of Brandor and the explicit instructions to guard it—never let it leave the tower.

Darius sighed and continued up the steps, reaching the highest room. It was circular and not very large, the ceiling above rising to a sharp point. Small windows opened in all directions along the stone wall. A magical barrier prevented anything from entering except a soft spring breeze, but it was a spectacular place in which to view Brandor and all its surrounding areas. But Darius had seen these sights many times before. It was the center of the room that drew his eyes solidly in a gaze. No matter how many times he had seen it, he continued to wonder at its splendor. Atop a small pedestal covered with velvet cloth of the deepest purple lay the book, and poised above the open pages was an enchanted quill.

An important relic, the magical book held the town's history and, in some strange way that Darius did not quite understand, its life. Written across its pages were the names and history of everyone who had ever lived in the town—everyone except Darius and his mother.

Darius watched, waiting for movement. If he waited long enough, he might catch the quill as it jotted down the next letter, word, or line of Brandor's history. At the moment, the quill floated motionless with only the soft feathers caressed into movement by the gentle breeze.

"Come on," begged Darius. All he wanted was to see it move, watch it glide across the page, but it remained motionless.

Disappointment was his only companion as he began to sweep the room, a chore he had done so many times before. When he finished, he paused before beginning the task of sweeping the steps—again, a task he had done more times than he could count.

Standing at the top of the steps, he looked one last time at the book. The quill began to move, and Darius dropped his broom, sending it sailing several steps downward toward the landing at Mr. Athus's door. He didn't care. He darted to the book and watched as it scribbled a few words. "Mr. Trim sold three bushels…"

Darius stood fascinated, not by the words being transcribed, but by the sheer magnificence of the feat itself. No one else in Brandor ever had the opportunity to witness such enchantment, and his body felt electrified as he watched the movement of the quill scratch across the page. It was a rare treat.

As quickly as it started, the quill once again stood still, and Darius paused. The exhilaration faded, and he sighed before walking down the steps and retrieving his broom. He had work to do.

When all the steps in the great tower were cleaned of dust, Darius swept the bottom floor, careful not to disturb Mr. Athus and his writing. Placing the broom aside, he picked up the pail of soapy water and began scrubbing the floor, thankful he had finished the upper room and stairs the day before.

It was tedious work, but he didn't mind. He enjoyed Mr. Athus's company and was often distracted from the monotony of his work by some story Mr. Athus would weave of the town and its current goings-on. Today, however, Mr. Athus remained quiet as he wrote, and Darius was left to entertain himself as he sloshed more soapy water onto the stone floor.

Dragons, he thought. A thin smile touched his lips as he envisioned their grandeur: fiery tongues threatening their prey, their massive legs pushing up from earth-shaken ground as they took flight, and the terror they invoked as they soared about, wings outstretched, dominating the sky around them and casting a shadowy darkness on those unfortunate enough to find themselves beneath them. And they were real!

So deep in thought, the crimson that rained down upon him seemed only part of his imagination, its blazing glow a remnant of the dragon's fire…until he heard Mr. Athus scream.

"The book!"

Darius eyes shot up, and he saw Mr. Athus running to the steps that led to the top of the tower. Jumping up to follow his master, Darius overturned the bucket of soapy water and almost slipped as he sprinted for the spiral staircase. Taking two steps at a time, he reached Mr. Athus's side just as they entered the tiny room that housed the precious book.

Breathless, Darius stood dazed at the sight. The room was glowing from the crimson rain outside, but the book remained untouched. Mr. Athus reached for the book when a fiery ball appeared from a rip in the sky outside one of the windows, and a fierce creature shrieked forth from its blazing carriage. The screech caused Darius to collapse to his knees in pain. Throwing his hands over his ears to muffle the shrill noise, he watched Mr. Athus straining to reach the book. Unable to withstand the sting of the piercing sound, Mr. Athus fell unconscious, helpless into a heap on the floor.

The creature swooped through the barrier of the window, and a wave of hot air pushed inward against Darius's face as the magical protection failed. With the fury of tornadic winds encircling him, Darius scrambled on his knees toward the book, clenching his hands tightly over his ears to avoid the same fate as his friend. The fiery beast turned its head toward Darius and hissed, its screams pulsing against Darius's hands as he tried to protect his ears.

The beast moved directly over the book, hovering as it flapped its flaming wings and never taking its eyes off of Darius. There was no time to think. Darius ran for the book, releasing his ears and grabbing the precious treasure of Brandor. Pain shot through his brain, but before he could even attempt to run from the room with the book, the beast seized Darius's hand with its talons. Hot fire burst through his hand, and Darius was frozen as he watched vines of crimson tendrils weave through his skin across his hand and over his wrist, forcing him to release the book. Before the book fell to the floor, the blazing creature snatched the book and shrieked once more. White flames filled Darius's eyes as the sound penetrated sharply into his ears. Then everything went completely black, and Darius collapsed to the ground.

When Darius finally awoke, he found Mr. Athus sprawled on the floor nearby. Darius crawled to his side.

"Mr. Athus. Mr. Athus!" Darius gently rolled him

over and patted his face.

Mr. Athus moaned and slowly opened his eyes, pain written across his face. Holding his head, he whispered, "The book."

"The book!" gasped Darius. In horror, he turned and stared at the empty pedestal. "Mr. Athus, it's gone! I tried to stop it, but…"

Mr. Athus pushed hard with his hands to force his body up, and Darius braced the older man to help him regain his unstable feet.

"Mr. Athus, are you all right?"

The older man dusted off his clothes. "I'm fine, son. Quickly! You must gather the village immediately. Now go. Run!"

Darius paused only a moment as he looked into his elder's eyes. In all the years he had worked for Mr. Athus, never had he witnessed such concern in his friend's eyes. Concern? No, fear! And for the first time in Darius's life, his safe existence shattered with danger.

"Go!" demanded Mr. Athus.

Shaken back by the command, Darius tore down the steps and slid to the tower door across the wet floor. Slinging it open, he ran outside. Sprinting farther up the hill, he skidded to a stop beside a large bell the villagers had erected shortly after the wizard left. It was to be used only in an emergency to call the townspeople to the town hall, and Darius could think of no greater emergency than the loss of the Great Book. Tugging with all his might, Darius set the bell in motion, and in no time the entire valley was echoing with its chimes.

Darius and the Dragon's Stone

Darius then raced through the village, yelling that the Great Book was gone. He reached the slope that led to the small cottage where he and his mother lived and rushed to his mother's side.

"Mother!" Darius screamed, trying to catch his breath as a sharp pain stabbed at his side. "Something terrible!"

"I heard the bell. What's wrong?" Miora stood silent as her son relayed the morning's events. "The Great Book...gone?"

"Yes! Hurry! They're meeting at the town hall to decide what to do!"

Darius, with his mother by his side, reached the meeting hall. It was built much like the houses of Brandor, but octagonal in shape. As they walked inside, Darius looked at the large room. A tall podium and chair were positioned in front of the wall opposite the door, and benches formed an angular circle around the room like spectator stands for an athletic event. But this was not a time of cheerful competition, and Darius and his mother quickly took a seat near the podium among the crowded villagers.

Mr. Athus entered and stood behind the pedestal. The room immediately fell silent.

"I am afraid the news is true," Mr. Athus said. "The Great Book of Brandor has been taken." Gasps filled the air as he told of the fiery creature. "If we do not retrieve it soon, all will be lost. As you know, the Great Book of Brandor holds our history. Until now, I could only surmise, but that book also holds our...lives. It was our protection, but now…"

Whispers filled the room until one villager asked, "What do you mean, lives?"

Mr. Athus shook his head and lowered his eyes. "The Harper's are gone."

"That cannot be!" Darius heard the voice of a gruff man seated across the room.

"Can it not?" snarled Mr. Athus. "Do you see the Harpers here at our gathering? Look! Look for yourself!"

The crowd filled with whispers and sobs as the room was scoured for the Harpers, and a lump formed in Darius's throat as he, too, could not find them.

Mr. Athus continued. "I know it is so, for I witnessed their house vanish before my very eyes as I came to this place, and the longer we tarry…" Mr. Athus closed his eyes for a moment before continuing. "We have always known that our land has been linked to the Great Book, a link provided by our wizard himself."

"It's their fault!" exclaimed Garp, an older member of the village, as he pointed his gnarled finger at Darius and his mother. "We let them stay, and we should have sent them away!"

Darius's mother began to tremble, and Darius put his arm around her shaking shoulder.

"That boy tried to save our book!" bellowed Mr. Athus, but his words were cut short as he looked at Darius. He slowly walked from behind the podium toward Darius and his mother, his eyes glued to Darius's hand.

Conscious of Mr. Athus's gaze, Darius removed his arm from his mother's shoulder and began rubbing his hand

and wrist. He had almost forgotten the incident. The intensity of the pain had subsided, but the vines of crimson left their mark, blood-red streaks embedded in his skin.

As Mr. Athus came closer, Darius said softly, "I tried to grab the book, but the creature…I couldn't hold on. I just couldn't."

The room was dead silent as Mr. Athus went to Darius's side. "Let me take a look at that."

Mr. Athus examined Darius's arm. Then placed his hand over his jaw, rubbing his mouth and chin in concentration.

"What is it?" asked Miora. "My son's all right, isn't he?"

Mr. Athus frowned. "I'm not sure. I've never seen such magic."

"It's dark magic, I say! He's been marked!" yelled Garp. "All the more reason to send them out before another of us disappears! We are being punished!" Garp's eyes burned through Darius, piercing his skin with accusation.

"The book is already gone!" Mr. Athus slammed his fist down on the bench next to Darius and then spun around, stomping to the center of the room. "Sending them away will not bring it back."

"Then what are we supposed to do?" grilled Garp.

The flurry of comments thrown at Mr. Athus came from all directions of the room, and Darius wondered if he should take his mother away from this place as the hostility filled the air like a thick, putrid fog.

It was only Mr. Athus's gaze that held him fast. Mr. Athus moved to stand directly in front of Darius and said nothing. The commotion continued until all eyes froze on the pair, and the only sound Darius could hear was that of his own heart pounding in his ears.

"We ask the boy." Mr. Athus's eyes did not leave Darius as he spoke with all calmness. "We ask the boy to retrieve the book."

Darius's mother gasped, and Darius was speechless.

"Why him?" asked Miora. "We have no connection here. As Garp said and others have concurred, we are barely even welcome."

Mr. Athus smiled gently at Darius's mother and laid his hand softly on her shoulder. "Perhaps...by some. But despite the cold reception you continue to receive, I believe you are meant to be here. Don't you see? Your mysterious arrival only days after our own wizard's departure cannot be coincidence. I believe you were destined to help."

"Destined? How?" asked Darius.

"That I do not know, but as Garp has so cleverly if not callously pointed out, you are marked—tagged, perhaps, to retrieve our book. Besides, we cannot send one of our own. What if they should be unwritten as the Harpers have been? No, it must be you, Darius."

Darius looked around the room, faces staring—some in fear, others in disgust—and tightened his jaw. He almost hated these people, but as he looked again at Mr. Athus and the kind strength that filled his gray eyes, he stood, his mother clawing at his sleeve. "I'll go."

"No! Darius! No!" Miora tugged vigorously at his arm.

"And what of his mother? We should send her as

well!" screeched Garp.

Mr. Athus wheeled about on his heels and faced Garp. His thin eyes were like daggers. "You will cease this talk! Have you no soul? Are you so cruel that you would send her away just as we ask her son to save us? No! She will stay, and we will thank her for allowing her son to endeavor on such a dangerous journey."

Darius sat back down and cradled his sobbing mother. "It's all right, Mother. Mr. Athus is right. I have to do this. Don't worry. I'll be fine." He silently hoped he'd fooled her as her face dropped limply into his shoulder, her body shuddering as she wept.

Chapter Three

The Shredded Page

Klavon set the book on the table and exited the secret room. He crossed his candlelit chamber to the window that overlooked his shadowed realm. In the distance, sunlight attempted in vain to break the wall of dark clouds, and he could see the shadow of Fraenir, in dragon form, circling the massive expanse of his kingdom, watching for any who would falter in their allegiance. That was as he liked it—domination and darkness.

"Klavon," the young girl said, her hair white as a newly woven spider's web, "it is done."

Sira entered so quietly he did not hear her, and a thin smile creased his lips. She was extraordinary, and he valued her skills, even if it did pull from his powers—not that she wasn't more than capable in her own right, but with a sorcerer, her powers grew tenfold. Besides, he was strong enough to maintain his sorcery and accommodate such a unique assistant.

"I have lit the beacon," she said, "and I'm certain the boy will see the amber light."

Klavon nodded and looked out beyond the boggy mire to the land beyond. Fourteen long years he'd waited...he could almost see her face.

"Shall I send Fraenir to make sure Prydon doesn't interfere?" Sira asked.

"There is no need," said Klavon. "Prydon is dead."

"But—"

"Do you doubt me?" asked Klavon, his voice venomous with a cold, steady conviction.

"Of course not. But his kind can be quite tricky."

"So you doubt Fraenir."

Sira didn't speak a word. Even without facing her, he knew what she thought—that while Fraenir's only talent was battle, he was no match for Prydon.

Her lack of response made Klavon laugh. "Prydon is dead, I assure you. Fraenir is stronger than you believe. The boy will make it here, and nothing will interfere."

Klavon did not see Sira leave, but he knew she would. She was not one to extend conversation beyond the words that were needed, at least with him. As he heard the quiet click of the door closing behind him, he walked slowly to a tapestry on the wall.

Slithering behind it, he returned to the hidden chamber, glided to the center of the room, and picked up the book. A wicked sneer curled along his lips, and with a wave of his hand, the book flew open. A single page ripped from the spine by some unseen force, and with another sharp twist of his hand, the page was shredded to pieces. As they floated to the ground, he could hear the screams of some distant voices...and he smiled, breathing in deeply of their pain.

He thought of tearing out another page, but no. He

would destroy Brandor's inhabitants slowly, leaving those behind to cower in the knowledge that they could be next. Instead, he set the book down and walked back into his main chamber, once again staring out the now completely darkened window.

"Soon, my sweet, they will all be gone, and you will have no one…but me."

Chapter Four

A Visitor in the Night

Darius faced Mr. Athus as he stood at the edge of town. He glanced back toward the direction of his home—and mother. "You'll watch out for her, won't you?"

"Of course, I will." Mr. Athus tried to smile, but his face became grim as he looked at Darius's hand. "Perhaps I was wrong in asking you to do this. Maybe we can find a way to remove the mark and—"

Darius placed his hand gently on Mr. Athus's arm and smiled. "And what? I survive while Brandor dies? You have no one else to send."

Mr. Athus sighed and patted Darius's hand. "Darius, why you have been chosen for this task, I do not know. But you are strong, and I have no doubt that you will find your way." Deep lines creased his forehead. "I'm sorry no one in the village would offer you their horse. Stubborn lot! Fools at that, but since our wizard left, they have been suspicious of everything outside the village, including you and your mother."

"I'll manage. Besides, it's one less mouth to feed along the way."

Darius's attempt at humor did not lighten Mr.

Athus's mood. He continued to frown and shook his head. "I can't offer a great deal myself, but I want you to take this." Mr. Athus reached inside his cloak and pulled out a small pouch that jingled with coins. "It's not much—"

"I can't possibly—"

"Yes, you can." Mr. Athus placed the pouch in Darius's hand, clasping it closed with his fingers. "I can't send you off without something, and I'm quite certain your wages will not suffice. Oh, and..." He let go of Darius's hand and again reached beneath his cloak. This time from under his robes, he pulled out a sturdy sword, polished and expertly made, and handed it to Darius.

"A sword?"

"It was left behind by the wizard. I'm sure he would want you to use it now."

Darius's eyes were glued to the sword as he accepted the intimidating weapon. Its blade was long, broad at the handle and thin at the point, with a subtle ridge running the full length of the blade along the center of both sides. He examined it carefully, and when he looked down the length of the blade, the forged metal resembled the shape of a diamond—a diamond with four distinctly sharp, distinctly deadly edges. It was a formidable weapon.

The shaft itself was tightly bound with a thin piece of black leather, and embedded in the very end of the grip was a rough yet completely clear stone. When Darius ran his hand over it, an obscure force tickled his palm, and he stared at it in awe.

"I've never seen anything like it," he said.

"I daresay you never will." Mr. Athus handed

Darius the sheath. "Now it's yours."

Darius returned the sword to its sheath, pausing a moment as he stared at the wizard's instrument. He nodded and fastened it to his waist, having no idea how to use it. Strangely, it seemed natural having the blade hang by his side.

"And I have one last thing." Mr. Athus removed a book from his bag and handed it to Darius. "I've always taught you things from books. Books give knowledge, some useful and some not. Let us hope this is useful."

Darius stared at the cover and read the elegantly inscribed words. "Spells, Old and New." He looked up at Mr. Athus with questioning eyes. "I don't understand."

Mr. Athus shrugged. "When I was searching for the sword, I found it, and I had a…feeling. I don't know. Maybe some of its words can help you defeat the darkness that has taken our book or, at the very least, allow you to have a better understanding of words that might be directed at you."

Darius placed the book in his bag with his other belongings and shook hands with his old friend. "Thank you, sir, for everything."

"No. Thank you." Mr. Athus smiled. "Take care of yourself, Darius."

It was the first time Darius had seen Mr. Athus show any sign of hope since the book had been taken. He breathed deeply. "I won't let you down."

Mr. Athus nodded, and Darius turned, never looking back. He knew his friend's eyes followed him, but they both remained silent until distance forced each to take their own path—alone.

Darius shivered as he left everything that was familiar and headed for the only known source of dark magic, the Drach Mountains. Once there, he had no idea what he was going to do or even what he was looking for. A fiery beast that appears from a rip in the sky is not a common occurrence, and he could only imagine how it would sound should he find someone along the way and ask, "Excuse me. Have you seen any fiery beasts about? The kind that leave red marks embedded under your skin and steal books?"

Still, he remembered vividly the crimson light that rained down around the tower and hoped that he might find its source in the mountains and ultimately find the book.

A long day of traveling, and thinking, left him with no more clarity, and now he stood silent before a damp, swampy mire. Darius sighed. For hours, he had watched it coming as he gradually descended upon it, its vastness preventing any reasonable route around. He stared out at the bubbling mud. He'd read about it in some of the books Mr. Athus had given him, but the words did not prepare him for the expanse that now lurked before him. Large trees and dense shrubs grew out of the wet ground, fed to engorgement by the nutrients they drank in this place, but to Darius it was poison. He touched the cured skin pouch that held his water, thankful he had filled it at the last creek crossing.

Darius whistled a breath through pursed lips. Weaving about like a scrambled web were thin, sloshy paths, barely wide enough for secure footing. He placed one hesitant foot on the slick ground and proceeded forward, careful not to slip into the depths of the slime. He had read that creatures unknown slithered about below the iridescent surface, and he had no desire to awaken them to his presence.

By evening, his boots were soggy, adding unwanted weight to his fatigued legs, and he was thankful to spot a small clearing of raised ground, protruding invitingly above the sea of muck like an oasis in a parched desert. Surrounded by trees, brush, and vines, he believed it would be a safe enough place to rest his weary body for the night.

He tossed his pack against the base of a moss-covered tree and began gathering some kindling. Once he piled the sticks just so, he tried to start a small fire, but the moist sticks and twigs refused to allow a flame to take hold. Defeated, he sat shivering. The ground was cold and damp. A spring rain had cooled the air, and the night came with much discomfort. Sitting on a rotting log at the edge of the small clearing, Darius thought of home and the comfort of the small room with the tiny fireplace. How he wished a fire blazed to warm his body and calm his confused mind.

He pulled out some dried meat and began chewing. He stared off toward a distant place he couldn't see, blocked by the trees of the mire, to the distant hills. Somewhere beyond those ridges lay the Drach Mountains, his destination. Shaking his head, he dropped his face into his hands and began rubbing his temples. He had no real plan. Somehow, he hoped he might simply steal the book back, unnoticed and never having to use the sword, which now lay undisturbed on the ground beside him.

He finished his bland meal and pulled his blanket over his shoulders, trying to get comfortable atop a pile of damp leaves. Closing his eyes, he pretended he was asleep in his own bed, but his fake sleep was soon interrupted when a flapping sound violently stirred the air in the trees above him. Darius sat up and silently unsheathed his sword. He'd been mindful of creatures of the mire, but he hadn't thought about animals of the air. What bird's wings could cause such wind, or was it only a delusion of exhaustion and the twilight of sleep?

A heavy thump shook his oasis, and he knew this was not a dream, though he would welcome a nightmare to the vibration of footsteps shaking the ground beneath his body. His heart pounded against his chest so hard that he felt he was being beaten like a dusty rug. The sound of trees cracking and wet soil squishing beneath large steps soon revealed an enormous shadow creeping into the small clearing. When the figure emerged into full view, Darius could not believe what loomed before him—a dragon.

Darius wished he had read his new book. But he did know something of dragons—that if it so desired, he would soon become a nicely cooked meal for the beast. How pathetic he stood as he wielded the sword, a serious blunder in his incompetent hands, but it was all he had. And as he stared up at the dragon, defeat showered down on him, failing Brandor and his mother all in less than a day.

The dragon circled in front of Darius and then sat down. With its enormous, clawed hands, it dragged some dead limbs into the small pile Darius had already made in his attempt to start a fire. Then, with a single breath, the dragon set a fire to blaze in the cold of night.

With his sword pointed squarely at the dragon, Darius's eyes were fixed on the beast. Its powerful body was covered with blue, leathery scales, the color of a clear, dark night. In the glow of the fire, drops of water glistened on its skin like stars. Its head was large, with impressive jaws that came to a blunt point where sharp teeth were visible behind thin, sleek lips. Its nostrils flared, and its almond shaped eyes glowed white in the firelight. Tufts of feathery fur created eyebrows that extended up like long, pointed ears, flowing over the crown of its head. Its wings were tucked along its sides and partly covered its massive hind legs. Its front arms were only slightly less impressive than its back legs, its hands strong with sharp claws. Along its back were two parallel ridges, extending all the way down the long tail, which was now curled around its thighs. To finish it off, spikes protruded from the end of its tail, and Darius was sure that with one swift swing, he would be skewered and hung to roast over the fire.

"Much better, don't you agree?" the dragon rasped.

"You…You talk?" asked Darius, still awkwardly holding the sword.

"Of course I do," answered the dragon. "Now, would you kindly lower that sword before you hurt yourself?"

Darius peered at the dragon through squinted eyes, the sword swaying slightly as the weight pulled at his arms. He tried to speak, but the words stuck in his throat like a dried piece of bread. He stared at the dragon with a thousand unknown questions swimming in his head, but only one reached his lips. "Aren't you going to eat me or something?"

The dragon appeared to grin as it tilted its head, one of the feathery brows raised. "I could, if you'd like. But my preference is not for human flesh. Now would you please put that sword away before you manage to sever a limb? Your limb, that is." The dragon's smile faded back to a nonchalant pose, but Darius did not move. "As you wish, but do not blame me if you cause yourself harm. My name is Prydon." The dragon lowered its head and peered deeply at Darius. "So tell me, Darius. Why have you left the safety of Brandor?"

"Brandor? What do you know about Brandor? And how do you know my name?"

Prydon laughed; at least that's what Darius thought he heard. "I know more than you realize. But you, my friend, appear to be quite confused about a great many things. Tell me, what do you know of dragons that you would continue to threaten me with a sword—a wizard's sword at that?"

"I..." Darius paused, staring dumbfounded at the dragon yet unable to alter his expression.

"I thought so. There is much you do not know of dragons, but you will find out in time. For now, accept that I am a friend, and I will help you find your way."

Darius stared at the fire, tempted by its warmth, and hesitated before lowering his sword. Accepting that he wouldn't even know how to use it against such a massive beast, he returned it to its sheath and squeezed his eyes tightly shut, waiting for a deadly blow. After a moment, he opened one eye to discover the dragon flicking some dirt from beneath a claw and shaking his head in disbelieving humor. Darius's tension eased, and he crouched near the flames, soaking in the warmth like a sponge.

The dragon moved closer, his face lowered near Darius's hand. "You have been marked."

"So I've been told, but no one knows what it means."

"I do."

Darius's gaze shot from the fire to the dragon, his stuporous state dissolved to determination. "You do? But...how? I mean, you're a dragon..."

"I am a dragon. And I am also the one who can answer your question. But before I do that, I must know all that has happened in Brandor."

Darius settled his sights on an orange flame and began telling Prydon all the events that had transpired since the book was taken: the fiery beast, the shrill sound it made, the village meeting, Mr. Athus's concern, his mother's fear, and finally the mark that now mockingly encompassed his hand like the threat of a bully on a playground, daring him to attempt to discover its secrets.

"I fear that this is only the beginning. The mark you bare is that of a dark sorcerer."

"I've been told that as well, but that still doesn't tell me what it means."

"It means you must face Klavon."

"Klavon?"

Prydon glanced at Darius's hand. "Klavon is the sorcerer who is responsible for all of this and for the mark on your hand. And that mark must be removed."

Darius looked down at the dark streaks that wound like vines around his hand, dancing in the reflection of the fire, and then he turned his eyes to Prydon. "How?"

"You must defeat the one who gave it to you. You must defeat Klavon."

"You mean…kill him?" Darius's hand shook as he stared again at the marks. "What happens if I don't? I mean, I was hoping to just steal the book back."

"That mark will stay until you have defeated it—defeated Klavon. If you do not, that mark will eventually poison your heart and you will suffer a terrible fate."

"I'll die?" The pulse of the streaks that infested Darius's hand and wrist throbbed as if laughing at him.

"There are worse things than death." Prydon said, adding some logs to the fire before he continued. "Klavon is a dark sorcerer who has done evil things. He killed your father—"

Darius stumbled as he quickly jumped up, and had it not been for Prydon's steady claw on his shoulder, he would have taken a painful swim in the flames. "You know of my father? You know of my father's death?"

"I do." The dragon paused and pulled a log up behind Darius. "Sit. This will take time. Your mother never told you how your father died?"

Darius sat back down and rested his back against the log, lowering his head and kicking a stick into the fire. It sizzled and popped as the moisture was forced from the wood. "No. She refused to speak about it. I guess it was too painful."

"Painful? Perhaps, but your mother is very strong, if shortsighted. I suspect she was trying to protect you from the same fate as your father. A motherly instinct, no doubt, but she cannot protect you from your own providence. Now you must face the same evil that drove you and your mother from your home."

Darius listened, waiting for the story he'd always wanted to hear. Heat glazed over his face like hot coals pouring across his skin, but the source was not the fire that burned in front of him. It came from within as he anticipated, or perhaps dreaded, the words that would come out of Prydon's mouth.

"Klavon was always jealous of your father. They grew up together, best friends, or at least that is what your father thought. When the time came for them to enter the Valley of Wizards—"

"Valley of Wizards? What's that?"

The dragon scratched his cheek with one long claw. "Hmm. Did your mother tell you nothing of where you came? Of who you are?"

"As I said, she wouldn't talk about it. She'd simply say, we were where we were safe."

"Yes, you were safe in Brandor, but no more. So I shall tell you all I can. The Valley of Wizards is a place where the young wizards, after years of training, go to receive their blessing."

"Blessing?"

"Blessing...or perhaps curse. The Valley of Wizards is a place where wizards of old dwell when their time in this land has passed. It is they who can read the heart of a wizard, reflected in two stones: one in their sword, giving them strength in battle, and the other in their staff, giving them the power to wield spells beyond compare."

Darius touched the sword's handle. "Is that what this is?"

"Yes, it is. You have a wizard's sword, but that stone…a dragon's stone…will not help you. It will only help the one for whom it was intended."

"I guess that's good to know," said Darius. "But you were saying…"

"Your father and Klavon trained for years, and when it was their turn to enter the valley, your father returned with stones adorning his sword and staff as clear as the purest water. Klavon, however, did not."

"Crimson? Like the rain that fell in Brandor?"

"Yes, exactly. You see, the color of the stone granted a wizard reflects his true nature—whether he is good, kind, compassionate—cruel, oppressive, evil. Crimson proved to all that Klavon was bitter in his heart, probably from the jealousy he had, for so many years, allowed to consume him."

"You said he was jealous of my father, but why?" asked Darius.

"Your father's strength, his kindness, his integrity. Perhaps it was your mother's love for your father. Perhaps it was all of these things that fed his jealousy, and I believe your mother recognized more than most the true nature of Klavon, watching the two as they grew up together. Sometimes it is easier to perceive the truth from a distance, as an observer. In any case, Klavon vanished, never to be seen again until that final day when Klavon returned and killed your father."

"So...my father was a wizard?"

"Yes, Darius, and I believe that is why Klavon has marked you, for his own purposes, though I do not know what those purposes are."

"You never said what would happen if the mark isn't removed. You said it would poison my heart—a terrible fate, but not death." Darius rubbed one prominent, wide vein of red.

"Are you certain you want to know?"

Darius replied, "Not particularly, but I think I should know, don't you? I mean, after all, it is my heart."

"That is true." Prydon bowed his head, his brows coming together. "You will become like the evil that has attacked you. You will be lost to all you hold dear, subservient to Klavon for all eternity."

The words stung like the moment he was seized by the fiery creature, but this time it was his heart that burned, not his hand. "So, now what? What am I supposed to do?" Darius tried to hold the tears swelling in his eyes. He failed.

The dragon turned away, as if trying to allow Darius privacy in his pain, and spoke softly. "I will see to your training as your father would have. You will become a wizard and fight Klavon. It is the only way to stop this curse and save Brandor...and yourself."

Darius didn't know what to think. His father was dead because of Klavon, and now the only town he'd ever known was being undone. And he had been charged with finding the book and returning it to Brandor as quickly as possible. Yet...something told him the dragon was right.

But as quickly as he felt he could trust Prydon, a soft, warm breeze blew against his ear, stark against the cold night. It stirred in his mind like a storm blowing across a sea, churning and growing.

"Your town is dying," came the soft whisper of a girl's voice. "Your mother will be next. Beware tricksters in the night. He means to sway you from your true path."

Darius shook his head violently. A balmy breeze swirled around his body, building his confidence in a blanket of warmth. Suddenly he became enraged.

"Are you kidding me?" Darius sniffed and wiped the tears from his eyes. "I don't have time to train! I need to get that book back now!"

Prydon tore around to face Darius, his tail slicing a clump of trees at the ground. He stared at the boy as if surprised. Then he shot back, "You would fail if you attempted such a feat. You are untrained and unarmed—"

"I have this sword, don't I?" A blaze of anger flooded Darius's cheeks and his eyes flared.

"That sword is useless to you. I doubt you could so much as cause a scratch to Klavon." Prydon stood tall above Darius, his brows curled in anger. "Do not be foolish."

Darius grabbed the sword once again and aimed it at Prydon. "Foolish? How dare you! It's not your heart that's in danger."

Prydon stomped the ground causing Darius to wobble. "This curse will not consume you quickly, unless you allow it! You have time to be trained properly. Months even, with proper discipline."

"Months? Brandor doesn't have months! Besides, how would you know that? You're no wizard. But...but I am, and I'll find a way. I have a book on spells. I'll learn those."

"You're coming with me to be trained!" demanded Prydon.

"Oh, no, I'm not!"

Prydon threw his head back, shooting a streak of flame into the dark sky. When he finished, he snapped his jaws at Darius. "Son of Thyre? No, a foolish child! I offer my help and you refuse. Instead, you choose death? Or maybe worse! So be it!" Prydon swung his tail into the fire, sending the burning logs out into the wet mire.

"Hey!" Darius yelled, as he watched the warm flames extinguish and the logs sizzle out of sight beneath the dark water.

Prydon roared, and Darius almost fell backwards trying to avoid Prydon's spiked tail as he swung around. With the flap of wings, a cold wind blew on Darius's face. Prydon pushed up from the ground and was soon swallowed by the sky...and the sound of the dragon's wings faded into the darkness of the night.

Darius walked to where the fire had been. The ground was still warm, and a few burning embers remained. He quickly grabbed some sticks, but again the moisture would not allow the coals to bring a flame to life. Darius sighed and raked what was left of the coals together with one of the sticks. He huddled closely and thought of the dragon. Why didn't he understand? How could he waste time when Brandor and his mother were counting on him?

A cold mist began to fall, and for a moment, he wondered where the warm breeze had gone. With a final fizz the coals darkened. Darius stared at the sky where the dragon flew away, wondering if it were anywhere near, lurking behind some cluster of trees, waiting for Darius to admit fault and beg him to return. Anger again swelled inside of him and he spat hard on the ground.

"I don't need him," he snapped out loud, hoping Prydon would hear. "I have my book and this sword."

But the dark of night kept him from reading, and the rain fell even harder. Darius curled up on the ground where the fire once blazed, the warmth quickly fading, and pulled his blanket over his body. Tears came once again, and Darius chided himself for such a childish display. He lay there motionless, except for the shivering caused by the damp cold, until exhaustion—and doubt—overtook him.

Chapter Five

The Pile of Bones

Sira appeared just outside the courtyard next to the castle. Above, Fraenir circled, and she could see a young man, no more than eighteen, kneeling in front of Klavon.

She tilted her head and paused—Klavon would not be pleased. For her to go against his wishes and look after the boy…look for Prydon…had been a risky move and one she did not endeavor upon lightly.

Years before, it was Fraenir who almost died—at the clawed hands of Prydon—and even though Prydon had been deeply wounded, she was not so prideful, as Klavon and Fraenir, to believe him dead.

And she was correct—Prydon lived, and had she neglected her instincts, the boy would have listened to Prydon's counsel, and Klavon would have lost his prize.

Stepping out into the courtyard, she inhaled deeply, knowing what she must do. She quietly approached Klavon who ignored her, glaring down at the young man.

"You will never speak against me again," said Klavon, "or you will die…"

"My death it nothing compared to your cruelty," said the young man. "If I have convinced but one—"

"Then your father will die!"

At this, the young man hesitated. "You are a coward, threatening an old man's life."

"Perhaps, but I think not. Now, do we have a deal?" sneered Klavon.

The young man's jaw tensed, and reluctantly he nodded agreement.

Sira stood silently by—she would not interfere. She had seen Klavon exact his punishment on many—the pile of bones at the edge of the courtyard his trophy—and now was no different.

"Sira," said Klavon.

"I have news," she said, not looking at the young man.

"Speak then. What is it?"

"This is news best fit for private discourse," she said.

Something compelled her to glance at the young man. He looked up at her, and for a brief moment, he held her gaze. In his eyes, she witnessed his thoughts. She could not label it, but the closest she could come was to say it was…resolve, unbreakable and strong. Then he lowered his eyes and remained focused on the ground in front of him, in expectation of the sorcerer's wrath.

Curious. Most in the region knew that if they were brought before Klavon, it was not likely they would leave…alive. And the fear they exhibited was unmistakable. Their bodies would shake and their faces would beg mercy. But this one…

Sira had never been bothered by Klavon's need to

vent his frustrations out on the local peasantry, but for a moment, she felt...compassion? She brushed her thoughts aside and looked at Klavon.

"It is of great interest to you, I am sure. Perhaps you should send this one on his way. You have more urgent matters," she said. She was slightly amused at her own words. But no, it was not compassion she felt—it was respect, and it would be a shame to see such strength vanquished.

Klavon raised a brow and said, "This one has spoken ill of me. You would have me release him?"

"Was that not your agreement?" Sira said, glancing only a moment at the young man, her eyes showing none of her desire. "But do as you will, and do it quickly. Trust me when I say there are more urgent matters."

Klavon hesitated, tilting his head at Sira. He stared at her, and without looking at the young man, he said, "Leave. Remember what I have said. And know that there will be no compassion should we meet again."

The man hesitated, looked over at Sira, and then rose. He backed away a few steps before turning and walking slowly and purposefully to the edge of the courtyard.

Klavon's scrutiny broke from Sira long enough to see the man retreat, and he laughed.

"Prydon lives," she said deliberately, drawing his gaze back to her.

Klavon's eyes widened and his jaw tensed. "How? How would you know?"

"I went to the mire. To watch...just in case."

"So you did doubt me!" Klavon yelled.

"No, I did not," Sira said calmly. Behind Klavon, she could see the young man disappear into the woods. "I simply felt it was wise to be cautious. This is too important to leave to—"

"So you believe me unwise and incapable of recognizing the importance of this?" Klavon raised his staff and looked at the trees where his prisoner had escaped.

"Of course not!" Sira shot back, louder than she'd intended.

A moment's pause caught Klavon's breath, and he glared at her.

She raised her chin slightly and she added, "I want only to help you…to serve you. Your energies are better served dealing with Prydon."

"You think me so weak that you would control my actions." Klavon yelled. "Fraenir!"

Sira closed her eyes for a moment and then watched as Fraenir dove into the trees. She heard a scream, not of fear but of pain, and the beast appeared above the courtyard. His claws pierced the shoulders of the young man, and for one brief instant, Sira saw the man's face as he struggled to break free…still no fear.

Fraenir shrieked and dropped the man as lightning blazed from the end of Klavon's staff. In a matter of seconds, bare bones fell to the ground, adding to the already mounding pile.

Sira looked at Klavon with a vacant expression. "Pity. Had you been able to convert him, he would have made a strong addition. In any case, as you wish…as always. I care not." She bowed and turned from the courtyard. Before she entered the castle, she looked back at the pile of bones. Such a waste.

Chapter Six

A Peculiar Meeting

The morning air was sharp, the sun still hanging low on the horizon. Darius yawned, arched his back, and stretched his arms out to the sides, relieving the aches the cold had bitterly deposited in his muscles. It was Prydon's fault; had he not obliterated the fire the night before, there would be no dampness, no cold, no pain.

The morning dampness of the mire was miserable. The swampy slime combined with the intense rays of the sun proved to be a perfect recipe for extremely wet nights.

Darius grumbled and stood tall, and the blanket that ineffectively shrouded him the night before fell to the ground in a soggy, wet heap. He picked up the heavy cloth, shook it, and snapped it into the air, flinching as cold beads of water slapped his face and arms. He popped it again, but the blanket remained laden with moisture; his desire to throw the thick cloth over his shoulders to keep warm was quickly squelched. Instead, he rolled it up and bound it with a leather strap.

He was miserable. His clothes were soaked, his bag was soaked, and the sun mocked him, staying hidden behind dark clouds on the horizon. There was no picturesque sunrise, and Darius longed for the warmth of his own bed.

In an irate fit he kicked the ashes that were left from the night before. They stubbornly stuck to his boots like wet clay, and he cursed the dragon. "I'm glad you're gone!" he yelled toward the vacant sky, shaking his feet about in an attempt to dislodge the masses of ash that seemed determined to remain a permanent fixture on his boots.

An instant later, he thought he'd heard the flap of the dragon's wings, but it was only a flock of birds stirred by some unseen foe. Darius drew his sword and sited a shaking bush with the point of the blade. A snake slithered lethargically from the edge of the brush, and Darius immediately severed its head.

Filled with a sense of triumph, his resolve was momentarily strengthened by the small victory. He would read the book on spells, he would practice with the wizard's sword, and he would…he would…. Darius glanced at the crimson tendrils on his hand and wrist, and his head dropped. He looked at the snake's head and whispered, "I'm sorry."

Then he wondered if a true wizard could reverse the mistake, but death was permanent. Prydon had said he was to kill Klavon—he'd never killed anything until today, and it made his stomach turn. Why had he done that? Why was he so angry? Pulled down by the weight of a difficult reality, he wondered if he'd made the right choice.

Odd…the anger. It was unlike him to react so strongly. Even when he was younger and the boys in the village taunted him to fight, he rarely reacted. He remembered the look on his mother's face when he showed up home with a bloodied lip, and he hated the heartache her expression relayed. Their lives in Brandor were hard enough. He vowed not to add to it by engaging bullies in a senseless fight.

As a result, he learned very young to control his emotions no matter how much he wanted to respond to their unkind words…their false accusations about him, his mother, and his dead father. So why did he kill the snake…and why did he yell at the dragon?

He gathered his things and walked to the edge of his overnight oasis, glancing back only for a moment at the evidence of actions. He had made his choice, and there was no rush of wind, no dragon's wings, to save him. He sighed and looked out at the path ahead of him, heading out in search of the crimson light…and Klavon.

The mire promised no more safety than before, and with the dampness of the morning, the paths threatened even more treachery. As the sun finally gave up its hiding place behind the clouds, shadowy figures passed through the water, constant reminders that with one slip, with one improperly placed step, he would be swallowed forever in failure.

The heat baked down upon him, and steam spiraled up into the air from the mire, creating an eerie effect across the entire surface of the swamp. The only benefit was that his clothes were drying—all except for his boots, which were continually saturated by the bubbling ooze that splattered up onto the path.

And then it happened. His footing gave way, and he slipped. His bag and bedroll went flying, and he grabbed at the air, hoping beyond hope that he could take hold of some invisible savior. No. He plunged backwards, into the mire, cutting the steamy fog as he fell, sinking far into the depths of the murky water. He struggled as shadows instantly moved closer. Panic overcame him, and he clawed upwards, his heart beating so fast he could hear it echo in the ears. Finally, his head broke the surface, and he was able to gasp a huge breath of welcome air. He reached for the path, flailing, clawing, digging deeply into the mud. He grabbed a dead root, but it broke free from the slime before he could even attempt to take hold. He grabbed again at the path, the muddy grass, leaves, anything, but...a tug at his legs and something pulled him under once again. A thousand hands were grabbing him and he sank deeper and deeper. He kicked and shoved, yanked and punched, trying to break free. The panic he felt before was nothing compared to now as he felt jagged claws against his legs and arms...face.

And then suddenly, as suddenly as he had fallen, he was being hoisted from underneath up, up, up, out, and onto the path. He spat and threw up water—poison—filling his lungs with huge gasps of air. He turned to look back at the water, his chest heaving as he continued to breathe frantically. A dark shadow floated beneath the surface and lingered for a moment, but as it shot away, a white flash of something caught his eyes. White...he sat for a moment and stared.

Slowly, he stood and looked around, his legs

shaking beneath him. His bag was snared on a nearby limb, easy enough to reach, but the bedroll was lying halfway in the mire. He retrieved the bag and hesitated. He bit his lip as he stared at tied-up blanket, and after what seemed forever, he used a limb to snag it and drag it closer. When he leaned down to pick it up, he began to slip and sat hard on the path, his feet stuck in the muck at the water's edge. A shadow appeared in the distance and moved in closer. Against a suction that felt like shackles, Darius tugged, and just before he feared hands would grasp his ankles, he freed himself and fell backwards onto the path.

For several minutes he sat, inhaling, exhaling, until his pulse returned to a more desirable, steady rate. More dark shadows returned, and he carefully stood. Darius breathed deeply and attempted to ignore the threatening shapes. Cautiously he trudged on, his bedroll dripping at his side, his wet hair sticking to his face, the foul water stinging his eyes, and his drenched clothes sagging dangerously at his feet...his unsteady feet. It seemed an eternity that the paths slithered about, and he set his sights on the distant horizon where rest would be available, and the swamp would finally relinquish its hold on this land. He could make it—he had to.

Darius guessed it had been about an hour before he finally reached the edge of the damp swamp, its noxious claws unable to penetrate the grassy slope and solid ground beyond. He gladly took his last step away from the slippery path into the shelter of the forest. A solid canopy of intertwined tree-limbs covered the trail, and shade blanketed the ground. It was the first time since his fall—

perhaps since he entered the mire—that he felt safe.

Darius stopped and looked back. He had made it, thanks to some unknown presence, and he wondered what it had been. He tossed a rock into the mire as if to call the white specter that had saved him. The splash was greeted by a dark shadow that turned sharply toward the bank where Darius stood. He jolted back quickly, almost tripping as he scrambled away from the mire's edge. The shadow hung near the surface, and Darius stood frozen, staring at the shape. It almost seemed to be dancing as the waves ebbed toward the mire's edge, but it was a dance that created fear, daring him to step into the water. After a moment, the figure retreated deep into the bog. Darius hesitated, afraid to move, and then slowly and cautiously continued up the shaded trail. He wanted to rest, his body begged him to rest, but he trudged on, determined to put as much distance between him and the mire as possible.

When he reached a small nook in the path where a bubbling stream crossed and settled in a small pool of pristine, clear water, he stopped. With the slimy ooze covering his body and clothes, he jumped in, scrubbed his face, and then lay exhausted at the water's edge. He wasn't sure how long he slept, but when his eyes opened, the sun was high overhead—noon. He stripped down and washed out everything that had been contaminated by the mire's goo. Then he hung his belongings on a nearby limb and tossed his boots up onto a flat rock, climbing up and sitting next to them. He tilted his face upward and enjoyed the warm sun. As he looked up into the canopy, glints of white sunlight bounced off the leaves. Birds chirped, and he inhaled a long breath as the wind carried the faint fragrance of fresh, spring flowers. He sat in the sun, on this warm rock next to a thick tree, and rested some more.

He closed his eyes and leaned his head back against the bark; he could almost forget the troubles that unfolded. Almost…but with a heavy sigh, reality returned. Still, it turned out to be an agreeable afternoon. Darius slipped on his dry shorts and settled beneath the tree to eat and wait for his other, heavier clothes to dry.

Another meal of dried meat was not very appetizing. He envisioned roasted chicken, steaming vegetables and potatoes, freshly dug from the garden, all smothered in gravy—all of which he might be having if he were home. He licked his lips and swallowed to prevent drool from running down his chin. Darius ripped a piece of meat with his teeth, his nose shriveling as he took the bite.

Chewing the leathery substance, Darius pulled out the book of spells. Even closed, it commanded respect, and he hesitated as he gently touched the edge of the cover. But then he thought of the dragon. He regretted the words he had spoken. Yet…if Prydon was such a friend, where was the dragon when Darius almost drowned in the mire? Why didn't he come to help? And where was the dragon now so that Darius could tell him that he would train after all?

Darius felt abandoned, and in his self-pity, he allowed the anger he'd felt toward Prydon the night before to return, the anger that had been fueled by some strange warmth. Now trying desperately to justify his refusal to train, he swiftly opened the book on spells, determined that he would succeed in retrieving the book. But just as quickly, he exchanged the book on spells for the book on dragons.

This book did not carry the same majesty as the other. Still the cover was elegant, a dark blue with the imprint of a silver dragon. Darius stared at the beast. Something about it agitated him; perhaps it was the eyes.

Ignoring the sensation, Darius flipped open the book and began to read. "Dragons are a stubborn lot." He laughed, a piece of dried meat shooting from his mouth into the water below where a tiny fish quickly retrieved it. "Did you hear that, Prydon? Already this book speaks wisdom!"

Darius looked into the sky through the trees, paused and listened, hoping the words would be carried by the wind and sting Prydon's ears! As he continued to read, he discovered more delightful tidbits of information.

"Dragons are not to be trusted, dangerous, and often prone to the delights of their own hearts, caring nothing for humans except to enjoy as an occasional snack."

Each time, Darius flamboyantly yelled the words into the air. A dragon—how could he even trust such a creature? And this creature wanted him to spend precious months training while pieces of Brandor's history were being ripped from existence. Feeding his own ego, Darius tried valiantly to convince himself that he'd chosen the correct path after all, a shorter path to victory.

Darius flicked a leaf that floated past his face and settled on the open page. He continued to read until the joy of bellowing insults into the air and the confidence of his own choice faded. The words began to melt into the page, and soon they became a puddle of ink floating aimlessly across the parchment. His mind wandered to the night before and thoughts of his father.

How did Prydon know so much? How did he know that Klavon was responsible? Was it all a trick to set him up, and had he foiled the plan by refusing to allow Prydon to "train" him?

For a moment, his heart began to race at the thought, but it didn't make sense. If Prydon were in allegiance with Klavon, why didn't he do away with him last night? Why didn't he skewer him for dinner as he so easily could have done? Was it the sword? No. Though Darius knew the sword was powerful, Prydon had more than enough opportunities to do him in, should he have so desired.

Despite the unanswered questions, one thing was clear. Darius had made his choice, and now he was going to face Klavon. And if he was going to face Klavon, he would need some kind of defense. He shoved the book on dragons back into his bag and grabbed the book of spells.

Besides, he was smart. He was a quick learner; Mr. Athus always told him so. And Mr. Athus gave him the book. Surely now that he knew he was a wizard's son, the words would expel more power.

Darius set the book on the rock next to him and put on his clothes, all the while staring at the book. When he was dressed, he sat back down and picked it up again. He opened the book as if it were the most delicate of flowers. A brush of wind brushed against his face as if some unseen power came forth from the book and swallowed him whole. It was not threatening…it was soothing. The pages were yellowed from age, yet strength exuded from each as if even a gale force could not tear them.

He began reading. After repeating the same spell over and over in his mind, words began to float from the pages into his memory. While still engrossed in the book, Darius attempted to put on his shoes, his nose buried in the pages. He slid off the rock and walked, still holding the book to his face, to where the now dry blanket hung.

Darius stopped and looked down, a slight discomfort cramping his feet. His face became flushed, and he glanced around in embarrassment, hoping that Prydon wasn't watching. He set the book gently on a rock and rubbed his temples. Leaning against a tree, he removed his boots, swapped them, and put them on again. He gathered his blanket and other belongings, picked up the book, and continued on his way.

He glanced up from the pages only long enough to make certain he was traveling in the right direction and then delved into the book of spells. The book was enthralling and time passed quickly. The sun traveled through the sky, casting long shadows across the path and diminishing the light, but Darius's youthful eyes took little notice. He continued to read.

Absorbed in the words, Darius was jarred to his senses as he stumbled on a root that invaded the path. With belongings cascading down upon him, he found himself sprawled at the edge of a field covered with tall, dead stalks.

The sun dipped behind the mountains, and an eerie glow swam across the field like a thick fog. Darius stood slowly and brushed the dust off his knees, staring out into the dead field. A flicker of lights beyond the field caught his attention. His brow rose at the prospect—a village where he might discreetly gather information or at least find shelter for the night and, perhaps, procure a decent meal. His stomach growled, and he stared again across the dead field. First, he would have to pass through this disconcerting place.

Darius picked up his things, his eyes locked on the strange field in front of him. Perhaps it was the way the shadows played along the soil, battling each other for the last chance to survive in the fading sun. Or possibly it was the bare stalks, thick as his fingers, clawing upward as if begging the sky for moisture. The rain the day before left scattered puddles of mud, and the remainder of the ground, though dry, was not parched. So why was everything dead?

Darius glimpsed movement and tried to focus in the waning sunlight, but the dusk quickly encased the entire valley, and even his young eyes could not follow. His heart pumped faster as another movement yanked his attention, then another. Everywhere he looked movements drew his eyes, and every time his eyes failed him.

He blinked hard and slowly backed away from the field. The movements reminded him of the shadows darting ominously beneath the mire's surface. He stopped and shook his head, attempting to rattle his senses to reason. "So what are you going to do? Stand here all night? It's only the wind rustling the dead stalks."

But reason suggested caution. Darius stepped onto the field, resting his hand on his sword as the last of the shadows melted into the ground. As he advanced farther into the forest of dead stalks, the stone atop the sword's handle began to hum, and Darius involuntarily loosed his grip. Stopped dead in his tracks, he stared down at the sword. "That can't be good," he said.

He planted his feet firmly and attempted to draw the sword when the ground beneath him began to tremble. Before he could grasp the hilt, something snatched his feet and flung him onto his back, his breath forced from his lungs.

Rolling over and scrambling quickly to his hands and knees, he was greeted with a belt across his back. He plummeted to the ground, the dirt powdering his face like a dusty rag. Coughing and spitting out the grime, Darius wobbled to his feet and yelled, "Who goes there?"

Darius managed to unsheathe his sword before another attack came. He swung randomly from one side to the other, jolting as he spun in an attempt to discover who was there, but he could find no enemy, no target to hit. Another slap to the back of his knees sent him kneeling on the ground.

Almost instantly, he was back on his feet, screaming in frustration. Catching movement out of the corner of his eye, he turned just in time to receive a smack across his face. He fell backwards and looked up at his foe, the taste of blood trickling from his wounded mouth.

Had he more time, he would have pondered the situation. As it was, with another strike coming straight down from above, he rolled, grabbed the sword, and ran, flailing the weapon haphazardly.

His efforts proved futile. As he attempted to advance farther through the field of stalks, he was continually pounded; the stalks themselves were striking him as he passed, driven by a life of their own and determined to prevent Darius from escaping their torture. His sword proved ineffective against them. As he would fell one, another, looming up from the ground like a serpent ready to strike, immediately replaced it.

He tried yelling a spell he'd read, but the words floated around in his head, out of order, and making no sense. So Darius ran. As he continued, a non-ending barrage of pokes, stings, and strikes disoriented him, causing him to lose sight of the opposite side of the field. He no longer used the sword but frantically zigzagged through the brutal stalks, lost in a path of madness.

His motion was halted, however, by a strong tug from behind. "What are you doing?" the feminine voice yelled. "Are you crazy?"

Amidst further assault, Darius was dragged this way and that, until the force which pulled him threw him down onto a grassy slope, plopping down beside him. She sat as if nothing out of the ordinary had happened, her white-blond hair shining in the moon's glow.

"Who are you?" Darius asked.

"I am Sira," she said, pulling out a clean kerchief and wiping blood from Darius's face. "Who are you?"

Discomfort slid over him as she moved to his blood crusted lip, slowing almost to a stop as she ran the cloth along the outline of his mouth. He gently took her hand. "Thank you, but I can do that." Darius took the small piece of fabric and she shrugged, leaning back against the soft ground.

"Suit yourself." Sira's eyes froze on the stains spiraling around Darius's hand. "Interesting mark. And who did you say you were?"

Darius looked at her skeptically. She was beautiful…almost too beautiful. Her eyes were an emerald green accented by thin brows that slanted upward. Her dress was rustic, but the leathery cloth complimented her slender figure. She didn't look strong, yet she'd managed to drag him effortlessly through the maze of attacking stalks. And her hair. Something about the color, or perhaps the way it shone in the light, reminded him of the glimmer beneath the mire's surface, the one of the unknown presence that saved his life.

Darius didn't know what provoked him to do so, but he asked, "Have you ever been to the mire?"

"The mire? That dreadful place?" she asked. "Wouldn't be caught dead there. Or maybe I should say I would. That mire isn't a safe place. No, I prefer here, for the most part. Why do you ask?"

For fear of having said too much, "No reason. I just saw it as I was traveling. It looks interesting from a distance."

"Hmmm. You are a strange little fellow. And I still don't know your name." Sira smiled and blinked in a flirtatious manner.

"So, what are those?" Darius motioned toward the field in an attempt to avoid divulging his name.

Sira's mouth pursed in amusement and she bobbed

her head slightly. "Cautious. Very well, then." She tousled her hair and sat up. It fell perfectly in place when she stopped. "It's him."

"Him?" Darius's brows puckered.

"Klavon. The sorcerer who rules this land."

The name stung his ears. So, he was in Klavon's territory. Already? Darius looked out at the now still field. "Klavon? I don't understand."

"Klavon is our sorcerer. He cursed it. He has a barrier around his entire domain."

"Barrier? But why?" Darius's heart began to race. Had he, in his stupidity, tipped the sorcerer off to his presence?

Sira shrugged. "Don't know. To keep people out?" The edges of Sira's lips curled up slightly, and she gave a throaty laugh. "Or in, I suppose."

"Then how did I get through? And even more, how did you get out of there unharmed?"

It was true. Not a mark darkened her face, arms, or any other part of her body, whereas he was covered with scratches, bruises, and scrapes.

"You got through because I helped you," she said.

Darius was not impressed with Sira's expression of amusement. "Me? Allow a few tricks to cause me harm? No. Truthfully, it's not a very good barrier if you know how to handle it. You just aren't that smart."

The hair on the back of Darius's neck stood to attention. "Me…I…uh…"

"Oh! And articulate at that. So, listen. If you won't tell me who you are, you can at least tell me why you are here. Maybe I can help. You seem to need it."

"I do not!" Darius snapped quicker than he would have liked. "I was just lost, that's all. Look. I appreciate your help, getting me out of that field and all, but if you would just tell me where I might find the nearest inn."

"Midtown. On the left. I'd take you there, but I have other things to attend to. And since you think you don't need my help..." Sira emphasized the word *think* more than Darius would have liked. She stood and headed for a path, barely visible through the thick brush. "...I assume you can get there without getting lost?" *Lost.* Another word overemphasized. "And there aren't any more fields to cross, so you should be fine. Oh, but you may watch out for the wombuloes."

"Wombuloes?"

Sira laughed. "Just kidding. There's no such thing, but you should see the look on your face."

Darius stood, but before he could respond, the young woman vanished into the thick night.

"Nice sword, by the way." The words echoed up from somewhere in the night.

Darius sighed. His body ached from the attack, but it was nothing compared to his wounded pride. He looked out again at the field of stalks, motionless to deceive the next traveler. He shook his head in exhausted confusion. He returned the sword to its sheath and checked to make sure all his belongings were securely in his bag. Turning toward the lights of the distant town, he trudged along.

Chapter Seven

Sira's Report

Klavon had been angered over Sira's actions. He was furious that she had not believed him—had gone behind his back to see if Prydon was indeed dead. But, had she not, the boy would surely have followed the dragon to the training fields.

Sira had prevented that, and he had to admit that she had done well by him. As it was, he instructed her to continue to watch and to make sure that the boy reached his destination...and his death.

She had done just that, and now Klavon laughed cynically at the boy's incompetence. His own son, had he had one, would never have been so inept! Killing him would be too easy, unfitting of one so powerful, but it must be done. And Klavon would enjoy it, beneath him as it may be.

Sira stood beside him. She was petting a large cat-like creature. It resembled a panther, black and sleek, but its shoulders were larger, and it mouth was framed with two large fangs.

"It was quite amusing," she said.

"Did he know it was you?"

Sira laughed. "Did he know? He was so frantic as he was…drowning. I doubt he would have known had it been his own mother who saved him. No. He has no idea it was me who boosted him from the mire."

"Good," said Klavon. "And where is he now?"

"I sent him to the inn. He will be heading here tomorrow."

"Of course," said Klavon, "I could go to the inn and dispense of him tonight…"

"But that could cause panic in your subjects," said Sira.

Klavon laughed. "True…and I would not want my subjects to believe they were ever in any danger. I can wait until he gets here. In fact, I prefer it that way. This courtyard makes a wonderful battle arena, don't you think?"

Klavon glanced at the pile of bones and laughed again. He was distracted as Fraenir came into view and dove to the ground. Sira stepped back, and her pet stepped in front of her as if to protect her from the beast.

"Will you never learn?" laughed Fraenir. "I am the stronger."

The cat hissed, and Sira frowned. But then her face softened, and she said with a light voice, "Perhaps I should have him take care of Prydon for you."

Fraenir growled and thrust his face toward Sira, stopped by the long fangs of her cat. They fixed their eyes on each other, neither appearing to budge, but neither making any further gesture of hostility.

"Come, come, you two," said Klavon. "You are

both valuable. Have you found the wretched beast?"

Fraenir stood up but was still staring down at the cat, a rumble in his chest as if he would roast Sira's pet at any moment. "I have not, but if that dragon comes near, I will know…and I will kill him."

"Him, yes," said Klavon. "But Darius? He is mine."

Chapter Eight

The Lesson Learned

Darius stood at the edge of the dark village. The streets were worn, the businesses bland. Not a speck of grass was to be seen except clinging tightly in tufts at the base of buildings, trying to hide from the ravages of unwelcome footsteps. The hoot of an owl drew Darius's attention to a dying tree, and a black cat passed lazily by, pausing only a moment to stretch and express its boredom with the new visitor. Lanterns hung from doorways, lighting signs. Most informed Darius businesses were closed, and with the spiders and webs that found their homes among the crevices, he wondered if they'd ever been open.

Darius put on some gloves to conceal his curse and continued on. Exactly as Sira described, he spotted the inn on the left, midway down the dusty road. The two-story structure was covered with brown vines, and the windows stared down at him with their diamond shaped eyes. The wind blew the sign, *The Dusty Lantern*, and a soft squeak trickled into Darius's ears. It was soon drowned out by the much louder creak as he opened the door.

In front of him stretched a long bar with double

doors centered behind, from which a waitress came carrying two plates, steaming with hot meals. Tables were positioned all about, each one having a solitary lantern stationed in the middle. Most were empty. A staircase sat in a cove to the left, leading to the second floor. From the ceiling hung three candlelit chandeliers, spaced evenly throughout the establishment. The shadows they cast did nothing to improve the dreariness that enveloped the room. The few inhabitants in the inn busily chattered, but with Darius's entrance, the hubbub came to an abrupt halt.

Darius forced a smile and tried to amble casually to the bar. Intense eyes followed him, many glancing from his face to the sword, which hung inconspicuously at his side. He avoided all gazes save the one that watched him from behind the bar. He was a large man with dark hair and a dingy apron tied sloppily around his midriff, which he was using to dry a glass. His work did not falter with Darius's entrance, and his expression showed nothing.

Blood began pumping faster through his veins, and Darius asked, "Excuse me, sir, but would you have a room?"

"Yup." The burly man spit a brownish liquid into a bin on the floor. "Nice sword."

"Uh, yes." Darius felt the heat of several eyes boring into the back of his head. "And how much would that room be?"

"I don't know? Maybe that sword would cover it?"

The dried meat Darius ate earlier in the day began pushing upward on his throat. He swallowed hard. "I'm sorry. This was a gift."

Whispers floated about the room, and the man grinned. He paused his labors and leaned in toward Darius. One of his bushy brows raised in curiosity. "Must be some friend. Five gold then."

"Five?" Darius fingered the gold in his bag, Mr. Athus's life savings. It wasn't much, and five pieces would diminish his supply more than he liked. "Would you consider three?"

The bar tender laughed boisterously and then leaned down on one elbow, cupping his chin. "Tell you what. I'll let you have it for three if you tell me who gave you that gift."

"My old boss. He…died. His name was…was James."

The tender squinted and huffed. "James, huh? Common name. Very well." He slammed a key from beneath the counter. "Room 14."

Darius pulled the three pieces of gold from his bag, placed them on the bar, and took the key. "Thanks."

The barkeep grinned and spit another stream of brownish liquid into the bin. "Sleep tight."

Darius nodded. The room remained quiet as he headed for the small cove. He nonchalantly walked past the patrons, trying his best to appear as casual as possible. Climbing the steps to the second level, Darius heard the chatter of the inn return, and he leaned against the wall.

He was out of their sight, and with the release of a breath he was certain he'd been holding since entering the inn, relief washed over him. Following the narrow hallway, he turned two corners before reaching his room.

He inserted the key and opened the door. A simple bed lay in one corner, and a wash basin hung on the wall in another, supported by two wooden legs. Between them faded, yellow curtains decorated a plain wooden window. It was nothing like the more elaborate diamond shaped windows that looked down upon the entrance.

Against the wall next to the door sat a small chair and table that stood bare, except for a thick layer of filth and a small lit lantern. Darius removed his gloves and tossed them on the table. Dust stirred and he ran his finger along the dirt. He paused, wrote his name, and then wiped it clean, making sure to leave no trace of his identity. With dust-laden hands, he slapped his pant legs, transferring the powder to the cloth and the surrounding air; he coughed.

Darius slipped the thick strap from his shoulder and threw his bag down on the bed. A cloud mushroomed into the air, and Darius frowned. He picked up the pillow and went to the window. Opening it, he held the pillow outside and began to beat it with his fist. A shower of dust floated to the dead bushes below. When the haze diminished, he placed the pillow back on the bed. Moving his bag to the chair, he did the same with the blanket, popping it like a whip and holding his breath to avoid a lung full of dirt.

Satisfied that there was no more he could do, Darius pulled the blanket back inside but was jerked back to the window as something caught his attention. He squinted. The moon was high, the light shining brightly, but in the shadows indistinct forms remained hidden. Then he saw it; a flash of white color peeked through the bushes. In an instant it was gone, and Darius shot behind the edge of the window, peering around only enough to see the brush. After some time a stiffness invaded his neck, and still nothing revealed itself. Darius pulled the curtains closed and turned back to his room.

His stomach growled, and Darius thought of going back downstairs to procure a hot meal. Another thought of the patron's watching him made his decision; Darius ate some dried meat, put out the lantern, and threw himself back onto his bed. In no time, he was asleep.

An unfamiliar squeak pried Darius's eyelids open. A tiny sliver of light, originating in the hall, sliced across the bedroom floor through the small crack in the door. Darius held his breath; a hand slowly began inching its way inside. Panicked, Darius reached for his sword, and in a clumsy instant, as he drew it, the weapon slipped from his grip and shot across the room, lodging into the wood next to the arm that was now reaching for his bag.

With a sudden shriek, the figure was gone. Darius darted to the door and into the hall just as the heel of a boot disappeared around the corner. With his breath challenged, Darius returned to his room, slamming and then leaning heavily against the door. He slid to the floor where he sat in a daze. Looking up at the sword, he almost laughed at his own luck.

Darius tossed his bag next to the bed and wedged the chair underneath the handle of the door. And this time, he made sure the lock was latched. He walked to the window and peaked from behind the curtains. The moon had barely moved from its last position. The night was still young.

He lay back in the bed and stared at the ceiling. Surely it was only some common thief who noticed his bag when he came in. But he was sure he had locked the door. No problem. His blunder with the sword saved his belongings and possibly his life, and now the room was secure. What he needed most was a good night's sleep.

The next morning, Darius washed his face, gathered his belongings, making sure to grab his gloves, and went back downstairs. The inn housed fewer patrons in this early hour, which was perfectly fine with him. Some of the faces he'd seen before seemed even less pleasant than Mrs. Keedle's, if that were possible. Darius chuckled.

He returned the key to the bartender and plopped down at small table in the corner where he could have some privacy yet ample view of the establishment. He discreetly looked at the shoes beneath the tables, trying to recognize the heel, but it could have been any number of boots. His thoughts were distracted as the young lady, whom he had seen serving food the night before, approached him.

"What'll it be?" she asked, pencil in hand.

"Uh…"

"We don't have any."

"I mean…" Darius again fingered the coins in his bag, thankful it had not been stolen.

The waitress peered up from her pad. "You want the special. One bronze."

That Darius could manage. "Sure."

The girl whisked around and in no time returned with a plate of bacon and eggs, toast and butter. It was a wondrous sight, and Darius relished each bite, fighting the urge to inhale the meal in one quick gulp. The awkwardness of wearing gloves helped him attain that goal. When he was done, he left a small tip and walked back to the bar.

"Need another room?" the tender asked.

"No, sir. But could you tell me what is farther up the mountains? I noticed an interesting light up that way." Darius almost threw up at his inept attempt to sound relaxed.

At first, the bartender squinted his eyes until only the folds of skin were visible around them and leaned in close toward Darius. Darius forcefully swallowed a small bit of bacon he dislodged from one of his teeth and attempted a weak smile. To Darius's surprise, the bartender threw himself upright and began to guffaw so loudly, he almost seemed to choke on his own laughter.

"Have a taste for adventure, do ya'?"

Darius feebly chuckled. "Uh, yeah. That's me."

"Didn't think you were from around here. How'd you get past the barrier?"

"Barrier?" Darius faked a boisterous laugh. "That was a barrier?"

"Really, now?" The bartender snorted and slapped Darius firmly on the shoulder. "Well, you don't want to be going too far up into the mountains. That light you saw? You'd best stay clear of that. Our sorcerer doesn't much care for visitors, and he wouldn't take too kindly to a scrawny thing like yourself intruding on his personal space. I wouldn't go past the first ridge if I was you."

"Oh, I wouldn't dream of it. I was just curious.

Thought I'd do some camping before I settle into a job somewhere."

"Yeah...since your *old* boss is dead," laughed the bartender.

Darius feigned an amused smile and said, "You wouldn't happen to know if anything's available, would you?"

The bartender eyed Darius, and Darius struggled to maintain his smile. But after a moment, the large man seemed more relaxed as Darius continued to lie.

"There's a farm south of town a ways," nodded the man to some direction over his shoulder. "Man recently lost his son to, uh, well let's just say his son and the sorcerer had a bit of a disagreement. Anyways, he could use some help with his fields. 'Bout the only one left growin' stuff around here."

"South. Thanks."

Darius collected his belongings and headed for the door when the innkeeper called from behind. "Campin', huh? There's a deer path just west of town. Leads to a nice flat spot midway up the mountain. Makes for gooood campin'...or huntin'."

Darius turned. "Thanks. Sounds perfect."

Closing the door behind him, Darius exhaled the anxiety that had steadily filled his lungs with each new lie. This he was not accustomed to. He couldn't remember the last time he'd lied. All he could think of was the small fib he'd told when he was seven—something about cookies—but he'd received a stiff spanking for that. No. Lying was not in his nature, and he was glad to be rid of it.

He turned left and headed toward the mountains. He found the path the bartender suggested easily enough, and the clusters of trees that skirted the mountains proved no great obstacle to maneuver. Hours later, Darius reached the flat spot. The barkeep was right; this would be a great spot to camp, but that was not Darius's intentions. Still early in the day, he would pass as much distance between himself and the small village as he could, each step bringing him closer and closer to his destination, each step binding him to the task to which he was committed.

Darius headed for the upper side of the clearing and was about to enter a slender path he assumed had been forged by wild animals when a large figure bounded in front of him, blocking his way.

"And just where do ya' think you're goin', lad?" asked the unshaven man.

"I, uh—"

"Not so fast," came another voice from behind. Darius turned to face a man who bore a striking resemblance to one he'd seen in the bar the night before.

As Darius inched his way to a midpoint between the two, other men emerged from numerous hiding places and into the clearing, surrounding him with a web of teethy grins and bulging muscles.

Darius reached for his sword and slowly unsheathed it. "Look. I have no beef with any of you. I'm just exploring a bit…before taking a job."

"Likely story."

Before Darius could negotiate any further, the men lunged forward. Darius swung with the sword, managing to keep a few at bay, but a hand from behind grabbed Darius around the neck and pummeled him to the hard ground, seizing the sword as he fell. Another man jerked the bag from Darius's shoulder, flipping him face down.

With the side of his face planted in the dirt he could just make out a figure, hidden behind a thick bush at the edge of the clearing, with white hair!

His attackers released him and began throwing his bag from one to the other, toying with him.

Darius jumped up and stared at the bush. "Sira?"

"Sira? Who's Sira?" asked one of the men as he held out Darius's bag, taunting him.

"Please! You can't do this!" Darius pleaded, and he squinted at the thick bush—the white flash was gone, or maybe it had never been there at all? He couldn't decide, but he had no time to reflect.

"Oh, yes we can. And we did," laughed the unshaven man.

Darius began chasing the men as if he were some child in a bully's game of keep-away, zigzagging this way and that as the bullies tossed the wanted belongings to and fro. Shaken, he thought of the book on spells. He closed his eyes and remembered the words to cause a tremor that just might knock the thieves off their feet.

A hard slap on the ground caused the mountain itself to shake, and Darius and the others were upended.

"Did you do that?" asked one of the thieves, a nervous edge in his voice.

Darius grinned, and he stood a bit taller. His lip trembled in self-awe. "I did."

"Actually, I did."

A ring of fire instantly blazed above—all of them, even Darius, crouched low to the ground.

"And I believe the boy is right. You can't do this. Return his belongings!" Prydon marched amid the fallen group as the men clambered for footing.

The unshaven man attempted to run away, carrying Darius's sword, but Prydon tripped him easily with his tail. He roared and snapped at the man as he stood to run.

"I'll take that, if you don't mind." Prydon picked up the sword and used his tail to aid the man in a quick descent down a not-so-clear path.

Another man who clenched Darius's bag to his chest paused with wide eyes, staring at Prydon.

Prydon raised a brow. "Well? Would you prefer my aim be true? Of course, I have no desire to roast the bag…"

The man hastily dropped the bag and stumbled after his cohort in crime. Others scattered as Prydon breathed fire along the side of the clearing, setting several trees ablaze.

Soon only Darius and Prydon remained. Darius stood and, as he took back his things, could think of nothing to say. His ego was deflated as he realized his attempt at the spell had failed, that it was only the landing of Prydon which so violently shook the ground, and that had it not been for Prydon, he most likely would have been beaten and left for dead by the thieves.

"Climb on," Prydon said, no patience shrouding his words.

Darius began to obey, but backed away as warmth

again filled his head and unwanted pride took over. "No. I can't! I have to find the book!"

Prydon let out a shrill cry, and he lunged at Darius. "Look, you fool. You are coming with me whether you like it or not!" With that, Prydon scooped Darius up and threw him between the two ridges right above his shoulders. "And I suggest you hold on!"

Darius couldn't even begin to protest. In the blink of an eye, he was in the air until the clearing below was nothing but a speck of red where the fire continued to burn. His body began to slip, and he grabbed Prydon's ears...brows.... Darius wasn't sure.

"Not there!" Prydon rasped. "My neck."

Darius's arms could not reach the full expanse of Prydon's neck, but he leaned down, nestled between the ridges, and held on with all the strength he could muster.

Dipping up, down, and around, Darius lost all sense of direction, and when the flight finally stopped, Prydon unceremoniously deposited Darius on a rocky patch of bare ground overlooking a small valley.

"Ouch!" Darius screamed, but Prydon ignored him and began to walk solemnly toward the edge of the small shelf of land on which they stood.

"Hey! You! How dare you! Take me back this instant!" Darius yelled, almost immediately regretting his harsh words.

As quickly as Darius spoke, Prydon lunged and snorted angrily in Darius's face, his dragon's breath muggy against Darius's skin. Darius halted and jumped back. Prydon's eyes narrowed, his chest heaving as if he would release a wave of hot fire, but he said nothing. Prydon turned and continued on his way. For a short moment, Darius hesitated and then quickened his pace. He could do nothing but follow Prydon, avoiding the slow-swaying tail and the spikes that adorned it.

Prydon stopped, gazing forward as if staring at a distant time and place. Darius followed his eyes and settled on a village below, left in ruins. Many rains washed away the blackness of fires, yet wrinkles in dissolved wood echoed their violent past.

"What happened here?" Darius's voice was quiet.

"This is your village."

"What? Brandor?" Darius scoured the area but could find no signs of the gentle slopes or trickling stream with which he was so familiar. Puzzled, he looked up at Prydon. "No, it's not."

"Not Brandor. This was your father's village…and yours."

"But—"

Prydon's ice blue eyes turned hauntingly toward Darius. "This is the destruction that Klavon left when, after killing your father, he could not find you and your mother. This is what Klavon is capable of. You cannot hope to defeat such strength, and it is why you must be trained."

"But, I can't. I have to get that book before Brandor vanishes," said Darius.

"If you die, Brandor has no hope at all."

"I won't die!" Darius snapped, but his words were weak, and he felt no sincerity in them.

Prydon's eyes flashed and he lunged toward Darius,

lowering his snarled teeth directly in front of Darius's face. "You couldn't even stand up against a small band of thieves! You think you can handle Klavon?" Prydon's chest heaved, and the rumble in his chests seemed as if at any moment, fire would end it all. Instead, Prydon growled, and the rumble subsided. With a glare, he forced Darius to the edge of the ridge with one of his clawed hands and held him fast. "Look at it! This is what Klavon did! This is his power! You are nothing compared to this!"

Darius lowered his head, his eyes shifting from the ground beneath him to the ruins below.

Prydon leaned his head in close to Darius. "If you die, you lose not only Brandor and your mother, but you destroy the whole reason your father died. To protect you."

"But this curse...and more of Brandor is vanishing every moment."

"There is nothing you can do about that...yet. You must learn to defeat Klavon. You have no choice."

Darius stared at the ruins. Several minutes passed, and Prydon stood quietly by his side. He thought of Brandor, barren spaces hollowed out where structures once stood. He thought of the mire, and the strange presence that had saved him. He thought of the field of dead stalks and the young woman who came to his rescue. He thought of the inn and his blunder with the sword that had been the only reason he still retained his bag, that and Prydon. He thought of the thieves...and the spell that didn't work.

Then he thought of the warmth that filled him with a desire to defy Prydon. It inched its way back into his mind. It seemed so...strange...as if it possessed some control over him—control he didn't want it to have. Against his will and better judgment, he wanted to argue further.

Darius closed his eyes and shook his head, fighting the words that wanted to roll off of his tongue. They finally faded, and he sighed. "You're right."

Chapter Nine

The Foiled Plan

Klavon's anger roared like a violent ocean. "Why did you not stop him?" he yelled.

Sira stood motionless, almost passive in her response. "I tried. The thieves interfered—easy enough to deal with—and although my influence was sound, Prydon—"

"Prydon be cursed to the depths of the underworld! I care not of Prydon!"

Klavon seethed. His plans had been thwarted by a band of common thieves? Had it not been for them, the dragon would not have come…and his prize would be close upon his doorstep, awaiting his final breath!

"Bring them to me! Now!" he screamed, and Sira vanished.

He stood atop his courtyard next to the pile of bones, fresh still from his last victim. In anger, he flung his staff, and the pile turned to ash. No more would he clutter his surroundings with trivial casualties. His sight was now set firmly on only one—and now he was long gone to train. That changed everything.

A while later, the thieves stood before him, Sira

standing behind. The time had only served to heighten his anger, and he turned, a red light glowing from the end of his staff.

"Please, sir," one thief said. "We knew not what he meant to you."

The others nodded, stepping back from their leader.

Klavon laughed cynically, and then his face turned to stone. "Sira, go and prepare my lab. It will take strong magic to break into the training grounds."

Sira nodded and headed into the castle, her cat-creature following.

"Sir, we didn't…"

"We were going to bring you the spoils!"

The thieves begged for mercy and pleaded their ignorance, but with a wave of Klavon's staff, their bodies shook.

There was no need for Fraenir. Clutching frantically to each other, the band of men was lifted off the ground. As their cries rang through the air, the thieves were no more, joining the others as ash in the wind—meddlesome fools!

Sira watched as Klavon prepared the serum. Only a sprinkle on the barrier, and she would be able to slip inside undetected—so Klavon believed. Of course, no one had ever tried, and if discovered, there would be no mercy shown by Barsovy to the intruder. Barsovy was an enigma and the keeper of the fields…and he was most powerful. Sira would not dare to confront him.

She wasn't concerned, however—she had other plans. Ever since she had met Darius, saved him from the field of dead stalks to gain his trust, she wondered at Klavon's intention to kill the boy…disagreed. A klutz for sure, but there was something else she detected in this handsome youth. He could be of use to Klavon, she was certain—of use beyond death.

"Here," said Klavon, interrupting her thoughts.

"Are you certain this is wise?" she asked.

"You doubt my ability again?" asked Klavon. "I certainly hope this isn't becoming a habit. That would be most unfortunate…for you."

"I do not doubt. All of my intentions are to further your power and reign. As always, I am your servant," she replied.

Klavon laughed. "You are servant to no one. We both know that."

"My allegiance then. I merely wish to ensure that you do not become detected, bring upon yourself and your realm the wrath of the one called Barsovy."

"Barsovy is nothing. Parlor magic. No, this will work. And you will convince the boy to continue on his quest for the book—without training." A satisfied sneer crossed Klavon's lips as held up his sword, turning it slowly in his hands. "Blood is such a beautiful shade of red…"

Sira watched her master as he obsessed. She recalled the first time she had met him—at the end of the blade that had just killed a powerful sorcerer in whose service she had been attached.

It was true. She was servant to no one, and although she was willing to align herself with a sorcerer, it was selfish. Her talents were many, but the energy she absorbed when aligned with a sorcerer? She was almost as powerful as…a wizard.

She could not, however, turn against the one whose energy on which she relied, not that she would ever want to. However, Klavon's decision to kill the boy could not be allowed.

Klavon, still turning the blade in his hand, nodded toward the serum. Sira bowed in turn, quietly picked it up, and left.

Chapter Ten

The Valley

Gusting waves of icy cold brushed past Darius. The blanket tied about his neck did little as the dragon soared higher and higher into the sky. Drops of moisture stung at his face, and his breath was challenged by the thinning air. The clouds had long since thickened, and it seemed hours since the ground below had been visible. Darius would have welcomed the swamp or even the dead stalks that had pounded him outside Klavon's kingdom to the frigid air that now whipped past his shivering body.

"Where are you taking me?" Darius screamed, his lips quivering from the severe cold, but Prydon didn't answer.

Darius wasn't surprised. Even he could barely make out his own voice amidst the bursts of wind howling past his ears. Or was it the echo of his own thoughts as he attempted to yell the words? He couldn't be sure. He was numb—mind, body, and soul. Darius gave up his desire to communicate and buried his face between the ridges on Prydon's back.

He closed his eyes and tried to envision a warmer place. His thoughts settled on the gentle slope of land above his home in Brandor, where he would spend lazy afternoons lying on the soft hillside and chewing the sweet end of a tall piece of grass. When he was a young boy, his mother would pack a lunch, and they would lie in the grass together and pick out shapes in the clouds. They would make a game of it to see who would be the first to discover a flower or a ship or some other predetermined shape. He wondered why they ever stopped playing the game.

Darius opened his eyes and looked at the thickness of clouds around him. There were no shapes here—no flowers, no ships—only the expanse of white fog as they flew through the mass of unending cold. His heart ached for home, and his arms throbbed from clenching Prydon's massive neck.

Just when he thought he might lose his grip, his friend began to descend. Soon, the white sea of clouds became a ceiling, and a small shelf of snow-covered land appeared. Most of it was surrounded by walls of mountainous rock which rose sharply and faded into the blanket of clouds above. On one side, however, a lower curtain of clouds replaced the mountain, and the shelf vanished deeply into an abyss of fog below. The entire powdery white shelf appeared to be floating in a bubble of clouds.

As they neared the ground, a wave of energy washed over Darius's body. The pulse almost felt warm, but he couldn't be sure as it faded as quickly as it had come.

"What was that?" he asked, this time clearly heard.

"A barrier." Prydon's landing was markedly less

rough than when Darius had been dumped onto the plateau above his father's village. This time, Prydon delicately placed Darius on the soft, snowy ground.

"Barrier for what?" Darius looked around at the walls of rock and the drop-off on the opposite side.

"A barrier to prevent those unwanted from entering here."

"Like the one Klavon has."

"That," Prydon frowned in distaste, "is a feeble attempt at best. This, however, is the real thing."

"I thought you said Klavon was powerful." It was a sincere comment—Darius's voice echoed his trust in Prydon's previous words of Klavon's strength.

Prydon nodded, "Yes. He is, but the barrier that surrounds this place is beyond the ability of any wizard or sorcerer. It was formed long ago by the combined power of many wizards. Even Klavon could not match—or penetrate—this."

Darius shuddered. "It's freezing! With all that power, you'd think they'd have blocked out the cold weather as well." The bitter wind stung like needles against his bare arms, and Darius gripped the blanket more tightly in a vain attempt to offer himself protection.

Prydon's lips rose slightly on one side, and he chuckled as he turned and headed for the rock wall. Darius stumbled along behind him, knee deep in snow and falling with every step. He was pleased when the mountain wall blocked the wind.

Prydon turned behind a large boulder and disappeared. Darius quickened his pace, and as he rounded the large rock, he stood at the opening of a rather large cave, at least large enough to hold him and Prydon with room to spare. Prydon nodded him in, and Darius entered, standing next to his friend. It was still terribly cold, but at least he no longer felt like a slave being flogged by his master with an icy whip.

"So now what?" he asked, picking up a stone and letting it supinely roll from his palm. It fell to the ground, creating an echo as it cascaded over a small pile of rocks.

Prydon ignored his question and stared at the farthest wall. A low rumble began to shake bits of rock loose from the ceiling above, and Darius instinctively bolted for the opening of the cave. A large tail slapped in front of him, blocking his path.

"Watch," Prydon said, standing firm and calm as if it was the most natural thing in the world to have pieces of rock falling all around.

Darius turned, and with the rumbling noise of waves crashing in the ocean, the back of the cave slid open to reveal a lush, green valley. A gentle wind caressed the cold off of his skin, and Darius leaned toward the entrance, breathing in the heat and filling his lungs with the warm breeze. It was the first time in hours he'd felt any relief from the bitterness.

As he followed Prydon into the valley, the wall behind them sealed shut, leaving no sign that it had ever been opened. Darius stopped and stared out into a vast valley. Clusters of trees filled with birds chirping in the sunlight scattered his view. Colorful flowers grew everywhere, and even more colorful butterflies fluttered about. A large lake resided in the center, glistening like jewels as the sun above in the cloudless sky danced across the surface. Shelves of mountain all around were draped with green vines, atop several of which small buildings sat. Higher up, the shelves appeared vacant, but Darius couldn't tell from this vantage. He envied the birds that flew across the sky and longed to have Prydon join them so he could witness the scope of what spread out before him.

"What are you doing here?" An old man sprang in front of Darius's view, causing Darius to stumble and fall back against the ground. "What do you want?"

Darius sat dazed, perplexed by this odd man who appeared from nowhere. He didn't seem to be of any significance. In fact, he looked the part of a common gardener. The man was dressed in a loose, pale green shirt that tied at the neck. His pants were brown with a drawstring waist. About his neck was fastened a thin, tan cloak. His hair fell far below his shoulders, tied back in a single ponytail and gray from root to tip. Darius couldn't make out the color of his eyes as they were merely slits burning into Darius's face as he looked up, still sitting on the ground where he'd fallen.

"Well? What do you want?" The old man's eyes widened as if he were trying to force an answer from Darius's lips, and they flashed ash gray in the sunlight.

"I…" Darius paused. All words had been yanked from his tongue.

"He is here to train," answered Prydon, stepping toward the man.

"Humph. Where is his staff? He has a blade,

but…that is not his blade to have!" The old man pulled a long stick from where Darius knew not and began jabbing it at him. "Thief! Scoundrel!"

"Hey!" Darius shouted. He threw up his arms in an effort to shield himself from the invading stick. Prydon stepped in front of him, but the man simply persisted in stabbing the stick at Prydon.

Darius stared, completely befuddled by this ridiculous man. Watching him poke Prydon with the staff was almost amusing. The dragon stood like a fortress being pelted with toothpicks. But somehow Darius could sense that residing inside this old man existed fortitude beyond this pretense of weakness.

"Who are you?" he asked from behind Prydon.

"Why have you brought this phony to my valley?" the man screamed, still jousting with the dragon's massive thighs.

"Enough, Barsovy! You are not the fool you pretend to be!" Prydon pounded the ground with one of his clawed hands, and the old man halted.

Barsovy's eyes returned to the slits Darius earlier witnessed, and he moved closer to Prydon. The man's stance confirmed Darius's earlier thoughts. No longer a small, feeble man, Barsovy stood tall in front of Prydon. Prydon lowered his head until their noses almost touched.

"I know you, but this cannot be. Confirm your identity and your right to be here?" asked Barsovy, his lips closing to match the slits in his eyes.

"I am Prydon, old friend."

Barsovy stared at Prydon. A thin smile touched his

lips and he bobbed his head in agreement. "I heard you were dead."

"Obviously, I am not," replied Prydon.

"And for that I truly am thankful. How did you—" Barsovy began, but his question was cut off by a quick snap of Prydon's jaws.

"Our discussion is about the boy. Let us save talk of my exploits for another time, shall we?"

Barsovy rubbed his bearded chin and nodded toward Darius. "And why would you bring me a child of no real significance to train? A thief at that—a thief marked by evil."

Darius's eyes shot to his glove-covered hand and as quickly back to the old man's face. "But...how could you know this?"

Prydon turned to Barsovy. "Darius is the son of Thyre. He is no thief. He has been charged with saving Brandor from the sorcerer Klavon, and the sword was a gift from the town as their wizard has long since been gone."

"Utter nonsense. Gone is not the proper choice of words. Did he not leave protection? A book, I believe?" A strict brow arose on Barsovy's forehead, and Darius was overcome with the impression that the old man was blaming him for the wizard's strange disappearance.

Prydon sighed, seeming to read the same accusatory impression. "Klavon has stolen the book. The town is fading. And the boy knows nothing of the wizard who once resided in Brandor."

"That sword was not theirs to give, and the boy's ignorance is no excuse." Barsovy walked in small circles, staring at the ground and stroking his beard. He halted and grunted. "And what of the mark?"

"You know as well as I that he has been touched by Klavon, although for reasons I do not know. Perhaps to force him into confrontation."

"Does the boy know what that means? Does he know the dangers that he must face to overcome such a challenge, if indeed such a challenge can be overcome?" Barsovy's head swung back and forth, and his tongue ran across his bottom lip.

"He knows enough, and he will learn more, but for now he must be trained. You and I both know the consequences if he were to face Klavon without proper instruction."

Barsovy continued with his circling and again halted, snapping his staff firmly against the ground. "Has he had any training?"

"No."

Darius's mind was a blur. "Wait a minute! I've read some on spells." Darius's voice faded and his words slowed. He recalled the failed attempt when he had been confronted by the vagabonds and the necessity of rescue by Prydon at the uselessness of his words.

Barsovy continued his questioning. "Why does he not have his staff?"

Were it not for his recent acknowledgement of his own failure, Darius might have been offended by the inconsiderate tone Barsovy maintained. Nevertheless, it was irritating to say the least to have this old man continually speak of Darius as if he were not standing three feet away.

"As I said," answered Prydon, "he knows nothing of his past. Do you not agree that it would be dangerous to ask him to retrieve the staff at this time?"

"Hmm. Dangerous for whom? All who train here must first face danger." Barsovy stroked his beard even harder, running his hand over his face and head until settling on the back of his neck. He stood there several moments, almost as if he wasn't breathing until a heavy sigh broke the silence. "I will have a word with you alone, Prydon."

Darius's mouth shot open, but Prydon nudged him. "Patience. I know that is a difficult task for you, but trust me. It will be all right."

Several paces away, Prydon stood tall above the old man. They spoke in hushed tones. Occasionally, Barsovy would glare at Darius. Other times, one of his gray brows would raise and he'd shake his head, although Darius didn't know if the nods were for or against him. With one last nod the old man turned and walked away. Prydon made no attempt to follow and waited respectfully until Barsovy vanished. Then he turned and in a few paces stood once again at Darius's side.

"So? What happened?"

"You will train." Prydon held out a pair of coarse leather gloves. "Barsovy has demanded that you wear these at all times."

"Why?" asked Darius as he removed his old gloves and replaced them with those Prydon offered. They reached almost to his elbows.

"Your gloves have no power to shield your mark from the curiosity of unwanted eyes, at least not all of them."

"Oh, so that's how Barsovy knew about the mark," Darius said, "because he's a wizard."

"Yes." Prydon nodded agreement. "These, however, possess an enchantment that will guard your secret. Barsovy does not wish the others to know of your mark, and I concur."

"Others?" Darius glanced up at one of the shelters on a nearby ledge.

"There are others in this valley who are training. Now follow me." Prydon began walking down a wide path, and Darius followed.

"Will I get to meet them?" The prospect of making friends, real friends, ones who were wizards like him, was interesting to Darius.

"With your situation, your mark, and Klavon, that would be unwise. No, we will remain as isolated as possible while we are here."

A small amount of disappointment entered Darius's thoughts, but Prydon's response did not bother him. He was used to being alone, having grown up that way in Brandor, and was content to leave it be. "Where are we going?"

"We will take our residence in one of the shelters on the far mountain cliff, as far away from the other students as possible. Now follow but say nothing more. Any conversation between us can wait until we reach our lodging."

"No talking?" Darius was certain he must have

misheard his friend.

"No talking," Prydon responded slowly.

"None?" Darius questioned. "But why? I have so many questions."

Prydon stopped and turned to face Darius. His massive jaws were clenched tight as if forcing patience. "Keep your eyes forward and hold your head high and with confidence as we will soon be passing others in training. It would be unwise to appear weak in their eyes. Can you do that?"

"Yes, of course. But I still don't understand why?"

Prydon sighed and scratched his forehead with one of his claws. "You are unfamiliar with all that is happening here, right?"

"Well…"

Prydon raised his brow. "Asking me questions would be perceived by others as lack of knowledge. A lack of knowledge would be perceived as a grave weakness. In this world, knowledge is power."

Darius's face wrinkled with confusion.

"Darius, you have no way of knowing which of these wizards will become evil and which will not. Any weakness you show now will be remembered and used to their advantage, should they believe it in their best interest to do so. Another's weakness is often exploited by those seeking power."

Darius nodded slowly and bit the side of his lip. He no longer felt an equal to his peers, potential friends with those like himself, but beneath them. He came to this valley with nothing, neither knowledge nor equipment. All he possessed were a book on spells he couldn't cast and a second hand sword which wasn't even his to have.

Prydon appeared to read his mind. "You will learn, and you already have one advantage of your own."

Darius's brows pulled together, and his head jolted ever so slightly back. "I do?"

Standing taller, Prydon smiled. "Yes. You are not alone. You have me. And that is no small feat, even among wizards."

Darius returned Prydon's smile, and Prydon turned back down the path. Following a few paces behind the spiked end of Prydon's tail, Darius obeyed, his lips secured in silence.

Soon they passed along the edge of the pond. It was as soothing as when Darius looked upon it from afar, and sunlight continued to play in the ripples that floated across its surface. Small barren fields bordered the path around the water's edge, sectioned off by trees intertwined with thick vines. A sturdy fence could not have provided such privacy.

In each alcove there was a young man, close to his age, and.... Was he seeing this right? Barsovy? Several Barsovies? He recalled Prydon's words and held his tongue. Instead, he concentrated on the dragon's tail, strained to breathe steadily, and absorbed what was around him only through his periphery.

Some students stood in conversation with their master. Others were sparring Barsovy, and still others sat at rest, watching Barsovy perform some spell or maneuver. On occasion, a student would stop cold and stand in awe as they stared first at Prydon and then at Darius. To this, the Barsovy in their presence would soundly rap them across the head with his staff and yell choice words of which Darius could not quite make out.

Darius clenched his jaws together and successfully, albeit with extreme difficulty, resisted the urge to inundate Prydon with a thousand questions. It seemed forever they continued with this facade, but in time, they exited the opposite side of the valley, leaving the pond and training fields behind, and were again passing along a shaded path.

Darius opened his mouth to speak, but Prydon looked back and shook his head. Silence was his companion until they arrived the base of a small cliff that reached at least fifty feet up. Prydon nodded toward a rough ladder, and Darius began climbing. A rush of wind blew against his back followed by a thud from above, which gently shook the ladder he was climbing, and Darius knew that Prydon had already flown the ascent and had landed somewhere above.

By the time Darius finished his climb, his limbs were aching, having already been weakened from the long, cold ride. But the scenery was tremendous, and he walked to where Prydon was perched and sat down.

"Here," said Prydon, handing Darius a small plate of food. Darius's brows raised and Prydon chuckled. "Barsovy wants food on your stomach before tomorrow. It will be a long day for you."

Darius took the food and stared at the scene that stretched before him. He would have immediately thrown questions at Prydon, but the view held his tongue. He breathed the fragrant air and gazed out at a valley so vast and so beautiful that for a moment he never wanted to leave. He wanted to forget his troubles, forget his trials...forget his failures. But thoughts of his mother entered his mind.

Darius wondered if she was hanging clothes as she always did, or was she sitting in their house, crying for him to return? Were the people of Brandor showing her any kindness in her sacrifice as they frantically awaited his success? Or perhaps they were expecting his failure, watching their neighbors disappear and wondering if they would be next. And here he was, helplessly waiting to be trained. With all the questions Darius had repressed as they passed through the valley, one thought emerged. "Prydon? Will I ever be able to save Brandor?"

Prydon leaned down, his muzzle very near Darius's face. "As careless as you may seem, you are much like your father. And although I cannot say as to whether you will succeed or not, I will say this. Brandor could not have chosen more wisely. You are their best hope."

Darius paused. *Their best hope.* With Prydon so close, Darius almost believed the words his friend spoke. But he wondered if his conviction in that strength would hold firm if Prydon were not near. Still, there was no alternative, and Darius tried to focus on his current task—to learn all he could in this strange and wonderful place with an even stranger master, Barsovy.

"Prydon, why were there so many Barsovies as we passed through the valley?"

Prydon laughed. "Oh, trust me! There is only one

Barsovy! But he does manage to spread himself around quite easily for one so old, wouldn't you say? Now, it is time to rest. We can talk more tomorrow."

"But I have so many questions. I mean—"

"Rest first. Experience will answer most of your questions and probably much better than my words can explain." Prydon stood and walked to a small structure. "Good night, Darius."

Darius wanted to protest, but when he opened his mouth, he had nothing to say. His shoulders slumped, and he simply said, "Good night, Prydon. Thank you."

"You are welcome, my young friend," said the dragon.

Darius entered the hut and looked around. Only the bare basics decorated the modest shelter: a cot, a small wooden table, a pitcher of water, a cup, an empty basin, and a chair. Two windows opened on each side, but the back wall was the mountain itself into which smooth ledges, decorated with books, formed shelves. Darius picked one up and thumbed through it but returned it to its shelf. He looked outside at the soft glow of light. Prydon was already curled up, the sun setting behind him.

Although it was not quite dark, Darius was exhausted. His body melted as he lay down on the soft cot. For a few minutes he stared up at the ceiling, watching a moth as it lazily awoke from its sleep, bouncing from crevice to crevice, readying itself for a flight in the moonlight. Darius's eyes drew shut and his breathing slowed. His mind relinquished his thoughts, and he fell into welcome darkness.

Chapter Eleven

The Barrier

Sira reached the edge of the barrier. Although she knew she was bound to try, she would not convince the boy to come back. No. His power must grow in his strength as a wizard. Only then would he be able to stand at Klavon's side—not as his equal, but as his dedicated servant—the curse complete in its corruption.

And her power would be secure. With two wizards from which to pull, she would be unstoppable. She was a master of manipulation and would guide them both exactly as she wished, shrouded in the deception of her allegiance. It would be a perfect arrangement, and the three would coexist quite nicely.

And, of course, the boy was attractive, perhaps a suitable distraction from day to day business. With her guidance, he might even become strong. She smiled as she thought of him, again, slipping into the mire. Yes, she would guide him, and Klavon would be pleased.

Sira held out the vial and poured the contents onto the barrier. Nothing happened. She tried yet again, but as before, the barrier held strong, not even a hint that the serum had any effect.

"Of course. Even Klavon is not all-powerful." She laughed. "No matter."

Sira softly whispered mysterious words only she could understand, raised her head to the sky, and became a white wisp of wind, penetrating the barrier.

She floated about, unbeknownst to Barsovy and the others—a trait of her kind that allowed anonymity beyond compare and a trait she would never divulge to Klavon.

When she found Darius asleep, she lingered, suspended above him. She could invade his dreams, create a world so real, so sensual that he would be defenseless against even the slightest suggestion, but no. Instead, she floated just above his lips until she could feel his breath against her clouded form…and waited.

Chapter Twelve

The Training Field

Darius's body jolted like a dreamer suddenly falling and waking with a sharp jerk, only he wasn't dreaming. He landed with a thud, his face flat on the dirt floor and the cot next to him overturned. Outside, Prydon's massive chest heaved as he stood roaring with laughter.

Darius rolled over and smeared his hand across his lips, spitting out the excess dirt and leaving a streak of wet dust behind. "Was that really necessary?"

"Yes," said Prydon, his shoulders square as one who was quite confident in his response.

Darius sat up with his arm resting on one raised knee. "You couldn't find a gentler way to wake me?"

Prydon smirked. "I tried…several times, in fact."

Darius thought of his mother. She often had difficulties waking him and devised some creative, if unpleasant, means of accomplishing her goal: a splash of water, a pop with a belt, a stray cat thrown atop his chest. He looked sheepish. "Sorry."

"Don't be. I quite enjoyed the method. Shall I save time tomorrow and make this a daily ritual?" Prydon was still laughing.

Darius ignored the question, stood, and walked over to the small basin where he washed his face and rinsed his teeth of the grit. "So you're a wizard, huh?" he said, looking into the small mirror perched above the basin. He tilted his face side to side, eyeballing the soft hair that was barely visible along his jaw line. "Well, you don't much look like a wizard."

"Have you ever actually met a wizard?" asked Prydon, his head just poking through the window opening. "Other than Barsovy, of course."

"Well, no. I guess not," said Darius.

"And just what do you believe a wizard should look like?"

"I don't know. Robes. A hat. A long beard, the kind that makes you look distinguished and wise." Darius struck a pose and grinned at his description.

Prydon shook his head and smiled. "And where did you hear such rubbish?"

"Books! Wonderful books! I've learned everything I know from books."

"Hmm," said Prydon. "It is quite apparent that not all books provide truth. And in this case, you need a much better source of instruction. Before you begin, however, you must eat."

Darius stepped out into the morning sun and spotted a table where breakfast awaited. It was a feast compared to anything he'd ever seen. Eggs, bread, meats, fruit—the variety stunned Darius, but he ate quickly, anxious for his first day of training and answers to questions he could only imagine would swim into his mind.

"Slow down," said Prydon. "Your stomach won't appreciate such haste."

Darius tried to slow his pace, but the sensation brewing in his stomach was not an aversion to eating quickly. He was nervous and scared yet excited and hopeful at what awaited him below in his own field. Would he practice spells, use a sword or staff, or even spar with the old man?

Within a short time, he found himself standing at the edge of a vacant alcove at the farthest edge of the training fields. An instant later, Barsovy appeared next to him.

"So, you know some spells," commented Barsovy.

"Yes, sir." Darius's eyes bulged with surprise. He hadn't thought Barsovy was listening when he'd mentioned it the day before.

"Let's give it a go, shall we?"

The old man walked into the clearing and turned to face Darius. Darius glanced at Prydon who nudged him forward, and the training began. Hours later, Darius was quite certain that there was not one spot on his body that hadn't become intimately familiar with the hard sting of the ground beneath his feet.

The entire morning passed slowly, devoted entirely to defense, and Darius failed more times than he succeeded. Until today, he had never been levitated in the air and dropped to the ground, a sensation he gladly would have gone his whole life without experiencing—by mid-morning, he had been knocked backwards, forwards, and any other -wards he could think of, and even some he couldn't have imagined at all. He was aching, and there was no hiding it.

"Very good," said Barsovy. "Now you break for lunch."

Before Darius could acknowledge his master's declaration, Barsovy flourished his hand and vanished. Darius walked, or rather limped, over to where Prydon sat patiently, quietly watching.

"Very good," Darius said, a definite hint of incredulity in his voice. "Very good? Are you kidding me? I stink!"

Prydon sniffed the air. "Well, you could use a bath, but after all of that, did you expect to come out smelling of flowers?"

"That's not what I meant," snapped Darius.

Prydon's head tilted, and a patient smile crossed his scaly lips. "I know what you meant. Truly, did you expect to come in here the first day and own the field?"

In the short span of one morning, what pride Darius did have had been quickly deflated. He sat slowly but then shot back up. Prydon laughed and produced a small pillow.

"Thanks. You always carry a pillow around?" asked Darius, taking the pillow and placing it on the rock as he gingerly sat down next to Prydon.

"Only when I know what is coming, and you're welcome."

Darius began to eat a small lunch, prepared for him by whom he knew not. After a few bites, his hands fell to his lap, still holding his sandwich.

"Prydon?"

A long silence hung in the air before Prydon coaxed him further. "Yes?"

Darius breathed in deeply, trying to suck in words that would adequately express his thoughts. He sighed. "Do you think I'll ever learn enough to beat Klavon?"

Prydon paused, which did not help to alleviate the anxiety that pulsed through Darius's body, then said, "In time, yes."

"In time?" Darius jerked and dropped his sandwich on the ground. "And what of Brandor? And what of this curse?" Darius ripped the glove from his marked hand, exposing the streaks as if showing them to Prydon for the first time.

Prydon glanced toward the other alcoves. "Put your glove back on. No good will come if anyone here is made aware of your mark."

Darius followed Prydon's gaze and looked toward the closest alcove. As other students had been awed by the sight of a dragon, Darius knew they had attracted quite an audience, and the young boy who occupied that alcove was frowning. Darius returned the glove to his marked hand, and the boy turned, slowly disappearing behind the wall of thick trees.

"Let us hope that was just innocent curiosity." Prydon took a claw and patted Darius's leg. "As for your ability regarding Klavon, you will learn, in time."

Darius's heart sank into the pit of his stomach. Why couldn't Prydon just lie?

Prydon nodded slowly; he seemed to read Darius's mind. "That is all I can offer. Unless you would rather I fabricate some statement solely for the purpose of alleviating your concerns."

Darius watched as a small animal shot out from underneath a nearby rock and stole the remains of the sandwich. "No, I guess not."

Prydon sighed. "Darius, what help would it be if I were to tell you that you will learn all you need to know, you will overcome this curse, and you will save Brandor?"

"What help?" Darius turned toward Prydon, his brows raised. "How about a little support here—that I'm not a total failure?"

Prydon smiled, but it faded quickly. His eyes filled with a mist of seriousness. "If I were to deceive you solely for the purpose of filling you with a false sense of security, the urgency which now drives you would be lost. That urgency is what will make the difference between success and failure."

The word *failure* filled Darius's head as Prydon continued.

"Your determination would be weakened, and the swiftness with which you achieve your goals would be diminished, thus decreasing the likelihood that you will save Brandor and yourself."

Darius looked up at Prydon, a sudden wave of defeat etched in his face like a crumpled piece of paper.

Prydon lowered his head close to Darius's face. Those eyes, the ones that had glowed white in the firelight the first night Darius had met him, now shown of azure blue. The gaze caused Darius to freeze.

Prydon spoke with all conviction. "You have the

power and the ability to do this, but I will not fill you with false hope. That is for weaklings, and you are no weakling. You must fight for this as it will not be easy. You must work harder than you have ever worked before, and you must push your body to its limits and then some. Then and only then will you succeed."

Prydon raised his head, and Darius stared at the place where the small animal had earlier fled. He wasn't looking for the creature but looking for answers to all the questions that were crowding his already taxed mind. Beside him, he heard only the steady pace of Prydon's breathing. He soaked in the words Prydon had spoken, and in that instant, he knew what he must do.

Darius's limbs ached, his head pounded. Every inch of his body screamed for relief. He pushed himself up from the rock and handed Prydon the pillow. Stirred by the conviction in Prydon's words, he smiled. "Thank you, Prydon."

"You are welcome."

When Barsovy returned, there were no breaks. Darius accepted everything Barsovy could throw at him and still begged for more.

At nightfall, Barsovy yelled, "Enough! We will stop!"

Prydon chuckled, "Barsovy, you aren't implying that Darius has tired you out, are you?"

Barsovy glared at Prydon. "The boy needs rest, or tomorrow he will be unable to train." With that, Barsovy vanished, and Prydon laughed even harder.

"I want to keep training!" Darius yelled where

Barsovy disappeared, seeing no amusement in what had transpired.

"Barsovy is correct, Darius. You must rest."

"But—"

"But, nothing," interrupted Prydon. "You will rest. Now climb on."

Darius hesitated, but Prydon lowered his body to the ground and gestured to his back. With one last glance at where Barsovy vanished, Darius slid on.

Dinner awaited them when they reached their housing. It was even more extravagant than breakfast, and Darius tore into the meal of grilled meats, breads, steamed vegetables, and potatoes. He hadn't realized how hungry he'd become, and for a moment he thought of the little animal-thief that had taken his lunch. He grinned to himself. That would not happen again.

As the sky became aflame with the setting sun, Darius sat next to Prydon perched at the edge of the cliff and looked out over the valley. He stared at his hand. With the gentle fading of light, the crimson streaks appeared black. Somehow they seemed less threatening that way, but Darius would not be fooled by the illusion.

"Prydon, how do you know I have months before this curse could take over?"

Prydon's head turned toward Darius. "Such a spell must seep into the very soul of the victim."

"Why didn't he use a spell that would work more quickly? I mean, I'm glad he didn't but—"

"Klavon's desire was not to kill you but to consume you. If he possessed knowledge of a spell that was instantaneous but would spare your life, he would have used it, but such spells do not exist, to your advantage. Klavon's spell must tear down your will to resist before it can take over. You are strong, and your soul is well protected deep inside you, but—"

"I will never stop resisting!"

"Do not underestimate the strength of that mark. One who has been cursed as you have been, no matter how strong and determined, can become vulnerable in time."

Darius pounded the ground next to him. "But I won't let it take me. I can't!"

"Your conviction is strong indeed," said Prydon, lowering his face near Darius's, "and as long I have breath in my lungs, I will do whatever I possibly can to ensure that you remain strong. And the first step in doing this—"

"Is to train." Darius looked again over the valley. Small torchlights dotted the land like fireflies. There was no movement except for the brush of wind across the tops of trees. Yet even amidst this peacefulness, his head filled with unease.

As if to respond to Darius's disquiet, a thrash of movement tore through a nearby bush. Darius turned, and a boy's eyes flashed as he pounced toward Darius.

"You!" he screamed. "I was right! You have been marked by evil yet you are allowed to train?"

Prydon immediately poised himself between the two boys, but behind his massive body, Darius could make out his opponent. Almost as tall as Darius, the boy appeared close to his own age. It was the young boy from the training alcove closest to his.

The boy stood with broad shoulders, his face framed with sandy blond hair. Ice blue eyes shot daggers at Darius as he spoke. "Barsovy must be mad! Or...he doesn't even know!"

"Enough, young one," demanded Prydon. "You have no business here."

"And you. A dragon. Never does a wizard train with a dragon!" The boy raised his hand, attempting to strike, but Prydon swung his tail and knocked the boy's feet from beneath him.

Splattered on the ground, the boy quickly stood and attempted again. Prydon flicked him over with his claw, but before Prydon could toss him farther, Darius jumped between them. "Stop! Stop this!" Darius reached down toward the boy, hand outstretched to help him up.

The boy leaned up on one elbow and glared intently at Darius. "You think I would allow you to touch me?"

"Fine," snapped Darius. "Then get up yourself."

"What of your dragon? Won't he just knock me down again?"

"First of all, he's not my dragon. He's a friend, and if you'll cease this idiocy, I'm quite certain he won't bother you again."

The boy stood. "Are you sure? Are you sure your nursemaid won't protect you?" The mocking sneer across his face reminded Darius of the boys from Brandor.

"You insufferable little snot!" said Darius. "How dare you? You don't know me or my situation, yet you come in here as if you own this valley? As if you are in charge? What arrogance! If you ask me, your arrogance is a much more dangerous condition than my current plight!"

Behind him, Prydon laughed and moved farther away as if to let the boys handle their own fight.

Darius glanced back at Prydon and, as a result, caught a solid punch square across his jaw. The fight ensued with the two boys piled one on top of the other, fists flailing. To Darius, it seemed only an instant and Barsovy appeared. With a white crack of light, a spell sent both boys flying through the air in opposite directions. Darius moaned as he landed solidly; no pillow protected him. He rolled over and slowly hoisted himself off the ground, wiping the small trickle of blood from his lip. The other boy was no better, swelling already apparent around his left eye.

"What is the meaning of this?" demanded Barsovy.

"He started it," snapped Darius as he and his newfound enemy both approached their master.

"He's marked!" yelled the boy, pointing at Darius's hand.

"And what concern is that of yours?" demanded Barsovy. "And how would you have known had you not been intruding in this camp? You know the rules. All are to respect each other's privacy."

"I didn't intrude. I saw him earlier in the training fields...at lunchtime. It was as plain as the daylight around us!"

"You removed your gloves?" Barsovy's eyes burned intently into Darius as he spoke with a determined restraint. "You are never to take your gloves off outside of this camp!"

"So...you knew?" stammered the boy. "And...and

yet you let him train?"

"Loklan, be quiet! Now...what to do about this." Barsovy paced, a sight that was becoming quite familiar to Darius. "Young man, you have intruded on things you should have left alone. I will ask you—I will demand of you to utter not one word of this to anyone else. Do you understand? And if you refrain from intruding on others as you have done tonight, that should not be a problem."

Loklan stood for several moments. His lower jaw shifted from side to side as he appeared to be chewing words he couldn't speak. He spat. "Fine."

Barsovy turned to Prydon. "Prydon, I would have thought you, most off all, would comprehend the seriousness of this."

"Prydon? Of Thyre's village?" Loklan's eyes bulged.

"You know of my father?" asked Darius.

"Father?" asked Loklan. "Thyre was your father?"

"Enough of this!" yelled Barsovy, holding both hands up as if to block any words from being spoken further.

Darius could not be sure that it wasn't a spell, but as hard as he tried, he could utter nothing.

"Loklan, you will return to your camp. I will discuss this with you later. And remember, not one word about this to anyone, or the consequences will be dire indeed, I assure you."

The Barsovy Darius now witnessed was no longer the strange Barsovy who had danced at the valley entrance, ridiculously jabbing at Prydon's legs. This Barsovy wasn't even the same Barsovy from the training field, one of incomparable capability yet shrouded with obvious restraint. This Barsovy was truly powerful, demanding in his very presence. Although his hair was still gray and wrinkles still etched his face, years seemed to fade from his whole being. He appeared taller, stronger, commanding in his stance. It was all very intimidating, and spell or no spell, Darius had no desire to utter even one word…or sound. Come to think of it, he almost didn't even want to breathe.

Loklan's arrogance completely faded. With his head lowered and his shoulders sagging, he now seemed a confused child. "Yes, sir," Loklan said, so quietly that Darius almost didn't hear him. With no other words, Loklan turned and retreated into the same bush from which he had previously appeared.

Barsovy waited until Loklan was adequately gone before he spoke. "Loklan's father was Norinar."

"Was?" Prydon asked.

Darius couldn't help but notice the surprise in Prydon's voice. "What? Who's Norinar?"

"Norinar," said Barsovy, "was a very dear friend of your father but regretfully has left this world—a tragic accident which has now left his village unattended while Loklan trains. Loklan went home only long enough to bury his father."

"That is regrettable," said Prydon, and Darius could see the sadness in Prydon's eyes.

"Yes, it is. So you see, Darius, Loklan was raised hearing of Thyre and the atrocities that transpired in your village. He had been told that Miora died, lost in a winter storm, her unborn child suffering the same peril. It is no wonder he is confused. And you have made things very difficult, very difficult indeed, allowing him to learn of your mark." Barsovy's brow became as one, linking over the creased valley formed above the bridge of his nose. His breath became forced.

Darius lowered his head, helpless to offer any resolution to a problem that, in his unguarded anger, he created. "I'm sorry," he said, but the words were blatantly inadequate.

Barsovy shook his head and exhaled a final gust of air. "No matter. I will deal with that right now. As for you, should you remove your gloves and cause such problems again, I will no longer train you. Klavon or no Klavon! Is that clear?"

"Yes, sir," answered Darius. Suddenly, he felt quite young...and foolish.

With a stiff nod, Barsovy vanished.

Darius hesitated only a moment before he quietly said, "I really am sorry, Prydon. And I'm sorry to get you in trouble, too."

Prydon chuckled. "I'm not in trouble, Darius. Barsovy is not my master. But perhaps it would be more prudent for you to temper your emotions, at least when there is a possibility of others to witness your lack of control."

"Perhaps I should temper my emotions regardless," Darius added.

"Words of wisdom?" Prydon smiled. "You are

growing up, Darius."

Darius nodded and said goodnight to his friend, and with no more words, Darius lay down on his cot. He stared up at the ceiling where the moth had appeared the night before, but his eyes were not seeking the small insect. With restlessness consuming his mind, only the fatigue from the day allowed him to finally fall asleep.

Chapter Thirteen

The Wait

Klavon paced. Where was she, and what was taking her so long?

He halted suddenly by the worn table, covered with vials of liquids and mortars of powder, and stared down at the book. The serum would work. He had prepared the potion exactly as required, but it had never been used on such a place.

The valley was secure, and Barsovy was not to be underestimated, but Klavon's vanity prevented him from admitting that the serum was likely to fail. Certainly, with the help of Sira, the potion would allow her to penetrate the barrier and complete her task.

The barrier—and Barsovy—had, since the beginning of time, protected those within. It was the nature of it, and no one had ever questioned it. It simply was, had always been, and would always be.

"But then again," Klavon said, muttering out loud to strengthen his own resolve, "Barsovy has never encountered anyone as powerful as I."

Sira was patient. She floated in the winds above the training fields and watched. Darius was stronger than she'd imagined, and he was learning quickly. She had thought of influencing his thoughts during training, but that was too risky. Being so close to Barsovy, she very likely would have been detected. And Prydon...he was always nearby, and although Fraenir and Klavon were willing to underestimate him, she was not. No. Timing was everything. All she could do was watch and wait.

And now there was another player in the game, a young boy named Loklan. It was almost amusing, watching them fight. Perhaps she could use Loklan's condemnation to sway Darius. With the mark, the curse, no one would ever understand or accept him. Yet if she could convince him that the mark was not a curse but a gift—convince him that Prydon lied to keep him from discovering his real strength—she could secure a place for him beside Klavon.

There was so much to consider. She would watch Darius, and Loklan, and determine the best way to undermine Prydon.

Sleep would be the best choice. Prydon would be unaware, and Darius's mind would be most easily influenced. And the dreams must be effective, planned with utmost care. That night, Sira rode the wind in the starlit sky and decided to let the boy sleep.

Chapter Fourteen

Alone

The next morning, Darius could hardly move. His muscles felt as if they'd been pounded, stretched, and ripped by some enormous giant. There was no need for Prydon to dump him from his cot to wake him as the soreness and unease from the events that occurred the night before induced a light sleep at best.

"Are you ready for another day?" Prydon stuck his nose through the window, grinning at Darius. "Shall I dump you out of bed?"

"No!" Darius said quickly. "No, thank you." He stretched his arms. The pain that shot through his limbs as he raised them made him feel like an old plow that sat too long, rusted, stiff and struggling to turn its blades.

"Do you need assistance?"

"I'm not sure that would help, but if you have some strong beverage that would make the pain go away, that might be welcome." Darius looked through the window at his friend with a devilish grin.

But it wasn't only pain Darius wanted to squelch. His thoughts of Loklan and Klavon lingered. There was some connection between Loklan's family and his own...but that life had been destroyed by Klavon, and only remnants of a shattered past were left behind. An unsettled knot rolled around in the pit of his stomach. Perhaps a strong drink would help that as well.

Prydon laughed. "I don't believe that exists, at least not a drink appropriate for one so young. In any case, the stiffness will subside as you move around."

Prydon was right. A drink would only mask his disquiet. He needed to focus on the task at hand. For the time being, he would place the incident with Loklan and his thoughts of Klavon in the back of his mind. There they would remain, still ever present and a motivation to do well in his lessons yet a shadow in the background, unable to hinder his progress.

By the time Darius reached the training field, the stiffness that earlier crippled his movements had somewhat eased. At least he didn't look like an old man, struggling to walk without his cane. Nevertheless, he was determined not to land as he did the day before and have need of the pillow at lunchtime. No, he was determined to guard that vulnerable—and tender—part of his body.

As training progressed, he jumped, dodged, and made every possible attempt to defend himself. His body screamed in anguish, but Darius was acutely aware that the pain of being shot through the air and dumped to the ground would have been much worse. He was also acutely aware that with each passing day, more of Brandor could be at stake, and his pain in comparison to their loss was nothing.

He clenched his teeth, enduring the soreness until,

as the morning progressed, the stiffness faded. The training was grueling, but he refused to complain. He would not be weak.

When lunchtime came, Prydon handed Darius a sandwich and held out the pillow.

Darius smiled, taking the sandwich. "I'm good," he said as he declined the cushion. He sat down and tentatively tried to find some position that would not remind him of the day before. He shifted, winced, and shifted again.

Through slit eyes, Prydon grinned and handed Darius the pillow. With a sigh, Darius took the offering and sat with more comfort. Nibbling on his sandwich, he glanced at Loklan, who was barely visible at the edge of a group of trees. Darius thought Loklan offered a slight smile, but he couldn't be sure as Loklan quickly turned his head and avoided Darius's gaze.

"I'm quite certain he will say nothing," said Prydon. "Barsovy can be very persuasive."

"Prydon, tell me more about Loklan and his father, Norinar," Darius said, turning his head back toward Prydon.

Prydon paused then began to speak as if his eyes were watching the past. "Loklan's father and your own were close friends, neighboring villages. When Klavon attacked your father, echoes of the battle rang in Norinar's town. There was nothing anyone could do, although they tried. A three day journey. By the time Norinar got there, it was over, and the land rained in ash and embers. The village lay in ruins and no one could be found."

"No one? Were there no survivors? None at all?" asked Darius.

Prydon smiled. "You and your mother. I suppose there were others, but they would have long since scattered. I'm quite certain any who did survive, not wishing to attract Klavon's attention, sought shelter where they could and remained in hiding, perhaps even to today."

"Why in hiding? Klavon wasn't after them."

"Loyalties, even in a village protected by a wizard, are never certain. Knowing Klavon's power and reach, no one would wish to invite his wrath and thus would remain silent. Should he have discovered any who survived, he would certainly seek them out and question them, perhaps even torture them, to discover your whereabouts."

Darius couldn't imagine an entire village gone.

"Norinar searched for days," continued Prydon. "He never found your mother. No one even knew she had already given birth. Stories circulated, but since there was no sign of her—and you—they assumed that even if she had been able to escape the village, she surely had been lost to the harsh elements of winter or even harsher animals of the wild."

"What about you? How does Loklan know you?"

Prydon's head lowered, almost as if pain pulled it toward the ground. "Your father and I were also close friends. That is uncommon for most wizards. In fact, most, as your book concurs, believe we are dangerous and unpredictable. In any case, news of your father's friendship and mine traveled far, much farther than Loklan's village. So it would make sense that he would know of me."

Darius thought back to the day they arrived and the expressions he witnessed as they passed through the valley. "Is that why everyone here seems so surprised to see you? To see a dragon?"

"Yes, my friend. That is exactly why."

Barsovy appeared almost as Prydon spoke. "Prydon, I need to have a word with you."

Darius finished his sandwich while the two walked to the edge of the alcove. He watched as Prydon shook his head and overheard something about not wanting to leave. Certainly Barsovy wasn't talking about sending him away after all because of the fiasco concerning Loklan. Certainly he would be able to complete his training. He looked at the glove covering his hand and chided himself for his lack of control, his lost temper, and his childish response to this entire situation.

Prydon's chest heaved as he released a resigned sigh, and Barsovy, with one last look at Darius, vanished.

Prydon hesitated then walked slowly back to Darius, so slowly that Darius wanted to scream out, "What?" But he didn't. Instead he waited for what seemed an eternity for Prydon to return to the shade.

When Prydon finally sat once again next to Darius, he spoke quietly. "I must leave you for a while."

"What? Why? Is it because of my hand?" Darius's voice sounded like a siren, low at first and then becoming progressively louder. Beads of sweat formed across his forehead as concern gripped his mind. "I won't take the glove off again. I thought he was going to give me another chance."

"Calm down, Darius. You will stay and complete your training, but I must run an errand. I will be back. Three weeks. Perhaps a month."

Darius should have felt relief. After all, he was staying. But the news of his friend's departure…"You're leaving me here? Alone?" Darius looked up at his friend.

"Do not think I am abandoning you. I assure you that if it was not of the utmost importance, I would not go."

Darius's heart dropped. "A month?" He thought of how long a month was. For an instant, he thought of how many lives could be lost in Brandor in that time. But that was quickly overwritten by thoughts of an entire month spent without Prydon by his side. He stared blankly at the ground beneath his feet.

Prydon nudged his shoulder. "You will be very busy, and it is necessary. Trust me."

Darius turned his gaze to the rock where the small animal was hiding and said nothing. He waited for an explanation, but none came. A rumble shook the ground, and as wind churned dust and Darius shielded his eyes, his friend was gone.

That night, Darius ate alone. He picked up a grilled chicken leg and took a small bite. The food sat still in his mouth, and he his eyes set vacantly on the horizon. Even as he attempted to fill his stomach, emptiness grew deeper in his thoughts. He blinked, finished chewing, and swallowed the meat. The food had always been exquisitely prepared, flavors melting in his mouth, but tonight, he tasted nothing. The sun was setting with deep reds and golds, and he thought of Prydon somewhere beyond the borders of this now quiet valley. *You are not alone.* He would hold on to those words, but at the moment they were of little consolation.

In all his time growing up in Brandor, he had no friends, so he was used to being alone. Yes, his mother and Mr. Athus were always there for him, but those were the relationships of a mother and son, a mentor and student. Although he confided in them to a certain extent, it wasn't the same as that confidence one discloses only to a closest friend, the kind of close friend with whom he could earnestly tell his wildest dreams and deepest secrets. Even though Prydon was a dragon, Darius considered him his best friend, and he had grown accustomed to his company. And now he was gone. *You are not alone.* Darius sighed and tossed the chicken leg onto his plate.

That night, Darius sat at the edge of his cot. The evening was warm, warmer than normal, and it sunk into his skin. His eyes shot to his arm where he felt it had entered. Strange, and he rubbed it, unsettled by the sensation. It was almost like in the mire and in Klavon's realm when he had been humiliated as Prydon had to save his hide. It felt…weird, and he threw his legs up on the cot and closed his eyes.

As Darius slept, warmth invaded his mind and dreams haunted him, framed in past events. He was standing in the middle of the charred remains of his father's village. It was quiet, empty, desolate. A shriek rung in his ears, and he threw his hands up to cover them as a fiery beast flew overhead, casting flames upon the already burnt buildings, bringing the fires to life once more. An instant later, the creature and his painful siren were gone, but burning timbers fell around and upon him. Darius tried to dodge them and looked up as he heard the laughter of a young woman. The white-haired girl calmly shook her head from side to side as she mocked him, dancing her way through the village and effortlessly avoiding any falling debris.

"You don't need my help? Suit yourself," she said, and she blew a kiss at him and vanished behind a burning building.

He stood confused, but the shatter of glass drew his gaze to windows of nearby buildings. Thieves poured out, their thunderous laughter filling the air, carrying bags of plundered goods. Darius ran toward them and tried to stop them, but they played a cruel game of keep-away as they tossed the bags over his head.

"Gold? You think you can take my gold?" said one.

One of them held up a sword. It was the sword Mr. Athus had given him.

"That's mine!" Darius yelled. He lunged forward but lost his footing and fell to the ground as a violent thud shook the ground.

The thieves disappeared into thin air, their laughter echoing in the distance. Darius propped himself up and stood slowly. When he turned around, Prydon stood at the end of the street, and Darius relief washed over him. But his relief was short-lived.

"I must leave you for a while," Prydon said flatly.

As Prydon took to the air, Darius heard a sharp laugh emanate from where his friend had just stood. In

Prydon's place towered a man in dark robes, holding a wizard's staff and sword.

"You are alone. And now you are dead," he said, and with one thunderous crack, Darius was thrown backwards.

Darius awoke on the floor of his hut, panting and in a cold sweat. He sat up, propping his bent elbow on one knee, his head resting on the tips of his fingers and thumb. He paused for a moment before getting up and walking to his door. It was still dark, but stars dotted the heavens like fireflies.

He picked up his pillow and went outside. A warm breeze brushed across his face, but it felt good as it evaporated the beads of sweat. Darius stretched out upon the ground and looked up at the sky.

Then he heard it and sat upright. That soft voice in his mind snaked in and out of his thoughts. *Prydon has lied to you. That mark is a gift, not a curse.*

Darius felt the tendrils begin to burn in his hand.

And now Prydon has abandoned you. You are alone, but you don't have to be. Train, and when you return, you will stand at his side, his equal, and he will treat you as his son.

Darius clenched his fists, pressing them into the side of his head. "No!" he shouted, in a fit of anger. "You will not tempt my thoughts."

Tempt? Return and stand with Klavon, and you will no longer be alone. You will stand with power, and—

"Stop!" demanded Darius. He stood and whirled around. In a sudden rage, he halted, threw his hands in the air and yelled, "Stooooop!"

The echo rang through the valley, and resting birds left their nests, filling the dark sky with a shadow of wings. Then silence fell, and Darius stood, breathing rapidly. He glanced side to side, wondering if he would see the warmth as some form, but...the warmth was gone. His mind was at peace, the tendrils in his hand stopped burning, and his beating heart slowed.

The warm breeze became a sweet cool caress against his face, and he closed his eyes. Whatever it was, he knew it would not bother him—not shroud his mind in anger—ever again.

He walked back to his pillow and lay down on the ground, staring into the beautiful starlit sky. Crickets chirped in the background, and he could hear a soft trickle of water from the stream that fed the big lake. A single cloud swirled quickly past, and he thought of his mother and the times they would lay in the fields of Brandor and search for shapes in the clouds. The cloud faded, and the sky was left looking like an indigo sheet of satin dotted with sparkling diamonds. In place of clouds, he used the stars to define his shapes: a flower, a ship...a dragon. Perhaps it was fatigue, but the dragon seemed to soar across the sky, staying within the confines of the valley, keeping diligent watch. He thought once more of Prydon's words—*You are not alone*—and he believed it.

Prydon watched from above. Darius was restless,

but the dragon knew he must not linger. The boy would be fine—Barsovy would make sure of that.

With one last circle, he vanished above the clouds, leaving behind a starlit outline, a gift from Barsovy to offer the boy some solace.

Barsovy was strong, and in a way, he was the human equivalent of Segrath, the one Prydon must now face…if only Barsovy could have offered him some sort of protection. But it could not be helped. Where Prydon had to go was a place beyond even Barsovy's reach…or power.

Chapter Fifteen

The New Plan

Sira was thrown from the valley. How was that possible? The dragon was gone, and the boy was easy prey, a mind so easily manipulated that every dream was exactly as she'd wanted. She stood in shock, angered at his...strength. How had he managed it? Her powers, her influence, had never been denied, except by a sorcerer or wizard of great power. No!

She faded into the familiar wisp and shot toward the barrier, but like a ball thrown against a sturdy wall, she bounced back onto the ground, back into her solid form. His vulnerability had allowed her access before, but now the barrier held fast.

"Agh!" Sira screamed.

How? Why had he stopped her? How dare he! How dare he refuse *her*! Then suddenly her angered face softened, and a devious smile crossed her lips. So he was strong. And with training, perhaps he would become as strong as Klavon. Klavon could not deny the value in that. And with two sorcerers, her strength might be...invincible.

She would remain in allegiance with both of them, and Klavon's realm would be a strong as ever. And she would never have to search for another, with plenty of power available to her.

She hesitated and began pacing, her eyes searching for some distant detail, something she might have missed...but no. Her plan was sound, and if she could convince Klavon to let him live, it could still work.

And in regards to the boy, she may no longer have the ability to enter his mind, but she was clever, much more than he. And who knew.... A thin smile touched her lips as she remembered touching his, when he pulled away. She was, after all, quite enticing when she wanted to be, and he couldn't stay in training forever.

She laughed out loud, and disappeared into the night, planning what she would say to Klavon very carefully. Then she reappeared outside Klavon's chamber, and knocked.

"Come," she heard behind the door, and she opened it and stepped inside.

"I tried," she said flatly. "It did not work." She did not want to tell him she had been able to pass through the barrier. He would not understand. Besides, the boy had found a way to repel her intervention, and it was no longer of any significance. "I tried several times...until the serum was gone."

Klavon's eyes burst in flames.

"But sir, I believe this may be for the best."

"The best?" he yelled.

"If you kill him, she may never forgive you. But with the curse...you could convince him to join you. And that would only serve to bring her by your side."

Klavon raised a brow as if deep in thought. "You are truly an excellent aid to my leadership." He walked to her and behind her back. She did not move. "But I do wonder at your true motivations, Sira. Surely you do not think me a fool. Perhaps you believe that with two of us."

She flinched ever so slightly. "Two? He would only serve to strengthen you—"

"You are powerful," Klavon laughed, "but you can only take that power that I give. Two will not enable your independence...or are you thinking manipulation? That level of cleverness is not in your kind. You will forever need me. I, on the other hand, do *not* need you!"

She felt the cool steel of the sword against her throat, firm enough that she dare not even swallow.

Klavon whispered in her ear. "Should you ever attempt to undermine me, I will not hesitate to slit your throat."

Sira felt the blade fall from her neck, slowly, deliberately. As Klavon rounded back in front of her, she could feel sweat trickle down the back of her neck.

"The boy will die, and even with his instruction—even as a wizard—my powers cannot be undone. I will destroy him." Klavon turned his back to her and walked to the window. "Yes, perhaps this is better. It would be beneath me to kill him without his training. And you will fully comprehend my power when I tear him down."

Sira backed silently out of the room. Once the door closed, she ran down the stairs, all the way to her quarters. Staring into her mirror, she could see the slice left by the impression of the blade. Blood came to the surface and made a thin line along her neck.

Her reflection spewed anger at her error. She was strong, but Klavon was a sorcerer. She could leave, abandon him, but that would reduce her power to nothing more than a bag of tricks. She may be more clever than Klavon, but he was more powerful.

Composure replaced the anger, and with a wave of her hand the blood necklace disappeared.

So she did not have the power to sway his mind. But Miora did. A thin smiled faintly crossed her lips, and she closed her eyes, willing the image to come to life.

Klavon held the sword and practiced moves against an unseen foe. Splashes of moonlight illuminated the sharp blade and cast shadows across the floor. Suddenly he stopped—he saw her face in the shadows of his mind, a sad face full of sorrow. He reached out to her image, and she pulled back in tears.

"But you must understand. If he lives, he will hold your affections...not me," said Klavon.

The image turned her back to him, her shoulders heaving with the weight of pain. Klavon stared at the figure until it vanished.

His desire had been to kill the boy. But Miora's face haunted him...a face that could never love him—not with her son dead. With an obsession that had grown for fourteen years, Klavon could not risk it, and panic washed over him as he envisioned the boy's death and her response. Over and over it played in his mind until he could stand it no longer.

Sira was smart, and even though she had her own motives—as ridiculous as they were—she may have been correct.

That night, as he tried to sleep, he dreamed of Miora, falling into deep despair at her son's death. As Klavon reached for her to ease her pain, she fell into his arms…dead.

Klavon jerked awake and spent the rest of the night staring out the darkened window, across the mire toward Brandor.

The next morning, he summoned Sira back to his chamber, and she entered, her cat following close behind.

"I am glad you took care that," he said, pointing to her neck. Sira only nodded. "And I am glad that you questioned me. Let us take a walk."

Klavon motioned toward the door, and the two made their way out of the fortress and into the courtyard.

Fraenir circled above, and Klavon stopped to stare at him. "He is magnificent, and he will defeat Prydon, but the boy…"

Sira said nothing, skepticism shadowing her eyes as they scoured his face.

"I assure you, my anger has subsided. So you believe it is best that the boy not be killed…that he stand beside me."

Sira stood tall and with conviction said, "I do."

"You believe she will never be mine if the boy was to die."

"I do."

Klavon walked a little further into the courtyard and turned back to face her, nodding. "You have done nothing but serve my best interest. We will make it happen—the boy, here with me—and you will always have your place here. You know that, don't you?"

Sira's face brightened…slightly. "Thank you, sir. I will do all I can to ensure that happens for you."

"It would be beneficial to both of us," laughed Klavon, and he watched Sira's expression closely to read if there was any disloyalty. He saw none. "We must test his strength, before he enters the Valley. I have a plan, but I need you to prepare my arsenal."

Sira nodded, and Klavon called for Fraenir. The large dragon-beast landed so close that Sira and her cat had to jump back out of its way.

"Sira, go to my lab and begin. I will be there shortly," said Klavon.

Sira passed Fraenir and slowed, glaring up at him. Her cat hissed bitterly and then followed his master, retreating into the castle. Klavon waited until the door was securely shut before he spoke to Fraenir.

"I want you to go to Mount Tyria," said Klavon.

"Why?" Fraenir asked, his dragon eyes narrowing.

"There is a place there," said Klavon. "I'm sure you have heard of it."

"Yes," replied Fraenir. "It is where wizard's travel to collect their staff and sword."

"It is where Segrath makes the dragon's stone." Klavon ran his hand across the stone at the end of his staff.

It glowed a brilliant blood red. "While I am strong even without this, the dragon's stone magnifies my power. I believe it could do the same for you."

Fraenir growled. "I can kill hi—"

"You've had your chance!" snapped Klavon. "And you failed!" Klavon composed himself and walked up to Fraenir, placing his hand on his neck. "You are truly magnificent, but we cannot make the same mistake. I, as much as you, hate dragons, but we cannot underestimate their strength again."

Fraenir roared flames into the air and across the ground. Klavon did not flinch. It was acceptable for Fraenir to vent his anger. In fact, it was preferred.

"Fraenir, there is no shame in this. The dragon's stone only amplifies what you already are—and you are powerful. Can you imagine how much more you would be, though, with a dragon's stone?"

Chapter Sixteen

The Shadow

The long days passed slowly. In the morning, Barsovy would teach Darius defense, and in the afternoon training would switch to offense. At lunchtime, Darius sat under the same shaded tree he had shared with his friend, Prydon. He would glance at Loklan, exchange a faint smile, and turn to his own thoughts. Loklan would turn and, Darius assumed, do the same.

Darius wondered what Loklan's story was—what happened to his father, Norinar. Knowing a conversation with the young man would be forbidden, especially since the altercation they had exchanged, Darius instead focused his attentions on his own studies.

The small animal that had stolen Darius's lunch that first day now made a habit of greeting him. Its head would poke out from underneath the shelter of the rock, its nose twitching, and Darius would toss a bit of bread or meat to the ground. The creature would then amble toward the food, sit back on its hind legs, and begin to eat. It no longer retreated to its protective home and would sit with Darius as long as food was made available.

"So, how's your training coming along?" Darius

smiled when the animal squeaked as if it understood. "Is that so? Maybe we should practice together sometime. No? Well, I suppose that is for the best. You look a formidable foe if I ever saw one."

And so the conversation would go until lunch was over. The animal would withdraw back into the shade of its rock, and Darius would head back into the heat of the field.

A week later, Barsovy appeared at the field holding a sword and staff. "Since you have no sword or staff of your own, I am providing these training weapons. You can use all manner of techniques and spells, and you will do no harm to me. We will start with the sword. Are you ready?" Barsovy propped the staff against a tree and handed the sword to Darius.

"Ready?" A guarded trepidation came over Darius as he stared at the weapon. The last time he'd tried to use a sword, he'd been a complete failure, a fumbling idiot in his opinion, and he hoped he wouldn't display the same inadequacy now.

"Indeed!" and Barsovy began his attack.

The response happened so quickly, there was no time for Darius to protest, and for over a week, Barsovy challenged Darius's abilities. Barsovy wielded his weapon with ease, a man of incomparable skill and honed technique. At first, Darius flailed about, dropping his sword and, had it not been for the protection of the training spell administered on the weapon, threatening to dismember a toe or two. He even managed to skewer the rock where his newfound friend met him during lunch each day. It was several days before Darius could entice the little animal to come out to eat with him again, and Darius wondered if he'd ever learn to safely handle this deadly weapon.

As the week came to an end and Darius became more intimate with the feel of the sword, Barsovy began to show him advanced techniques and strategies and how to discern the subtle movements of an enemy to anticipate their next move.

"It's not enough," panted Darius after an intense session of sparring. "I'm still too slow! I'm not reading your moves well enough!"

"You are progressing just fine," snapped Barsovy. "What do you expect?"

"I expect I need to train more," retorted Darius as if it should have been obvious to the old man.

Barsovy's lips skewed to the side, and he stroked his beard. His eyes became thin slits, and Darius wasn't sure if his words had pushed Barsovy too far. Speaking to his master with such disrespect surely would gain him nothing but retribution.

"There is something I can do," said Barsovy, finally. "I will give you my shadow."

Darius paused. Was a shadow some form of punishment? Darius wanted to say something, but what would be appropriate? He squeaked, "I'm sorry I snapped at you," still concerned about what the shadow might be.

"Pish-posh! Now go. Eat. I will meet you later." And with that, Barsovy vanished.

The old wizard's habit of appearing and vanishing without warning was something Darius wondered if he would ever get used to. He smiled, shook his head, and with an amused sigh went traveled the short hike back to his hut.

As always, a delicious meal was waiting for him. He sat and ate, but his curiosity and excitement about a shadow held his attention, and he hardly tasted the food. He continually looked around, waiting for Barsovy to emerge. After some time, however, the excitement began to wane. The food was gone, even though Darius didn't recall eating it. But his stomach was full, so he went to the ledge and sat as the sun was setting. Darius had almost given up when the old man appeared.

Barsovy said nothing but drew a circle around himself on the ground. He closed his eyes and held his hands up to the sky. Barsovy's lips moved ever so slightly, but Darius heard no words. Suddenly, with a clap of thunder, Barsovy threw his hands downward and slammed them against his thighs. When he stepped from the circle, a smoky image of himself stood silently, completely still as if it were waiting for something.

Darius, his jaw dropping, stared.

"With this, you may train," said Barsovy as if he had done nothing more than hand Darius a training sword.

Darius choked out one word. "What?"

"My shadow," answered Barsovy. "As I can obviously not be with you every moment of the day, you may use my shadow to train in the evenings. But do not overwork yourself. I expect the same energy and effort when you are with me on the training fields as any other day!" Barsovy's brows frowned at Darius as if threatening him to defy his command.

"How...how does it work?" Darius asked.

"It is only a shadow. Any strike you make will pass right through it. Likewise, any attack it makes will pass through you. No harm. No pain. Nothing. But, you will be able to practice technique." Barsovy waited for no response but instantly disappeared into the night.

"All right, then," Darius responded to the spot where Barsovy no longer stood.

The shadow stood there, its eyes empty as if it was a misty statue, unaffected by wind or anything else. Darius moved closer and ran his hand through the figure. The shadow remained unaltered and motionless.

"Well, let's see how you...work," said Darius, walking to the hut and retrieving his sword.

When he faced the shadow and raised the blade, ready to spar, the shadow abruptly came to life. It quickly lunged and skewered Darius. The young wizard leapt back with a scream and examined his midsection. While Darius rubbed his stomach, the shadow again attacked, this time beheading him. Well, it would have if it had been effective.

"Whoa!" yelled Darius, and he took stance and immediately returned the blow.

Practice continued. He was surprised that when he or the shadow did manage a block an attack, it was as if an invisible force prevented the swords from passing through each other. It was only when a block failed that the other's sword would pass through its opponent.

For over an hour, the volley continued. Darius was tired and thirsty, but he wasn't sure how to make the shadow stop. He could imagine himself sitting on the cliff's edge to rest while the shadow danced behind him, slicing his body. That had the potential to be quite annoying. Darius contemplated the situation, but as quickly as it had come to life, the shadow returned to its original state, a smoky statue standing next to the clearing. Somehow the shadow knew that Darius was done.

Darius lowered his sword and paused only a moment as he turned away, to make certain the shadow wasn't planning another attack. "All right, then," he exhaled, this time to Barsovy's shadow, and he went and sat on the side of his cliff.

Darius sipped some cool water and glanced over at the shadow Barsovy. Even though there was no real contact when they sparred, the practice was effective, and he was confident about the training. His eyes turned back to the serenity of the valley. It was as it always was—peaceful. Darius closed his eyes and breathed deeply.

His eyes flew open when he sensed there was someone near, someone other than the shadow. He turned around to see Loklan emerge from behind a small cluster of bushes.

"Hello," Loklan said, scuffing the toe of his boot in the dirt.

"Hello," said Darius. Loklan stood there in awkward silence until Darius finally added, "Well, come sit down if you want."

Loklan sat and glanced back at the shadow version of Barsovy. "Do you think he'll know?"

Darius squinted and looked around his shelter and clearing. There was no sign of the real Barsovy, and the shadow remained in its dormant state. "I don't think so."

Loklan looked down toward the valley, and it was several moments before he spoke. "I…um…I wanted to tell you I'm sorry for suspecting you. Barsovy told me of your curse…and Klavon."

Darius only nodded.

"So where's your dragon?" asked Loklan. "I mean, your…friend."

"He had something he needed to do. I don't know," replied Darius, and both boys became quiet, staring at the valley below.

Finally, Loklan broke the silence. "Does it hurt? The mark?"

Darius held out his hand and inspected the red tendrils that weaved so decidedly around his wrist and hand. "Sometimes…at least it used to. I think it's worse when I'm angry as if I'm letting the poison into my blood… if that makes any sense."."

"That's horrible. Everyone gets angry sometimes," said Loklan.

"Yes," said Darius. "So maybe it's not the anger itself but my reason for the anger. Like if I'm being foolish or feeling sorry for myself and I take it out on someone or something around me."

"So you really have to go fight him? Klavon?"

Darius nodded, and Loklan's head swayed as if trying to solve some sort of mental puzzle.

"I'm scared," said Darius. Then he looked away, surprised at his own admission.

Darius had long since pushed that feeling aside, but

something about talking to another wizard his own age, going through what he was in training, and the connection between his father and Loklan's simply felt like he could trust the boy…could call him "friend." He could see from the edge of his vision that Loklan was looking sideways at him.

"It's going to be alright," said Loklan. "Barsovy will make sure you are ready. And you have a dragon to help as well." There was a moment's pause as Loklan sat back upright, and then he said quietly, "And I'll help if possible."

Darius turned to face him. "I appreciate that, but I'm not sure how you can."

"What if we train extra at night…together?"

"That would be…nice," said Darius, glancing over at Loklan and then down into the valley.

The two boys sat, side by side, for several long moments. A true connection was born, and Darius felt much less alone. He smiled to himself, and then he looked at Loklan. He had been so focused on his own situation he had forgotten the very real pain that Loklan must be enduring as well.

Gently, Darius said, "I'm sorry about your father."

It was Loklan's turn to nod, and Darius thought he saw Loklan gulp back tears.

"I never knew mine," added Darius.

There was another long silence as the two boys sat overlooking the serene valley. Darius knew how it felt to lose a father, but his was an ache of loss that comes from years of never knowing—wondering what it would have been like had his father been a part of his life.

Loklan had those years, so his pain was new and sharp—a pain that can only be felt when someone is ripped suddenly from your life. And to add to his grief, Loklan wasn't even allowed the luxury of mourning.

His thoughts were interrupted when Loklan said suddenly, "So what is that? I saw you fighting it."

"Want to give it a try?" Darius asked.

"Can I?"

"Sure," said Darius, jumping up. He reached a hand down to Loklan, and unlike at their first meeting, the boy smiled and took his hand.

They walked over to the shadow, and Darius handed Loklan his sword. As soon as Loklan held it in his hands, the shadow came to life.

Darius laughed when the shadow sliced Loklan in half, and as Loklan grabbed his stomach in surprise, the shadow struck through his neck.

"Whoa! This is weird!" screeched Loklan.

"You'll get the hang of it," said Darius, smiling and leaning against a nearby tree.

It didn't take long, and Darius's new friend quickly figured things out. In time, Loklan appeared to tire, and as if on cue, the shadow returned to its dormant state.

"That's amazing!" said Loklan, breathless but grinning from ear to ear. "But, I'd best be off. If we don't get some rest before tomorrow, Barsovy will have our hides."

Loklan handed the sword back to Darius and reached out with his other in a handshake. Darius took both and returned the content grin.

"Until next time?" asked Loklan as he headed for the brush.

Darius smiled, "Next time, we spar together so bring your sword."

That night, exhausted, Darius slept. The shadow continued to teach him in his dreams, but somehow his sleep was sound. He awoke rested and prepared for another day at the field.

Day after day, Darius would learn much from Barsovy. Night after night, he would learn much from the shadow.

Loklan would join later, and the two would spar each other. And while the protective spell prevented either from harming the other, they still had bruises and scrapes to show for their efforts, sometimes comparing them as if each were glorious battle wounds.

Occasionally, the two would gang up on the shadow, but as the two sharpened their skills, so did the shadow. It was never easy, and the friends quickly became extremely proficient with the sword.

Sometimes, after Loklan had left, Darius would continue to lung and parry outside his hut, way above the valley and well into dark, as the starlit dragon hovered above, keeping diligent watch over him.

By the time Darius completed the sword phase of his training, he felt as if it was a natural extension of his own body. His movements were fluid and his technique honed. He could defend himself effectively against Barsovy, and Barsovy assured him that he was not holding back.

"Do you really believe I would pretend to be weak? And just how do you think that would serve you?" Barsovy would exclaim. "Enough of your self-doubt! If I say your swordsmanship is impressive, then it's impressive, and I'll not hear another word about it! Now, let's get to work on the wizard's lifeblood."

The staff. This was the true power of the wizard, and Darius grew to respect his fate where once he hated it. For the remainder of the month, with staff in hand, he practiced all the spells Barsovy taught him until they became second nature.

Barsovy modified his shadow, and instead of a sword, it now wielded a staff. "Each spell will have a distinct look and color," said Barsovy, and he went through the spells so that Darius would recognize them simply on appearance. "If it explodes upon you, then you failed to adequately defend against it. Likewise, if your spells explode upon the shadow, it has failed to adequately defend itself against you."

Darius gave it a few tries before saying, "I think I've got it."

"Oh," said Barsovy, "and one more thing. Loklan? You can come out now."

Loklan sheepishly appeared from behind some brush. "Um..."

"Um nothing!" exclaimed Barsovy. "Did you not think I would know? Either of you?"

Darius tried to offer an explanation, but Barsovy held up his hand.

"You both know this is against the rules, but I am also aware of the extraordinary progress you both have made. Given that yours is a special case, Darius, and that Loklan is somehow tied to your fate—"

"Tied to my—"

"Yes! Now, do not interrupt me again," said Barsovy. "...I have allowed this to continue unfettered. However, the staff is tricky and will require you both to apply the utmost concentration."

Barsovy drew a circle on the ground around himself as he had done before. Closing his eyes and muttering so slightly, thunder again clapped to the ground as Barsovy's raised hands slammed down against his thighs. When he stepped from the circle, a second smoky image of himself stood silently.

"As I said before," said Barsovy, "the staff is not the sword and will require individual training. Therefore, you both will have shadows with which to train."

"Thank you, sir," said Loklan.

"I assume you heard the directions I gave Darius regarding how this works?" asked Barsovy.

"Sir?" asked Loklan.

"You were in the bushes the entire time, were you not?" Barsovy said with some hint of exasperation.

"Yes...I was."

"Then I will leave you two to your training," said Barsovy, and in an instant, he was gone.

"Does that mean I don't have to sneak up here anymore?" whispered Loklan.

"You do not," replied a voice, from out of nowhere,

that sounded very much like Barsovy's.

The boys hesitated and then broke into hysterical laughter. It continued until both boys were holding their stomachs and wiping tears from their eyes.

"We should have known better," said Darius.

"Yes," replied Loklan.

The two soon turned toward their shadows and began their evening training.

While the spells cast were unable to inflict any harm, Darius knew what he was battling and if he was or wasn't successful. First he focused on defense, deciding which counter-spell would be most effective, and in time he learned to use his staff quite efficiently to defend himself.

Barsovy was correct. The staff required complete concentration, so he understood why he and Loklan had been indulged with a second shadow.

When Darius completed what he knew in defensive spells, he focused on offense, attacking the shadow and learning from its reactions. He discovered what spells produced what response and quickly learned how to select his next attack to maximize the previous.

At times, the boys would watch each other and offer suggestions. And as before, when Loklan would retire, Darius would continue to train.

On the training fields, he was soon better prepared to spar with Barsovy.

"Perhaps I should cast a shadow for all my students," Barsovy said. "Although I am not sure they possess the motivation that you enjoy, Darius."

Darius smiled. His time practicing at his hut

allowed Barsovy to focus on technique, a skill that would help Darius to cast without thought—a skill that would be invaluable in his battle with Klavon.

With Prydon gone, Loklan filled some of the void, but there were still moments of loneliness. Although Loklan was a dear friend, his battle with Klavon was one he would face alone, and this forever lingered in his thoughts. Even Prydon could not change that.

Darius sat at the edge of the cliff. The sun had gone to sleep, the far mountain its blanket, and as the sky darkened, fireflies slowly appeared from their hiding places. Campfires from other trainees soon popped up in the distance, and stars slowly begin to fill the deep blue sky, decorating the indigo backdrop with shimmering pearls. Darius lay back and looked up.

He smiled as he thought again of Loklan, but he knew that once training ended, so would their time together. With the curse and his impending battle with Klavon, Darius sighed and accepted his solitude. He wished Prydon were there. The dragon's company was comforting, and he dearly missed his friend.

He glanced over at the shadow. It was not a friend. It was simply a source of instruction. Strangely, more often than not, the instruction continued even as Darius slept. Darius wasn't sure if he liked it or was bothered by it. However, Darius was pleased that he was now able to predict most of its moves and spells, and it was quite possible that the dreams contributed to that success. It was a shame he would not have those colors and patterns to help him in his battle with Klavon, but he no longer needed the shadow or its instruction.

He thought again of Prydon. Perhaps his absence was a blessing, allowing Darius the opportunity to stand on his own and grow into a wizard independently of the dragon. There was no arrogance in this; Darius came to realize that Prydon's strength was a valuable asset to his cause, but it would be of no use to him if he were weak on his own. This was something Prydon had tried many times to instill in him, and now he understood. And with their combined strength, they would make an impressive and, if necessary, dangerous pair.

Darius stared up at the dragon form in the stars, more settled than he had been since the Great Book was stolen. He had concentrated on his studies, pouring heart, body, and soul into everything he learned, and he accomplished much. Even Barsovy was impressed and told him he was the fastest learner he'd trained since his father.

Darius smiled at the thought. He never knew Thyre, but the more he learned, the more he felt a connection to this man—a man he called Father. How Darius would have given anything to witness him standing regally in his wizardly robes, tending to the village with Miora at his side. He smiled again, but then he frowned. For the first time, Darius caught a glimpse of the depth of emptiness his mother must have endured all those years without him, and his heart ached for her pain.

That night, he fell asleep dreaming of his father and the life he never knew…the shadow allowed him that.

Chapter Seventeen

Segrath

Almost two weeks of flying, with sparse moments of rest, Prydon landed atop a mountain and stared at the fortress in front of him. Barely visible, even to those who were called to it, Mount Tyria was a place none would dare to enter. But he had matters that needed to be dealt with, and there was no point in delaying further.

Prydon circled the mountain to make sure no one else was there. Segrath would be much less inclined to hear him out if he were to disrupt a young wizard, struggling to discover himself and to receive his strength before training.

He found no sign of movement, so he landed just beneath a large outcropping of rock near the top of the mountain. He could feel the presence beyond the opening and slowly entered.

Prydon wound his way through the snake-like paths until he reached a large chamber. In the center stood a cauldron, as large and any human home, swirling with wisps of blue mist.

A young boy stood, bowing before…a dragon.

"You dare enter here, Prydon?" the dragon said, turning its head to look up toward the small ledge on which

Prydon was now standing.

With a few flaps of his wings, Prydon, in seconds, stood before the other dragon. "I come with matters of great urgency. I have no desire to interfere with the happenings of this great domain."

By this time, the young boy had moved to stand behind a large boulder.

"Do you know who I am? What I am?" the dragon bellowed.

The large dragon, nearly twice Prydon's size, began circling him, never blinking or taking her eyes off of Prydon's. Her scales were deep green, but when she moved, ripples of black seemed to form waves over the huge muscles that framed her entire body, and her eyes blazed red.

"You are Segrath, guide to those who enter here and maker of a wizard's staff and sword," replied Prydon, moving in unison with the larger beast.

"And you are not surprised that I know your name?" Segrath replied.

Prydon could feel Segrath's breath as the other dragon moved in closer.

"I would not insult you. You are the culmination of generations of our kind. You are the one who has sacrificed for the good of this world, never to find rest but ever to find respect in the eyes of those who would come to understand themselves as they travel these great paths."

"You flatter me, but I need no such words."

A rumble began to swell in Segrath's chest, and Prydon quickly replied, "I seek not to flatter. I speak only the truth. May we have conversation? Or am I to perceive your actions as an answer before you even know my task?"

Segrath stopped. "It takes great courage to enter here uninvited...or foolishness, but I will indulge you. Why are you here, Prydon?"

Prydon bowed and then looked up, directly into Segrath's eyes. "I am here to retrieve the staff and sword for Darius, son of Thyre."

"Only the wizard...or sorcerer...himself can retrieve such tools. Certainly you know this!" Segrath screeched out the words followed by a stream of black and red fire and steam.

Prydon flew into the air, avoiding the blaze. "You know why he cannot complete this task! You know of Klavon and the curse!"

"I know nothing!" Segrath shot into the air. "And I care even less."

Prydon flew in and out of pillars of rock, followed by Segrath, as she continued to spew flames that Prydon could feel scorch the tip of his tail. He swerved upward, a sharper turn than Segrath could make, and as he looked back to see where she was, he saw the fire, raining down into the cavern, and the boy, running to avoid each blast and seeking refuge behind the huge cauldron.

"Stop this!" yelled Prydon. "You will hurt your charge!"

As if forced beyond her will, Segrath turned to look at the boy and landed at once next to a small pool of silver water. Prydon flew down and perched on a small ledge across the chamber.

"Prydon, you will not move or interfere with what is to happen, or I will kill you," said Segrath. She then turned to the boy. "Come. Stand here."

Her charge approached slowly and bowed before her. She then took her clawed hand, held it over his head, and an iridescent net formed a cage around the boy.

Segrath reached into the cauldron and retrieved two stones, swirling with an opaque mist. She turned and sliced at a large wooden wall until a huge gash was cut into it. As she pulled her arm away, the tear mended itself, and in her hand, she held a wizard's staff. Segrath then took one of the stones and held it at the end, and with one breath, ice blue fire came from her mouth, fusing the stone into the staff.

The wood was left completely untouched, something that Prydon found quite phenomenal. A dragon's fire always burned, or so he thought as he glanced at the blisters at the tip of his own tail.

Next, Segrath turned and tossed the other stone into the pool of liquid steel. She closed her eyes and plunged her arms into the silver water. It began to boil, and Segrath screamed, shooting fire around the room. The boy stood still, not a single flame touching him, protected by the shimmering net.

When she opened her eyes, the pool had ceased to move. Slowly, Segrath pulled out her arms, and in her clawed hand, she held a superb sword, stronger and sharper than could be made anywhere else—a true wizard's sword, complete with the second stone, embedded in its hilt.

Segrath turned to the boy, and the net sparked and vanished. "You have completed your journey and are more aware of your own heart. I pass no judgment as to your destiny, be it wizard or sorcerer, but now you must train to discover your final place in this world."

Segrath handed the tools to the boy, and in a flash of blue light, the boy was gone. Prydon knew that at that moment, the boy, with sword and staff in hand, would be standing at the edge of the training fields—the same place he and Darius had first entered.

Segrath turned to face Prydon. "No one has witnessed such as you. But with the boy gone, you have no weapon to deter my wrath!"

She flew toward Prydon, her claws reaching to tear the flesh from his chest. Prydon soared into the air and spiraled again around the stone pillars, this time taking another sharp turn to prevent Segrath from following.

He landed on a higher ledge, and she stopped, looking up at him, slowly clawing her way to where he was perched.

"Prydon," she said with a hiss, "I know your past. I know your failure to prevent Thyre's death."

Prydon flinched. He could see it as if it were yesterday. Chasing Fraenir as far as he could, he had abandoned Thyre, and when he returned to Thyre's side, the wizard was already dead. Miora was nowhere to be seen, and Klavon was rapidly consuming the village in fire and ash. He stopped on a cliff overlooking the town…and cried.

His battle with Fraenir had weakened him greatly, and even wanting to stop the carnage that played out in front of him, there was nothing he could do—nothing but honor his promise and find and protect Miora and her child. So he left Thyre there, dead in the street with minions of every kind stomping his body until it was gone.

Many times Prydon had wondered. If he had stayed at Thyre's side, perhaps his friend would have lived. The safety of Miora and the baby did little to relieve the guilt of that one choice...a choice he could never undo.

"That is not why I am here," snapped Prydon. You know of Klavon and the curse placed on Darius...a curse that will consume him if Darius does not complete his training."

Immediately she shot toward him, shattering the pillar and ledge on which Prydon sat, and he crashed several feet, barely avoiding Segrath's claws. He exploded into the air, this time flying through the open cavern. Segrath followed him closely, threatening his life with every turn.

"You left Thyre's side," she teased. "Who knows what would have happened if you had stayed. And after he saved the life of your son."

Prydon curled around, flying backwards, "Stop it! I know my own guilt! But I am here only for the boy, Darius."

Segrath grinned, and her eyes became like half-moons. She said as if baiting his anger, "Yes, but had you stayed, the boy would have come here and retrieved these on his own, having spent a life being groomed by his own father. But you took that away from him."

"Enough!" Prydon screamed, and he flew to the ground. "If you would kill me, kill me with your claws, not with your words!"

Segrath hovered for only a moment and then landed in front of Prydon.

"As you wish," she said, and she plunged several sharp claws directly into Prydon's chest.

Prydon stared at her, surprised at her response, but could not move. He said weakly, "I am your kind."

"Yes, you are," she said quietly.

Prydon choked. He could feel his heart beating, the claws deep inside it…and then he saw nothing but darkness.

It felt cold at first. He could feel the memories of the past several weeks replaying in his mind. How odd he thought it was that to die, the mind must release old thoughts. Perhaps it was his essence leaving his body, allowing him only a glimpse of what his life had been. Then he laughed. His essence wouldn't have far to go, dying deep in the mountain, home of Segrath—his killer.

Fraenir sat coiled, a snake his choice of form, on the ledge above the opening to the mountain. Segrath would need to be dealt with delicately for she was more than a normal dragon. And although he did not want to admit it, Prydon had almost killed him. And Segrath was…more.

But Klavon was correct. A dragon's stone would prove most useful to him. He was powerful, indeed. And he believed he could easily destroy Prydon, but with the stone, there would be no doubt.

Fraenir began to slither from the ledge when he caught a glimpse of something. Prydon, his enemy was just a small stretch away and heading straight for him. For a moment, he thought he'd been discovered, so he quickly changed to the form of a small mouse and scurried beneath a rock just in the entrance of the mountain.

Prydon landed, his spiked tail only inches from Fraenir's hiding place, and paused. Fraenir knew why—he, too, would know the power of Segrath. As Prydon entered and made his way along, so did Fraenir, quiet and careful not to follow too closely.

This might prove to be most convenient, Fraenir thought as they entered the main part of the cavern.

Below, he could see her, and she was not amused with Prydon's invasion. During their first battle, Fraenir scurried down and ran stealthily behind the cauldron. Just then, a boot fell next to his head. The human child, in his fear of the two dragons and the fire that rained from above, had almost crushed him.

Stupid child! Fraenir thought, and he hid beneath a nearby rock to wait.

Somehow, Prydon had delayed her wrath. Segrath now reached into the boiling cauldron to retrieve the stones, and Fraenir cursed the process. How would he be able to attain one, with a fire so hot? Then he laughed. How ridiculous—he was from the hottest fires that burned deep beneath the surface of this world.

In a short time, the boy received his weapons and was gone, no doubt to the training fields—a stupid place were it not for the sorcerers it produced…like Klavon.

What happened next shocked him, however, as he watched Segrath plunge her claws into Prydon's chest. But there was no blood, and both dragons seemed to enter a trance, devoid of senses in this world.

Fraenir took advantage of the situation. The tiny mouse turned into a fiery beast—the same beast that had, on another day, retrieved the book from Brandor. It dove into the cauldron and in seconds, flew high into the cavern holding a dragon's stone. He grinned as he shot out of the mountain—Segrath and Prydon never knew he was there.

When Prydon awoke, Segrath was staring down at him, the red in her eyes now an emerald green.

"I'm...I'm not dead," said Prydon.

"Obviously," she said. "You care greatly for this boy, to come here and possibly meet your doom."

Prydon touched his chest. There was a jagged wound where her claws had entered. "I thought I had."

"It was the only way. I had to know your heart. But you must know...there is a great danger in what I've allowed. The boy might never find his way—be lost forever."

"I know this young man. I knew his father. He will not fail, and his heart is true."

"I know you believe that from reading your heart, but with the curse and his failure to journey here...if he faulters even the slightest, he will fail...or worse, join Klavon."

"This boy is the only hope. If he does not succeed, not only will it be the end of Brandor, but Klavon will not stop until he has destroyed every realm in existence."

Segrath tilted her head and touched the spot where she had pierced Prydon's scales. "That is exactly why I have done this. Be gone, Prydon, and never come here again…until you are dead."

Prydon woke, snow pouring down upon him, on the ledge he and Darius had first landed outside the training field. Beside him lay the wizard's sword and staff.

Chapter Eighteen

The Sly Suggestion

Sira watched in the shadows as Klavon methodically attacked and weakened Norinar's village.

"How convenient I killed him," Klavon had said when they were first devising the plan. "And now I can use this village, with no one to defend it, to draw the boy out."

Norinar was dead and his son was in the training fields with Barsovy, not due to be home for quite some time. It was a perfect opportunity, and Sira had to admit, his plan to test the boy's skills was sound.

Everything was happening to her liking. Klavon's desire to kill Darius had been thwarted, and she was curious to see how things would change once he stood at Klavon's side…and hers.

So Klavon had come for two evenings, disguised as a much younger sorcerer. He attacked Norinar's village and then left until the following night. No one had been killed—that would not serve his needs. If it had, Sira had no doubt there would be corpses strewn about. As it was, the town was left with a constant threat and fear of death…and no way to defend itself.

That was where Sira came in. She had been

watching, and there was one who always helped, standing her ground and protecting those weaker. This girl, Alara, was just what she needed.

That night, when Klavon left—as he did every night—the white wisp floated through the door, into the small home, and circled above Alara's bed.

"It is there," Sira whispered. "Travel to the fallen village, and you will find the wizard's sword and staff, left fourteen years ago."

Alara tossed in her sleep, and Sira pressed the image of the small home on the hill into the sleeping girl's mind.

"That is where they are," Sira said, "and with them, you can vanquish the evil sorcerer from your village forever."

Alara turned her head from side to side as Sira imprinted the path that would lead her directly to the small home.

When Sira was done, she left one last dream with the girl—a dream of great victory in defeating the invading sorcerer *if* the girl succeeded in retrieving the sword and staff.

Chapter Nineteen

The Past Relived

After a solitary breakfast Darius quickly readied himself and made the familiar trek to his more than familiar alcove. He stepped into the clearing, but Barsovy was nowhere to be seen. Darius began pacing the field, kicking at the dust beneath his feet. In all the time he had spent in this valley, within moments of stepping into the training area, Barsovy would appear. He was never late.

A bird flew overhead, casting a long shadow on the ground, and Darius looked up. The sun was peeking over the mountain on the far side of the lush valley. He walked over and sat underneath the tree where he normally ate lunch. He could not see Loklan and wondered if his Barsovy was present. If he were, Loklan would fast be in his alcove focused on his training. Darius thought of wandering over but quickly decided against it. Although he and Loklan had long since become great friends, he was sure an invasion of this sort would not be taken well by Barsovy.

The small animal poked its head out from under the crevice, sniffed, and returned to its sanctuary. Darius watched absently, his brows furrowed. His thoughts were elsewhere. By now, Barsovy was very late. A burst of concern churned in Darius's stomach, and he began to wish he hadn't eaten so much at breakfast.

A flush of wind blew dust in Darius's face, and an enormous thud shook the ground.

"Prydon!" Darius ran to his friend and threw his arms around the massive neck.

"Darius. I have missed you as well," said Prydon as he gently placed a clawed hand around Darius's back.

Darius loosened his grip. A knot tied his throat, and he fought back the tears that were threatening to engulf his eyes. "I'm glad you're back," he squeaked.

Prydon smiled. "I hear you have been doing well with your studies. I guess you have no further need of that pillow."

Darius laughed. "Not a bit."

In an instant, Barsovy appeared and stood in silence as Prydon pulled from beneath his wings a sword and staff.

Prydon's chest bulged and pride veiled his face as he ceremoniously held them out to Darius. "These, my friend, are yours. Careful, though. There is no spell of protection on these weapons."

Darius glanced from Prydon to Barsovy.

Barsovy's eyes nodded respectfully, and he bowed his head. "You are done here."

Darius reached slowly forward and gently took the weapons. As his hands touched their surface, a pulse of power surged out from him as if he were a small pebble dropped in a shallow pool. For a moment, a white light engulfed him, clouding his view from anything or anyone around him. A warm energy danced on the surface of his skin, and he felt at peace. As it faded, his surroundings returned to view.

"You are now bound as one," said Barsovy.

Darius looked at his newly acquired weapons. The exquisite stones embedded in the handle of the sword and perched atop the end of the staff came to life, and an opaque mist, void of any one color, swirled about, a murky shadow filling the stones.

"When a wizard takes a sword and staff," said Barsovy, "it is forever. They will never fail you, unless you fail yourself."

Darius's throat tightened and he swallowed hard as those words echoed in his ears—*unless you fail yourself.* With sword in one hand and staff in the other, Darius's eyes fixed firmly on what would now be a major part of his life.

"The bond will be permanent once you return from the Valley of Wizards," Barsovy continued. "But first, you must face your past, putting all questions, doubts, and concerns to rest once and for all. Else, your journey in the valley will not be as it should."

Darius frowned questioningly at Prydon.

Prydon nodded. "As I have told you before, the stones in your sword and staff will reflect your character. If you do not resolve your past, those stones—"

"I know," Darius confirmed. "But what of this mark? Can't that affect me as well?"

"Of that I am sure, but that cannot be helped," replied Barsovy. "Prydon?"

Prydon lowered his sleek body to the ground. "It is time, young one, to return to your past."

Darius climbed on Prydon's back. "Tell Loklan that—"

"Loklan will know," said Barsovy, and he waved as they took to the air.

Darius could see Loklan, busy in battle with another Barosovy in his alcove, stop and look up. Darius waved at his friend. Loklan hesitated and waved back, only to have his Barsovy knock him to his feet.

Darius laughed and waved again before the clouds obscured any other view of the valley. Soon he began to think of Brandor and wondered how he would resolve a past with a town that was vanishing. But he was excited to hug his mother once again. He could imagine the smile on her face when she discovered he was well…and a trained wizard!

The wind became cold as they left the shelter of the training grounds. Now, they were vulnerable, and Darius thought of Klavon. Would he sense Darius's accomplishments? Would Klavon be waiting for him in Brandor? Would he be forced to face Klavon before he could enter the Valley of Wizards? Before he had been blessed…or cursed? Darius shook the uneasy thoughts from his mind. There was no time to be insecure. He would receive a blessing because he needed to, and that was final.

Hours later, Prydon landed amidst the ruins of his father's village.

"Here?" asked Darius, a confused crease joining his brows. "But I thought—"

"Brandor is your present and not what you need to confront just now. This, however, is the past you need to resolve," answered Prydon.

Darius lowered himself off of Prydon's back and began to walk around. The putrid gloom of destruction still hung thick in the air even after all these years, and in a wave of unexpected turmoil, lucid visions of the fighting that destroyed this village came to life right before his eyes.

"Prydon?" he asked, but Darius's voice failed. His knees weakened, and he fell to the ground as ancient sounds became like new, and he looked up to watch two wizards deeply entrenched in battle.

Spells shot from one wizard to the other and screams in the distance echoed in Darius's ears. In between spells and, as the wizards came closer to each other, swords were raised and the sound of metal clashed like thunder. Darius didn't know how, but he was witnessing the battle between his father and Klavon. Prydon roared off to the side, heavy in combat with another much darker dragon. Prydon? Prydon was here? Then? With his father?

Klavon chanted strange words, and small creatures unfamiliar to Darius charged after a woman and her son. The creatures clawed at the boy as the mother screamed and yanked him into her arms. Darius's father, Thyre, immediately turned and cast a spell that pulverized the minions, and the lady with her son scrambled out of sight into a cluster of trees. Klavon, taking full advantage of the distraction, struck Thyre with his sword just as Thyre turned around, and a deep gash cut through his robes. Thyre, crimson dripping from his arm, was not deterred, and he raised his sword and fought back.

Townspeople ran everywhere as Klavon, at every chance, cast spells to disperse more minions throughout the village. Thyre would quickly counterattack, turning the minions into wisps of dust. It was at that time that Klavon would strike hardest at Thyre, but he would maintain himself and their fight continued.

Prydon's battle with the darker dragon proved equally intense. Although spells were not their advantage, the sheer massiveness of their strikes and the fire of their breath would easily bring a human to a quick end. But against each other, their powers were evenly matched and equally destructive. Although the dark dragon sustained comparable wounds, blood covered Prydon's arms, neck, and legs as deep gashes cried out with red tongues.

Darius's stomach soured as one unfortunate human, in her panic, ventured near the dark dragon. Prydon dove toward the woman, but the dark dragon was closer and devoured her with one, quick snap. Prydon cried and turned toward the dark dragon, shrieking in anger.

Thyre's attention was drawn by the death of one of his people, and Klavon sent out another barrage of minions. Thyre counterattacked, and as before, while he defended his people, Klavon struck hardest. He cast spell after vicious spell, and Prydon jumped to Thyre's defense only to be met with a slice across his back by the darker dragon.

With Prydon's help, Thyre eradicated the minions and turned his attention back on Klavon, and their battle ensued, as did Prydon's and the darker dragon. To Darius, it seemed to go on forever, swords, staffs, minions, claws, teeth, fire. But then the entire scene stopped, frozen like an audience anticipating the climactic appearance of the main character. Standing in a doorway up on a small hill stood a woman. Darius immediately recognized Miora, although her face showed fewer years than he ever remembered. She was holding a bundle of cloth and sobbing as she collapsed to her knees.

"No!" Thyre screamed.

The battle began to progress once again, but now it played in slow motion, every act painfully drawn out. Thyre yelled at Prydon, but the words were muffled beyond Darius's understanding. The dark dragon headed toward his mother, and she ran. Prydon followed, and soon both were out of sight.

Klavon laughed and sent forth such a surge of minions that the townspeople were beginning to fall all around. Thyre yelled again, but to whom Darius knew not, and turned back to Klavon. His attack on Klavon was like nothing Darius could have imagined. Screaming in anger, he cast spells, attacked with sword, and almost succeeded in taking Klavon's life until the cries of his people forced him to turn his attention once again on the minions. Thyre turned from Klavon, sending minions flying to oblivion, but without Prydon's help there were too many. Klavon laughed again and called more minions, and as Thyre attempted to save his people, Klavon raised his sword.

With a choked scream of anguish, Thyre froze. A dark red stain seeped through the fabric of his robes, and Thyre looked down at the tip of Klavon's sword, protruding from his stomach. Darius watched as his father raised his hands and clutched the blade of his enemy's sword. Gasping for his last breaths, tears filled Thyre's eyes. He dropped to his knees, and Klavon slowly walked around to face him. Klavon began to laugh, deep and wicked. Thyre looked into Klavon's eyes, a look of sadness as if he were looking at a lost friend. Blood began to trickle from his mouth, and with a final breath, Thyre fell to the ground.

Darius screamed, "No!" Clawing at the ground, he ran to his dying father, but when he got there, a dark cloud filled his vision. He awoke to the sounds of his own sobbing. His body was damp with sweat and his shoulders shook violently. Prydon stood over him, his head lowered in pain.

"You!" Darius yelled. "You abandoned him! You let him die!"

Prydon did not move. Darius found his feet and lunged at Prydon, pounding the dragon's massive body with his fists as hard as he could. Prydon did nothing, and Darius pummeled his hands against the scaled chest until he could pound no more. He fell back, sobbing once again.

When he found his voice, his sentence was broken between involuntary gasps of air. "How...could...you?" The gasps continued as he threw his hands over his face and allowed the pain to overtake him.

For quite some time, nothing was said. Prydon offered no response; Prydon, the one Darius had come to trust, the one he thought of as his friend, had allowed his father to die. It was more than he could stand, and he fell to the ground in a heap where his father had died.

Darius wasn't sure, but he must have cried himself

to sleep. All he knew was that his face was sticky with dampened dust, and his nose was runny. He sat up and wiped his nose on his sleeve.

Prydon was still there, standing in the same spot.

"I don't understand?" said Darius. He was hurt and angry, but his words were quiet, almost venomous. "How could you do that? I thought he was your friend?"

"He was more than my friend, Darius. He, at one time, saved my son's life. I would easily have given my life for him."

"Your son? So he saved your son, but you wouldn't save him?" Darius snapped.

"It was not his wish that I help him."

"What do you mean?" Anger began to boil under his skin, and Darius clenched his fists tightly shut.

"As Fraenir went after your mother—"

"Fraenir?" Darius interrupted.

"Fraenir was the creature I was fighting. As Fraenir went after your mother and you—"

"And me?" Darius interrupted again.

Prydon paused. "That bundle of cloth she was holding was you. Darius, your mother was in labor when Klavon attacked the village. Your father and I went to defend it, but he told me that under no circumstance was Klavon or Fraenir to get to her...or you."

Prydon sat down and shook his head, and Darius stared at him, waiting to understand the battle amidst whose ruins he now sat, the battle he witnessed so clearly.

"You saw the battle. We were doing our best, but when your mother appeared, Klavon sent his beast to seize her. I followed and was able to prevent Fraenir from reaching your mother. In fact, Fraenir was badly wounded and knew that it was only a matter of time before I would take his life." Prydon's jaws flexed, and he shook his head in anger. "He retreated and began to fly toward Klavon's tower. I followed for a short distance, but when he maintained his path, I returned to your father, knowing he would need my help."

"But you didn't help him." Darius lowered his head, the image of his father clenching the sword's blade still etched in his mind.

"I barely topped the houses at the edge of the village when your father demanded I stay on Fraenir. He demanded I save his child as he had saved mine. I tried to argue, but he would have none of it. And my discussion was only serving to distract him further from his fight with Klavon."

"Was that what he was yelling? For you to go?"

Prydon nodded. "I made him a promise. So I followed Fraenir. I was not in the best shape myself, and by the time I caught up with him, Fraenir had safely landed at Klavon's tower. A barrage of minions came to Fraenir's aid so I dared not enter. Knowing Fraenir was in no shape to leave, I returned here, to your father. But..." Prydon shook his head as if to toss some disgusting taste from his mouth.

"My father was already dead," finished Darius.

"Yes." Prydon swallowed hard. "And Klavon had called so many minions, the villagers, at least the ones who were still alive, abandoned the town. Klavon and his minions had already burned most of the buildings, I assume looking for your mother."

"Why didn't you kill him then?" asked Darius.

"I could have tried, but that would have been of no help to either you or your mother."

"No help?" snapped Darius. "We wouldn't be dealing with Klavon now!"

"Klavon called forth so many minions that I could not have hoped to defeat them. My wounds were severe. And if I died, you and your mother would have been left completely vulnerable."

"Ok, so if you didn't kill Klavon, what did you do?"

Darius's words were cruel, but Prydon responded quietly, as if he deserved the malice.

"I looked for you and your mother. I searched for days, but you were nowhere to be found. A terrible blizzard came in, and I was more frantic than ever. I was growing weaker, and I knew I would not be able to search much longer." Prydon closed his eyes. "My fear was that it had all been for naught. I was afraid I had failed your father."

Darius stared at the dragon. Prydon's eyes were still closed, and Darius thought of the deep gashes he had seen in his vision. For the first time, Darius noticed the scars beneath and between the scales that so beautifully armored Prydon's body. Why had he never noticed them before?

With a deep breath, Prydon's eyes opened. "The next day, I thought of Brandor. When I got there, I found Miora had sought refuge in a small inn. She was safe, as were you. I remained outside the village and watched."

Darius waited for Prydon to continue, but Prydon said nothing.

"You watched," restated Darius, but his words did nothing to aid Prydon in continuing his story. "Alright, so what did you do then?"

"Nothing. I knew the barrier would keep you safe as long as you stayed there, so I watched."

The continual breaks in Prydon's story annoyed Darius, and he sighed out loud. "For how long?"

"Until I met you in the marsh."

The sigh Darius released became a quiet gasp. He was speechless and sat dumbfounded for several moments. Then he asked quietly, "For fourteen years?"

"I made a promise." Prydon lowered his head. "A promise that cost your father his life."

Chapter Twenty

The Pathetic Village

Klavon continued his siege. Every night, he attacked. Even though the young girl had left—just as he'd wanted—he maintained his ruse.

His plan was working perfectly. Soon Alara would fulfill his needs—Sira had ensured that. He grinned as he summoned a fresh storm of fire, cascading down and terrorizing the town.

The villagers ran, tossing water on the flames, trying to save their pathetic little houses and shops. And as he allowed their success, he laughed. If only they had known just who he was—just how powerful he was—they would have cowered away, running in fear and abandoning their village.

All was working as planned. The curse would draw the boy to him, of that Klavon was certain. And the plight of the village was the first step.

Chapter Twenty-one

A Strange Assault

The night before, Darius and Prydon hardly spoke. Morning came, and even though Darius knew the truth, pain still hung heavy in the air like a weight around his neck. His father's death lingered so fresh—the blade, the blood, Klavon's laugh, all new as if it had occurred only yesterday. Darius wanted to remain angry with Prydon. He wanted to shout at him. He wanted to blame him for all those years without his father, all those years he could have been raised around people who loved him and whom he loved in return. Brandor was no such place, and for a moment, he wondered why he even wanted to save it. The red veins pulsed in his wrist, a reminder of evil, and for a split second Darius could relate. Then he thought of Mr. Athus and the kindness he had bestowed upon Darius all those years…and there was his mother.

Darius blinked, willing himself away from the temptation of hatred, and the veins slowed their pulsing rage. He glanced over the small fire at his dragon friend. "You were with me when I went to Klavon's village, weren't you," he stated, the fatigue of pain preventing emotion from projecting in his words.

"I have never left your side since I found you in Brandor." Prydon's gaze was intense. "Never, except to acquire your sword and staff."

Darius could not look at Prydon, a shadow who stood by him all these years. A silent guardian Darius knew nothing about. Prydon had done nothing wrong. He and his mother were alive…his mother, the one person whose love he never doubted. Darius couldn't imagine what it would have been like without her, and Prydon had kept her alive—kept them alive. Prydon sacrificed years watching him and his mother, and all for a promise he had made Thyre, a promise he kept even after Thyre's death.

"It wasn't your fault, you know—about my father."

"Thank you, Darius." Prydon stared down at the fire, his eyes flickering white in the glow.

Darius gazed at his friend. He could see pain, pain in Prydon's eyes, pain beneath each and every scar as if they existed only to be a constant reminder that Thyre was dead, and Darius wished he could say something that would remove all doubts from Prydon's mind.

Prydon looked up from the fire and smiled. "We make the best choices we can at the time. That is all we can do. At least you and your mother survived, and for that, I am truly grateful."

For the first time, Darius understood that some choices, even those you must make knowing the result will cause pain, can haunt you forever. He looked back at his own and wondered which ones would haunt him…if he lived. If only things had been different.

He looked out at the scorched buildings, recalling

the battle that seemed only yesterday in his mind. "Prydon, why didn't my father call minions like Klavon?"

"Did Barsovy teach you any such spell? To call minions?"

"No."

Prydon's lips tightened. "There is a reason for that. Those minions are vile creatures...abominations of the worst kind. They are called from the very depth of obscene wickedness, void of conscience or morals. Would a wizard with any degree of values use such a beast?"

Darius's response came all too quickly. "Not even to save himself and the village? To save Mom...and me?"

Prydon breathed slowly as if carefully formulating his words. "Even if he had wanted, he could not. Your father was a good man, a good wizard. Minions can only be called from evil by evil. A wizard would have to sacrifice all that is good to use such devices. Would you have wanted that of your father?"

"No. I suppose not," Darius said. "What about Klavon's dragon? I mean, I thought dragons were good, like you."

"His dragon? That was no dragon. Fraenir is a creature of pure evil, hater of dragons and an enemy to my kind. Of a most malevolent spirit, its kind dwells in the bowels of the earth, an astaroth, the crowned prince of hell. However, I understand your confusion. They are able to change their form, but most often they choose to take the form of a dragon, hoping to deceive those they hate most." Prydon stirred the fire and sneered. "But is it obvious to us. We can see through their guise, though their vanity would never allow them to admit it. They continue to portray themselves as dragons, aligning themselves with evil sorcerers such as Klavon. Sadly, in that way, they do us harm. Others, such as those who wrote the book you carry, believe the bad, and our reputation is marred."

Darius reached in his bag and pulled out the book. He'd forgotten completely about it. "Not anymore," he said, tossing the book into the flames. "At least not with me."

"A fitting end for such rubbish," Prydon laughed, "but enough of that. Now we must concentrate on your past so that you can then focus on your future."

"But I've already seen..." Darius swallowed, feeling as though he were trying to consume a rancid piece of meat. "I've already seen my past." His chin fell with the weight of the memory.

"True." Prydon looked up the hill at the remains of a house next to a once grand tower, and Darius's eyes followed. "But there is something more...something you should have."

"What?" asked Darius, looking back at his friend.

"Your father's sword and staff."

"*His* sword and staff?" repeated Darius. Looking at his own, he asked, "Pyrdon, how did you get these for me? Is that something my father was to do?"

"Not exactly," replied Prydon. "You see, when a young wizard is to train, he must first face the dangers of Mount Tyria. It is a journey like no other, in which a young wizard discovers much about himself. In these trials, a young wizard is compelled to face the reality of who he is and to respect the potential of who he can become. In the end, Segrath grants the journeyman a sword and staff, of no wizard power until training is complete, but powerful nonetheless. The sword and staff allow entrance into the training fields."

"But I never did that." Darius was puzzled.

"No, and it is the only time I know of in which Barsovy has trained before such a journey."

Darius looked at the sword and staff which Prydon so eloquently presented to him only days before. "So...how did you get these?"

Prydon laughed. "It was not easy, I can tell you. Segrath...well, we have a connection."

"A connection?" Darius asked.

"Segrath is a dragon." One side of Prydon's mouth curled in a humorous grin. "Well, I guess not exactly a dragon as the rest of us. She will never die."

"What? How is that possible?" Darius asked.

"Darius, those stones, the stones of all wizards, come from dragons. When we die, our bodies, our essence, returns to Mount Tyria. With that, Segrath lives on, and with that she creates the stones that adorn your sword and staff...the dragon's stone."

Darius stared at the stones, glimmering at the ends of his sword and staff...part of a dragon. "Then why do people think so badly of dragons? Why the book?" He glanced at the burning pages, still feeding the fire.

"Fraenir and others like him," answered Prydon. "And Segrath can be quite intimidating, especially to the young who face her. Segrath can give the impression that she is most dangerous, which she is. And while most wizards find the journey too personal to discuss freely, stories are told, and books are written." Prydon glanced at the burning book and then back at Darius. "Even so, she was most put out that I should demand the tools on your behalf. But with a little persuasion, I was able to get them for you."

Darius had no idea that the persuasion of which Prydon spoke was actually a sacrifice. When Segrath stabbed his heart, she not only learned about Darius but about Prydon as well.

Prydon had allowed Segrath to enter his memories, an invasive act that left him vulnerable. This was something no dragon would ever allow, but he had exposed himself and his deepest thoughts—all of them—for Darius.

Darius looked again at his staff and sword. "But if I have my own, why do I need my father's?"

"You don't need them, but you should have them nonetheless," answered Prydon. "We are here, and they are something of your father's to which you can relate…a common bond."

Darius looked to where his father had fallen. Pain tore at his face as there was nothing to be seen but ashes and dirt. "They were probably stolen, after all these years."

"They are here," said Prydon. He looked up at the remains of the old house.

"There?" asked Darius.

"Perhaps." With one swish of his tail, Prydon covered the fire with dirt, and the two headed up the hill along an overgrown path, faintly visible beneath the weeds that now covered it.

Darius entered the doorway, the roof of the house almost completely gone, now piles of rubble scattered against half destroyed walls. Prydon stood outside, staring down through the opening.

Darius looked up at him and then walked slowly inside. He heard a scuffle off in another room. Many creatures surely would find refuge in such a maze of debris, but Darius advanced with caution. He entered what was probably their main sitting room and was greeted by a rat as it ran past, carrying a small piece of rotting cloth. Darius watched as it scurried underneath a shattered table.

Darius laughed. "I'm wasting caution on a rat!"

"Caution is never wasted," replied Prydon.

Still amused with himself, Darius continued through splintered lumber and made his way to what would have been the master bedroom. Just as he stepped through the broken door frame, he heard a scuffle just to one side.

"Another r—", he started, but before he finished the words, he received a stiff greeting across the top of his head.

The sound of cracking wood rang like a crash of thunder in his ears, and his head swirled in a daze. He fell to his knees as two pieces of shattered wood seemed to guide him effortlessly to the floor. Before he could recover from the fog that filled his mind, a body was full on top of him, and he involuntarily rolled in the mass of ashes and wood. Ending up on the bottom, Darius looked into the eyes of a young woman right when a fist came full upon his face.

"Hey!" he yelled, grabbing his bleeding nose.

With a crash, Prydon entered, and suddenly, the girl was high above Darius. She hung upside down in the air, her red hair dangling like flames.

"Put me down!" she screamed. "I'm not afraid of you!"

Prydon raised a brow. "As you wish," he said, with satisfaction.

Darius snickered as Prydon dropped her from six feet high into a soft pile of ash. When she stood, she was coughing. The charcoal covered her face until Darius could hardly determine she was a girl.

She lunged at Darius, but Prydon grabbed the back of her shirt.

"I was here first! You can't have it!" she yelled.

"Have what?" asked Darius.

"The staff. The sword. I don't know. Whatever I find in this old, wizard's house!"

She ceased straining to get free of Prydon and was now attempting to adjust her clothes and hair, wiping as much ash from her face as she could.

"It may interest you to know," said Prydon, "that this young man owns this house."

The girl halted what she was doing and glared back and forth between Prydon and Darius. "This house," she said with venom, "this village has been abandoned for close to fifteen years. Even if I did believe you, and it is highly unlikely that I do, you would have no more claim to this place than I."

"And were I to agree with your assessment, and it is

highly unlikely that I do, just what do you believe you could do with a staff or sword anyway?" asked Prydon.

Darius laughed, and the girl shot him an icy stare. "I would use it to save my village!"

"Your village?" asked Darius, the humor lost.

"Yes, my village," she sneered. "My village is still alive. At least I hope it is. They're under attack, and we need help, any help, even if it is from some archaic sword and staff."

"Where is your wizard?" asked Prydon. He reminded Darius of Barsovy, his words shrouded with a serious power.

"Our wizard died a little over a month ago, unexpectedly. An accident of some sort."

"And you're under attack. By whom?" asked Darius.

"We're not sure," she replied. "He stands by and watches as his minions do the dirty work. Each night they come and scare the villagers. We've already lost several buildings, mostly businesses, but we haven't lost any people—at least when I'd left we hadn't. We did lose a barn with several milking cows, and it's only a matter of time before they start destroying houses, and that means lost life."

"How long has this been going on?" asked Prydon.

"A few days before I left, and it took me almost a week to get here." She stood tall and readjusted her clothing. "So, you see, I need this stuff more than you."

"It won't work for you," said Darius.

"How would you know?" she asked.

Prydon tilted his head, and a slight smile touched his lips. "Because he is a wizard himself."

The girl glared at Darius. "He's too careless."

"I...you caught me off guard," retorted Darius.

"Exactly!" The girl folded her arms in front of her chest and leaned heavily on one leg, her jaw set. "All right, then. For what village did you train?"

Darius looked from the girl to Prydon, and Prydon shrugged. "I...I guess Brandor."

"You guess? Some wizard," she snuffed. Then, as if she were stung by a bee, the young woman jolted. Her eyes were drawn to Darius's weaponry. "Wait a minute." Her weight shifted back to both legs and her jaw dropped. "Those are...are wizard's tools?"

Darius pulled his sword and staff from their resting place upon his back. "Yes, they are." He looked up at Prydon. "And apparently, I have more lessons to learn."

"Like respecting caution?" asked Prydon with a grin.

"Yes, and apparently I can learn them from a young woman," he said, bowing to the girl.

Darius's attempt at a compliment appeared to fall wasted on the girl as she clambered in the ashes.

"So you weren't lying," she said. "You really are a wizard? Then I don't need this stuff." She held up what looked like a broken staff, and for Darius the world screeched to a sudden stop.

"May I see that?" he asked.

The girl handed the broken staff to Darius. "Don't you see? You can come back with me and help our village."

The words were like a distant echo to Darius as he looked down at the staff, the pristine white crystal cracked and the wood fractured. His eyes swelled, and he sat down on the floor.

"What's wrong with him," the girl asked.

Prydon spoke quietly. "As I said, this is his house."

"But that isn't possible. The wizard who lived here died almost fifteen years ago, and his wife was claimed by a vicious storm. He never had any children."

"He did, and his wife escaped the storm, she and her newborn child. This is Darius, and he has come back to fulfill a destiny that has long been awaiting him."

"But the stories—"

"Were not complete," finished Prydon. "This is Thyre's son."

The girl knelt beside Darius, staring at him, and he looked up through blurred vision.

"I'm sorry," she said, "but I need your help. My village needs your help."

Darius looked up at Prydon. "The sword?"

Prydon uncovered a small pile of shattered timbers and pulled out a sword, bent completely in two. He handed it to Darius.

"No! How could this be?" asked Darius.

"Klavon. This could only have been accomplished by another wizard. No other would have that kind of power," said Prydon.

The girl was still sitting next to Darius. "Look. I'm sorry, but your father...well, that can't be changed, but you can still help me. So what if this staff and sword are, well, messed up. You have your own."

"So what! So what? How dare you! This was my father's! The only thing I had left, and now it's…it's—"

The girl stood defiantly. "It's in the past! But the destruction that is happening in my village is in the here and now! And if you would get over it and come help us, the lives of many—"

"The lives of many?" shouted Darius. "The lives of many are already being lost in Brandor! My obligation is to them!"

The words stung his throat as he said them. Never before had he cared about the people of Brandor, and why should he. They never cared about him or his mother—all except Mr. Athus. But that one man was the world to him, and he would not let him be lost. And what of his own mother?

"You selfish idiot!" she shouted. "Here you are, sitting amongst ruins of a past you cannot change, rambling about some town you think you trained for, and are you there helping them now? Nooooo." The girl waved her hands around mockingly. "You sit here like a spoiled brat while people may be dying. And if Bran— whatever it's called—is so important to you, why did you even come back here? You already have a staff and sword."

Darius stood, his eyes on fire as he stared at this girl. "How dare you judge me? You have no idea—"

The girl screamed. "Ugh! You egocentric little…. Give me those."

The girl snatched from Darius's hands the staff and

sword that belonged to his father and ran. Darius and Prydon were momentarily stunned by her actions. After blinking a few times, Darius followed, but the lead she had gained was too much to overcome in the debris. Before Darius could stop her, she tossed the broken weapons down a deep well.

Darius ran to the edge of the well, screaming, but the splash below deafened his cry, and he stood in silence.

"That good enough for you?" she snapped.

"Why did you do that?" Darius demanded, raising his hands as if he wanted to strangle this girl.

"Because you needed it. Wake up, you idiot." She slapped Darius square across the face. "This is real life here and people are dying. So what are you going to do about it?"

The sting still hung on his cheek, but Darius didn't care. "Me? Why is this all of the sudden my responsibility?"

"Because you are the only wizard around! And we need you!"

Darius opened his mouth to speak, but all that came out was a puff of air. He looked over at Prydon who stood behind the girl and shrugged his shoulders.

He looked back at the girl. "I can't. I have to go to the Valley of Wizards, and then I have to defeat Klavon."

"So, you can't spare even a short time to help us with our insignificant lives?" The girl's eyes rolled. "You're a wizard! You can fly your dragon to our town, get rid of the minions, defeat this wizard, and head back to your own more important life."

Darius looked again at Prydon. Prydon raised a brow but was silent.

"I…" Darius stopped.

The girl started to say something, but Prydon placed a claw on her shoulder. She was silenced, and Prydon bowed his head toward Darius and then looked toward the village below.

Darius turned and walked to the edge of the hill overlooking the charred remains. Only the night before he had watched as Klavon killed his father. And as his father lay dying, the ensuing conglomerate of broken lives, revealed now in the spots of ash and tinder, glass and brick, were the result of Klavon's minions and their vicious attack almost fifteen years before. His village had been destroyed, scattered…lost forever.

Darius's head fell to his chest, heavy and confused. His eyes shifted to the side as he thought of the girl standing only a few yards behind him. And now minions, exactly like Klavon's, were attacking her village, and her people were suffering just as his own people had.

He breathed heavily and his eyes scanned the wreckage once again.

Prydon moved to stand beside him and also stared out at the village below.

"What do I do, Prydon?" Darius asked quietly.

"That is a choice only you can make," he said.

Darius thought of Brandor and the disappearance of the houses. Then he thought of the woman, swallowed by Fraenir. "They could end up just like here," Darius said, nodding back at the girl behind them. "They could end up destroyed, in charred ruins and death."

"Yes, they could," said Prydon.

"But Brandor. It's disappearing, and I have to help them."

"Yes, you do." Prydon's gaze never left the village below.

Darius's head sank. "But what makes the people of Brandor any more important than the people of her village?" asked Darius, not expecting an answer, to which Prydon obliged with none.

"Well?" asked the voice from behind them.

Darius spoke softly, "Brandor has waited this long. I guess they can wait a little longer." He stood taller and turned around. "I'll do it."

The girl squealed, and Darius looked at Prydon. "Will I be able to fight without first going to the valley?"

"It is possible, but the consequences could be dire. If you fight before your character has been determined by the wizards of old, you risk everything. You must remain strong in virtue not in anger, never swaying as you fight."

"How can I not be angry?" asked Darius.

"Anger alone is not the harm; a certain amount of anger can strengthen your resolve. It is when you allow that anger to control that you risk losing yourself." Prydon paused and then said, "It will not be easy."

"Of course not," said Darius, shaking his head as if he really had no choice. "I only hope I can do this."

"Of course you can," said the girl. "So let's go."

Darius nodded slowly, and Prydon kneeled to the ground. Darius climbed on and held out a hand to the girl.

"Well?"

The girl nose wrinkled, and she bit her lip. "It's a…dragon."

"I am," said Prydon. "And I am your quickest way to get home."

Alara hesitated but climbed on behind Darius and held tightly around his waist. Darius leaned forward and grabbed on to Prydon's neck. With the familiar push up from the ground, Darius thought of Brandor.

Chapter Twenty-two

The Stolen Stone

Klavon heard the flap of wings as he exited his fortress and walked into the early morning light, shrouded as he preferred, in clouds.

Fraenir landed. "I have it. How are your plans at the village progressing?"

"Quite well," answered Klavon. "I will return tonight, but I believe any day now, we will have a better understanding of our young sorcerer's talents."

"And Prydon? Are you certain you don't want—"

"It is imperative that they not recognize me. For that to happen, there is no scenario where you could be present. Don't worry, my friend. I can handle Prydon," said Klavon. "It is only for a short time, and once I see what needs to be seen, I will leave—and no one will ever suspect it was me."

Fraenir nodded and bowed, and then he held out his clawed hand. As the fingers uncurled, in his palm lay a dragon's stone.

"Ahhh," said Klavon, and he took the stone from Fraenir's hand. "Are you ready?"

"I am," said Fraenir.

"I will not deceive you. This will be most

unpleasant, but I assure you that it will be well worth the initial pain."

Fraenir closed his eyes. "I am ready."

Klavon cupped the stone in both hands and whispered strange words. The words seemed to form an amber mist, swirling around the stone until they settled like a net, completely encasing it with its poison.

Klavon then raised his hands high above his head, still holding the stone, and thrust the jewel directly into Fraenir's chest. Fraenir screamed, fire shooting all around.

Klavon stepped back as the beast writhed in pain, stumbling and falling and then straining again to stand, raising his head and screaming a cry that only a dragon—only an astaroth can.

The sorcerer watched as the stone fused deep into Fraenir's scales. An amber net remaining as a cover almost as if it were a protective force, keeping the stone in place.

Fraenir continued to scream until he collapsed to the ground. Klavon walked over to him and spoke quietly into the beast's ear.

"You are going to be fine...extraordinary in fact."

Klavon placed a hand on the stone, and Fraenir's breathing slowed. Slowly the dragon's eyes opened.

"It is done," said Klavon.

Fraenir stood once again, no waiver in his step, and took a heavy breath.

"How do you feel?"

Fraenir nodded. "Good...better than good."

The amber-encased stone pulsed in Fraenir's chest, and red lightning began to spread through his veins, visible in streaks throughout his scales and wings. It was a threatening look, and Klavon knew that when Prydon saw this, that alone would cause him fear.

Klavon grinned and laughed. "You have power no other of your kind has ever had. Prydon will not know what hit him, the next time he faces you."

"But not the village?" asked Fraenir.

"Patience, Fraenir, patience," said Klavon. "The village is simply a tool of manipulation. Your time will come soon enough, and you will destroy Prydon once and for all."

Chapter Twenty-three

The Minion's Hold

Night had already passed before they reached the outskirts of the village, and the smoke-filled air bore witness to the previous night's destruction. Darius lowered himself off of Prydon's back and helped the girl down.

She began to cry. "So much destruction. Why does he keep dragging this out? Why doesn't he just finish us off and be done with it?"

Darius walked to her side and put his arm around her shoulder. "I'm sorry, um…What is your name?"

"Alara." The name was whispered through a choppy voice.

"I'm sorry, Alara. Don't give up. I'll do what I can." Darius glanced over at Prydon. "We'll do what we can."

"I have to get to my family. I have to make sure they are safe." Alara's eye swelled with tears.

"Go," said Prydon. "Tell them of our presence, and when the attack comes once more, we will be ready. Until then, we will remain here, hidden from your attacker's view."

Alara simply nodded and then ran toward her

village. Darius watched until she was no longer in sight. Sitting on a log, he stared down into a pile of dirt he'd been pushing around with his foot.

"Why does this sorcerer keep coming back? I mean, with my father's village—with my village—Klavon destroyed them in one huge battle. Why this?" Darius gestured at the tortured town.

"It is odd," said Prydon. "Perhaps this is a young sorcerer, one who has not yet achieved full command of his abilities. Or perhaps he simply wants to break the village, break their will to exist and not destroy it. With no wizard present, they are vulnerable to sorcerers who would wish to force them into subjugation."

"That doesn't seem right," said Darius. "I mean, why wouldn't a wizard make sure that his village is taken care of before he...you know, dies or something."

"I agree. Wizards always have a plan. It could be the protection of a neighboring wizard, an agreement with a wizard who has yet to take a village of his own, or even a son to take his pl—"

"A son!" exclaimed Darius, jumping up from the log. "Prydon, could this be Norinar's village...Loklan's village?"

Prydon hesitated and then said, "Alara would have known my name, and it was clear she did not."

"Maybe...but Barsovy said Loklan's father had died unexpectedly, and Alara said the same about her wizard."

Prydon nodded. "True, but most likely this is an odd coincidence."

"Why?" asked Darius.

"Because when a wizard trains, as is Loklan, the village for whom he trains is under Barsovy's protection."

Darius said, "I know Barsovy is, well, everywhere at the training field, but he couldn't possibly—"

"Barsovy acts with powers beyond those of normal wizards. His power comes from the valley and the wizards of old. With their strength, he places a spell to shelter a village whose wizard is in training," said Prydon. "Basically, they become invisible to any sorcerer wishing to take over a village already granted a wizard's care."

"So this couldn't possibly be Loklan's village," said Darius

"Unless…" Prydon's head swayed as if in deep contemplation.

"Unless what?" asked Darius.

"Unless the sorcerer attacking this village has no desire to conquer it. Unless his motive is only to attract the attention of someone else," said Prydon. "In that case, Barsovy's spell would have no effect. And even though a sorcerer's objective, by his very nature, is to conquer and rule, there is one."

Darius had never seen Prydon look so worried. "You think it's Klavon…and he's trying to get to me."

"Let us hope not," said Prydon, closing his eyes and shaking his head.

With a rustle of leaves, Alara appeared on a path from the village. She was carrying a basket of food. "My family is safe for now. I thought—"

"Was Norinar your wizard?" Prydon asked, his eyes now open.

Alara's eyes became wide and then her brow wrinkled with confusion. "What? Well, yes, but—"

Darius started to speak, but Prydon cut in, a brief glance telling Darius to stay quiet.

"We met Loklan at the training fields. It was mentioned his father was killed in an accident."

"Yes, he's my cousin," said Alara. "I only came to this village a few months ago, when my mother passed. Shortly after was when the accident occurred. I only saw Locklan for a short time, at the burial. Is he doing well?"

"Yes," answered Prydon. "He is doing very well. Is that food?"

Alara smiled and glanced at her basket. "I wanted to do something. It's not much, but…"

"Thank you," said Darius, taking the basket.

"I need to get back now," she said. She headed toward town but stopped and turned around. "Thank you. Thank you both."

Darius smiled, and Prydon nodded.

"Why didn't you tell her about Klavon?" asked Darius when she was adequately gone.

"There is no need. If it is Klavon, then telling her might cause this village to lay blame on you—lose faith in you. That is something we can not chance. They are counting on you…and it is, after all, only a suspicion."

"A huge, logical suspicion," said Darius. He sat back down on the log, the basket of food set beside him, and remained frozen. His breathing quickened as he thought about what Prydon said. "I'm scared, Prydon."

Prydon rubbed his chin with his clawed hand and

said, "Barsovy would not have given you that sword and staff unless he believed that you were ready."

"But the Valley of Wizards?" Darius asked, looking up at his friend.

Prydon nodded. "The valley is indeed a final step in your training, but it teaches you nothing more than the strength of your character. Your skills in battle have already been taught, and that is what you will need here."

"But what if I fail? What if I become angry and Klavon defeats me?"

Prydon smiled. "What if you succeed? What if you temper your anger and defeat Klavon? Then your task is completed, here, this very evening."

Darius sat quietly and stared out over distant hills.

Prydon continued, "A certain amount of fear in battle is healthy. It heightens your senses and allows you to embrace caution, a lesson I believe you recently learned. Besides, we don't even know for sure it is Klavon."

Darius bolted. "Prydon—Fraenir! He might be here as well!"

"I am prepared," replied Prydon. "I have my own debt to settle."

Few words were spoken the remainder of the day, and when evening came, he and Prydon walked to the edge of the village and waited in a veil of darkness behind the closest building. The villagers who passed by returning to their homes did not notice them, but anxiety hung thick and venomous in the air, connecting the villagers in a web of shared apprehension. And they were all depending on him and Prydon for protection.

As Alara predicted, minions began to appear.

"Remember our plan," said Prydon. "You will do well, Darius, and I will see you soon."

Without hesitation, Prydon flew to the other end of town to work from there, and Darius stepped into the street, wielding his staff and sword. They would do what they could to sandwich the enemy and devour them up.

Focusing his concentration, Darius breathed deeply and began extinguishing fires that were already ablaze. Alara was correct. They were now attacking houses, and Darius spent most of his energy defending those first. The minions were fast, very fast, and Darius began to wonder if he'd spend his entire night cleaning behind their path instead of confronting them directly.

As if on cue, the small demons split, and several headed directly for Darius. His attention now alternated between the fires and the groups of minions. A few avoided his attack and crept in close, growling with sharp teeth. Darius sliced with his sword as they lunged for him, and their tiny bodies fell to the ground. It was brutal, and no sooner would he disperse one group than another would appear.

As Darius held a spell to extinguish a large fire, minions enclosed upon him. He held his sword to keep them at bay, focusing his staff on the fire, while some of the villagers appeared nearby and formed a water brigade. The minions changed their target. They squealed and ran for the villagers, attempting to prevent them from dousing the flames. For a moment, Darius would be forced to decide between saving a second barn or destroying those minions. To his surprise, however, Alara appeared and took it upon herself to protect them. With a large club, she booted them away, sending them flying in a broken heap. One managed to weasel its way exceptionally close to Alara, and she punched it soundly in the face.

Darius laughed, thinking briefly of the first time he had met her, but this diversion was quickly interrupted as the roof of a nearby house began to cave in. Villagers appeared inside the door, a woman with several small children, and Darius waved his staff. The roof remained steady, and as if in response, Alara ran to their aid.

Darius strained, and it took all his concentration as Alara aided the woman and children from the burning home. From behind, however, a small band of minions clambered atop his body, and Darius could hold it no longer; the roof collapsed. Flames, sparks, and shattered timbers came crashing down, and Darius screamed as he lost sight of Alara and the villagers. He whirled about and with one strike, sent the minions to oblivion. Frantically, he sent a spell to douse the flames, and he ran toward the house.

Alara, the woman, and the children emerged from the smoke, coughing but otherwise reasonably in good health.

Alara stared at Darius. "Go!"

Darius hesitated. Alara's arm trickled with blood from a large cut, and her face was scratched. Anger began to swell within him. The stone in his staff began to pulse, and a flicker of red sparked deep within its cloudy surface. He blinked hard, remembering the words Prydon had spoken to him.

Alara shoved him soundly in the chest. "Go, I said! We'll be fine!"

Blood pounded through his heart, but he nodded. Leaving Alara behind, he focused his attention on one task; reaching the center of the town where he and Prydon had agreed to meet.

As he headed down the cluttered street, Darius was faced with a mob of demons. With a wave of his staff, the line of minions was sent flying, their high-pitched screams melting in the wind. He had no time to discern if Prydon had made any headway as a group of three attacked. One jumped on his back, while two others clawed at his waist and legs. A snap of his staff on the ground sent a shock wave several yards out, and all three were thrown against nearby walls of buildings. In a daze they lay there, and Darius's jaw tensed. He snarled, and with another flash, they were gone, pulverized into dust.

Darius continued to work his way toward the center of town as lines of evil creatures sent bolts of fire in every direction. The villagers were trying to douse the flames, but their progress was slow and they were losing ground. Darius did what he could between assaults to help them, but his main focus now was against the minions themselves.

No sooner would Darius send a line of the vile creatures to their graves than another wave would come. Several managed to break ranks, pouncing on him with the same results as before, but one managed to take a sizable bite out of his shoulder. Darius screamed in pain. He grabbed the minion around the neck and threw it to the ground in front of him. The minion laughed, Darius's blood dripping from its mouth, but in an instant it was no more, annihilated by Darius's spell.

Darius winced from the pain, but he pushed on. He wasn't far from the center of town where they had agreed to meet, and as he reached their rendezvous, Prydon was already in the midst of battling hordes of minions.

"Up there!" Prydon yelled as he slashed with his tail at a minion quartet attempting to climb his spine.

Darius looked where Prydon motioned. Atop a barn in the middle of the village stood a sorcerer. He was older than Darius, but still quite young, much too young to be Klavon, but Darius had no time to ponder it. The sorcerer's laughter echoed above the flames that shot about him as he stood, his image hazed by the heat of the fire.

Prydon roared, and Darius's gaze shot back to his friend. Several groups of minions attempted to engulf him only to become ash in his path, but many broke through. Prydon spun, and several others were skewered and slung by his massive tail.

"Prydon!" yelled Darius.

"No! I can handle this! You take care of him!"

Darius turned back to the sorcerer, who now appeared in front of the building facing Darius.

"So you think you can take me, do you?" Flames continued to surround the sorcerer as he slowly headed toward Darius. "No, I don't think so. Everyone will know of the power I have demonstrated here. Everyone will fear me!"

A dull punch in his stomach, and Darius was thrown backwards into a pile of firewood. His staff and sword were thrown from his grip and lay a few yards away. Darius hissed and scrambled toward his weapons, ignoring the stab of pain in his side, and bounced to his feet. He attempted to clear his mind and focus.

With his own staff, he attacked, but the sorcerer countered it, dispersing its effects into a cloud of dust. Returning Darius's attack, Darius was pleased to find his reaction instinctive, and he too dispensed of the sorcerer's blow. Barsovy's shadow would have been proud.

The sorcerer laughed. "Very good. You have some talent."

Darius would not take the bait. He had experience with this back in Brandor. Many times, some of the other youth would try to provoke him into a fight, to which end he was always laid complete blame. Punishment came swiftly from the villagers, and to keep the peace, his mother would promise likewise at home. Once home, however, she would sit him down and talk about how others who were cruel would intentionally use such tactics and that he must not allow it. It didn't take long for him to learn to turn away, which is one reason he grew up alone.

This sorcerer reminded him of the bullies back in Brandor, praying on those weaker than he and provoking those less able. But Darius was not less able, and he would not turn away—not this time.

With a confident smile, Darius said in a calm, cool, even tone, "Talent and brains, and a dragon."

The sorcerer scowled and brought more minions,

but with Prydon's help, Darius concentrated ferocious attacks on the sorcerer, only occasionally striking a stray minion with his sword. The sorcerer, forced to focus on Darius, began to lose his hold, and it wasn't long before the sorcerer's army began to diminish. All that was left was the final confrontation between Darius and the sorcerer.

Attack after attack, neither Darius nor the sorcerer gained any ground as one would quickly dissipate the other's spells. Some villagers huddled in the distance, too afraid to come any closer, and the volley between Darius and sorcerer continued.

After some time, Darius screamed, "Enough of this!" With sword in hand, he charged, and hand-to-hand combat ensued.

Darius's arms were sore, his shoulder bleeding from the earlier bite, and his ribs screamed for relief, but he did not stop. He dodged blows, made strikes of his own, and after what seemed an eternity, the sorcerer laughed and took a step backwards.

"You win," he said calmly and vanished.

Darius spun in circles this way and that like a top bouncing off bumpers. "Where it he?"

"He's gone," said Prydon.

Alara came running up and lunged at Darius with an enormous hug. "You did it!"

"Ow," Darius squeaked.

"Oh, sorry. Are you all right?" she asked.

"I will be. Prydon, is he really gone?" asked Darius.

Prydon scoured the village end to end with his piercing eyes. "It would seem so, but that was too easily accomplished."

"Easy?" Alara snapped. "That was the worse yet. It was a vicious battle."

Prydon frowned. "No, it was not."

"Is that why you left him to fight that evil thing alone?" Alara scowled. "Once the minions were gone? You just sat by—"

"Darius needed that battle," Prydon responded. "And I would have come to his aid had he truly needed me. In fact, I was expecting to, but as I said, this victory was too easily accomplished."

Darius nodded. Prydon had allowed Darius the opportunity to face anger and prevail, which was worth the wounds, but why did Prydon think it was easy? Pain shot through Darius's side, and he gasped for air.

"Darius?" asked Prydon, supporting him with his clawed hand.

Alara called for help, and Prydon carried Darius to a small house. A doctor appeared at the door and ushered Darius inside and onto a bed.

"You've broken a rib and bruised several others." The doctor said a while later, pouring a small amount of greenish fluid into a glass. "Here. Take this."

"What is it?" asked Darius, holding the pungent mixture up to his nose.

"Something to make you sleep. You need rest. Undisturbed rest."

"Is that really necessary?" Darius tried to hand the glass back to the doctor, to which he received a stern glare.

Alara smiled. "Prydon will wait outside and keep

watch. Don't worry. We'll be fine."

Reluctantly, Darius took the drink. With one gulp, his eyes glazed over, and he floated into an abyss.

Chapter Twenty-four

The Diversion

The curse was powerful, and if left to the curse, the boy would die, not of body but of soul. It was not as he had originally liked—he would gladly see the young brat dead at his feet—but Klavon smiled as he envisioned Darius, alive yet a reflection of the one he'd learn to call Father—no longer a legacy to Thyre but to Klavon himself. And Miora would see her son, his living body, and her smile would return.

The loyalty of Darius would ensure her love…and respect. But the final conversion still needed to happen. And while the curse strongly drew Darius to him, there was still the matter of the Valley.

If Klavon could convince the boy, somehow, to search for him instead of returning to face the ancestors, it would make his task much easier.

Sira walked up behind him, and he turned to face her.

"He fought well," she said.

"He did, and for that I am pleased. I am also pleased that despite his training, he is still no match for me—not that he ever would have been."

"But?"

Sira was perceptive, and he reached over and cupped her chin in his hand.

"You are very beautiful," he said. "I believe you could easily convince Darius to pursue his quest to find and destroy me." Klavon released her chin and nodded. "Yes, I believe he should come straight here instead of returning for his final evaluation."

"Will that be possible? With Prydon, I mean?" she asked.

"The boy is recovering, and his mind is more vulnerable to your suggestion. Not that you aren't sufficiently able, otherwise." Klavon turned away from Sira and looked out into the dark sky. "And, as I said, you are beautiful. Surely you have that to your advantage."

He said nothing else, but he knew that Sira vanished behind him, always eager to do his bidding. His eyes narrowed as a thin smile creased lips. Soon….

Sira floated about the room and waited. The girl she watched stirred annoyance in her spirit, and she felt…threatened. But there was no way this girl could threaten her. By comparison, Sira was easily Alara's superior. It would be like equating a wolf to a dog, and this girl looked every bit an incompetent mongrel to Sira.

Alara leaned over the sleeping Darius and ran a wet cloth over his forehead. Then she set the cloth down. Sira tensed when the girl gently kissed him on his cheek, and she wanted to leave her hidden state and rip the girl's heart out. It would have been easily done, but instead she endured watching this mutt tend to his needs.

It was necessary. There was that perfect time to persuade his thoughts, but she had to be careful. With the draft given by the doctor, her invasion could cause harm, and that was not to be allowed. If she waited too long, however, his mind would be strong enough to keep her out as he had done in the training fields.

No…but soon. For three more days, she waited until it was time. That night, after Alara fell asleep in the chair next to the bed, Sira floated down and into Darius's mind.

Chapter Twenty-five

The Decision

Darius had no idea how long he slept when he heard a soft voice invade his rest and confuse his thoughts.

"You were magnificent," she whispered, close to his face and into his ear.

He could feel the warm breath brush against his cheek, and he tried to force his eyes open. They were heavy as if made of lead. When he was able to wrench them open, the effects of the drink prevented him from focusing, but the outline of the figure and the color of the hair told him who it was.

"You?" he asked perplexed. For a moment he felt disoriented and didn't remember the fight, but then the stab of pain from his wounds brought vivid recollection of the events of the battle. "I'm in Alara's village. How did you...why are you—"

"Shhhh," Sira said, placing a single finger softly across his lips as she sat next to him on the bed. "She's insignificant anyway, in the great scheme of things. I've been trying to find you for ages."

"Wait. What?" Darius blinked several times, trying to encourage his eyes to work properly. The dizziness in his head made it feel as if the room was spinning, so it was not an easy task. In fact, it would have been much easier to lie with his eyes closed, but he fought to see what he could. "Find me? Why?"

"I saw the burglars. I followed them when you left the inn. I knew they were up to no good. It was that sword, you know, so I wanted to help you."

"You?"

"Yes, it was me there, and I was trying to come up with a plan to rescue you—you do seem to need quite a bit of that, don't you—but then your dragon came." She paused and cupped the side of his face. "And took you away."

Darius was speechless. With vision that was flawed, he felt for her hand and pulled it away.

Sira sighed. "Still shy, but I like that about you. Kinda growing on me." She smiled, stood up, and walked to the window, looking out. Darius could barely make out her feminine silhouette, a soft light shining somewhere beyond the glass. She continued, "Ever since I met you, I knew what you were." She turned back to him and sat in a chair next to the bed, still leaning closer than Darius would have liked. "That mark...and the sword. You had to be a wizard, and I decided it was time."

Darius realized his hand was exposed, allowing full inspection of the spiral marks, and he quickly pulled the blankets up over his arm.

"There's no need for that. Remember? I saw them when I saved you from the stalks. Even though you wouldn't tell me anything, I know that color. I know who gave that to you. And I know you need to face him to defeat that curse. So, as I said, it's time."

"Time?" Darius was disinclined to divulge any of his intentions, and he squirmed, trying to inch away from her but finding that his body was as uncooperative as his eyes. The medicine the doctor had given him was very effective indeed.

"Time for you to free our people," she said. "I know you've been training. That's what all wizards do. And of course, what with your problems with the barrier and then the thieves—and who knows what else since we last parted—you would *have* to train."

Sira was a professional at overemphasizing uncomfortable words, and now was no different. *Have* to train...Darius simply lay there and listened.

"And now this." Sira waved her arm in a gesture of the entire village. "I know you can defeat him now."

"I told you, I was just exploring," said Darius, but even he had to admit it was a lame explanation.

"Of course you were," Sira winked. "Listen. I know you are supposed to go back to the Valley of Wizards to have your stones blessed or something." She giggled. "Well, that is what you wizards do, right? Anyway, you've proven your abilities here, and if *I* know you are supposed to go the valley, then so does Klavon."

"So," said Darius, not willing to reveal anything.

"So...you go straight to Klavon! Skip the valley!" Sira held both hands up, palms raised as if all was obvious. "He'd never expect it, and you would catch him off guard."

Darius just stared at her.

"That's called an advantage," she said, raising an eyebrow.

"I know what it's called," Darius snapped, and he suddenly felt very much like the awkward boy she saved from the dead stalks.

"My sweet Darius," she said. "Yes, I know your name. I heard the dragon say it. Impressive creature, too. So is it a deal?"

Darius ignored her question. "How did you get here? I mean, you're pretty far from Klavon's land, aren't you? And someone must have seen you."

"Not a soul," she answered. "And don't worry about me. I have a cat, a very large cat, and he gets me where I need to go. But you need to rest." She touched his lips with her finger once again.

As if on queue, Darius's head began to spin, and he moaned. He could fight the fatigue no longer, and his eyes closed.

"Yes, my sweet," Sira whispered, this time her breath against his mouth, and Darius felt her lips brush back and forth across his, slowly before ending with a gentle kiss. "And I'll be waiting for you…"

He was helpless to respond and drifted once again into a very deep, dreamless sleep.

When he awoke, he was lying in bed with Alara sitting in the chair next to him, her head bent down as if asleep.

Darius looked around the room then spoke softly, not wanting to startle her. "Where is she?"

Alara's head picked up and her eyes popped open.

"I'm here...I've been here all this time."

Darius glanced around the room. His eyes no longer fought him, and he blinked several times to clear his vision. "No...wait...must have been a weird dream or something. How long have I been asleep?" Darius rubbed his hand across the linen bandages that encased his chest and ribs and tried to sit up.

Alara stood quickly and helped him, pulling extra pillows behind his back. "Three days. Pretty much, anyways. You woke for short periods of time, and I was able to get you to eat, but I'm guessing you don't remember."

"Not really," said Darius, still thinking of Sira.

"With the medication I'd be surprised," Alara said, laughing. She walked to a small fire and ladled some soup that had been warming in the flames.

That must have been it, Darius decided. He must have been hallucinating from the medication.

Alara walked back and handed Darius the small bowl of soup. "He bandaged you after you were asleep...thought it would be less painful that way. And he stitched your shoulder. A couple of weeks and you should be able to take those out—it was a nasty bite."

Darius steadied himself with one hand and took the warm bowl of soup with the other. "What about the sorcerer?"

"He hasn't come back. I think he's gone for good," she said as she helped him hold the bowl of soup.

Alara looked well. A bandage covered the gash in her arm, and her face, although scratched, was a pleasing sight.

"Are you all right? Your arm?" he asked, thoughts of Sira fading. "And the rest of the people? Did any..."

"I'm fine. It's just a scratch." Alara smiled. "And, no, we didn't lose anyone. A few minor wounds and burns, but nothing we can't take care of. You saved us—you saved us all, you and Prydon. Now eat."

Darius sipped the soup. He hadn't tasted anything that good since he'd left home. He closed his eyes and breathed the scent, pulling the bowl up to his face.

"Prydon told me about the mark."

Darius's eyes shot open. His gloves had been removed, and the crimson marks were clearly visible. "Uh—"

"It's all right. I understand. I hope you find a way to save your village, too." Alara's eyes shifted, and she idly removed a piece of lint from her clothes. "I guess it was selfish of me to ask you to help us, but I had no choice."

"You don't have to explain. You were right." Darius took a last huge gulp of soup and set the bowl on a small table next to the bed. "But I should get back now."

"But you're still weak," she said.

"I'll be fine. I'll get my strength back before I face him. But I really do need to go. Three days..."

Alara hesitated and then smiled. "Yes, of course."

"Um, my shirt?" He lifted the covers and glanced under the blanket. "And my pants?"

"Oh, here." Alara seemed to blush and walked to a nearby chest of drawers. She pulled out Darius's clothes, washed and neatly folded, and laid them on the end of the bed. "I'll just wait outside."

Darius dressed, the tension from the bandage challenging his movement, but when he finished, he joined Alara outside. The warmth of the sun washed over him, but the smell of burnt wood hung in the air—a reminder of the frail victory. His eyes were saddened as he scoured the village. The damage was severe—the structure that had fallen three nights before now sat in a mangled heap across the path—and he wondered if the town would have survived another strike.

Some progress had been made, however. Many villagers were bustling about, cleaning up the ash and repairing buildings. Others were moving more slowly, bandages covering various parts of their bodies, but they were all helping in any way they could. A few noticed him and greeted him with thanks and praise, but Darius felt inadequate. He wished he could have prevented more of the devastation. Soon, the entire village gathered nearby.

"I see you are up and about," said Prydon, landing with a thud beside him. Still new to the sight of a dragon, some of the villagers instinctively backed away.

"Brilliant observation, as always, my friend." Darius laughed, but a cough took over and he buckled at the pain.

"At least your wounds don't require the use of a pillow," Prydon said with a smile.

"Pillow?" asked Alara.

"Long story," replied Darius.

"And you appear to be back to your usual self, for the most part. That is good as it is time for you to return to the valley to finalize your training."

Darius thought about his dream with Sira—what else could it have been—but decided he'd tell Prydon later, when they were alone.

"What about the sorcerer?" Darius asked. "Alara seems to think he's gone for good. What do you think?"

Prydon's brows creased, and his eyes shifted in search of an elusive memory. "I have never seen him before, but he was, in some peculiar way, familiar. No matter. He believes you will remain to defend this village, and I doubt he will return."

"Especially when that wizard has a dragon." Alara laughed and handed Darius his staff and sword. She leaned forward and gave him a gentle kiss on the cheek. "Thank you. Don't worry. We'll be all right."

"And I suspect Loklan will be completing his training soon. However, I will inform Barsovy so that he can reevaluate his protective spell," added Prydon. He leaned down, and Darius climbed on his back.

The villagers expressed their gratitude with waves and kind words, and when all formalities were done, Darius said, "Perhaps we will meet again."

Alara smiled. "I hope so," she said. "I would like that. And let us hope it is under better circumstances."

Darius returned her smile, and Prydon set to the sky. Soon the village became a small dot on the ground, and Darius set his eyes toward the valley.

That night, Darius sat beside a fire Prydon had easily created just as he had done in the mire. With the direction they had traveled, it would be another day before they would get back to Barsovy, and his ribs and arms hurt terribly. Prydon had insisted they stop and rest, and Darius was in no condition to argue, nor did he want to.

"Prydon?" Darius said, gazing at a blue flame that danced among the red and orange. "What if we go straight to Klavon before going into the valley?"

Prydon looked genuinely surprised and said, "What would be the purpose of that? And...what of the danger? You do recall my warnings in the battle you just fought. The temptation of anger would be even greater."

"Yes, but we did think it was Klavon, and that didn't stop us there."

"You had no choice," said Prydon. "You had already committed—"

"I could have left, but you said I was ready," interrupted Darius. "Or were those just empty words?"

Prydon hesitated. "Darius, I do indeed believe you are ready, but why risk it when you are so close? What would bring about such a thought?"

Darius sighed and looked up at his friend. "While I was sleeping, recovering after the battle, I had a dream—at least I think it was a dream. Sira came to me and asked me to help her people overcome Klavon."

"Sira?" asked Prydon. "I do not know that name."

Darius had, in all the time they had spent together, neglected to mention the strange, alluring young woman named Sira.

"She is from Klavon's land. She saved me from the barrier—"

"The stalks," interrupted Prydon.

"Wait," said Darius. "You know about that?"

"I saw them. I also saw the white-haired girl. That was Sira?"

"Yes," answered Darius.

"Was it also she who saved you in the mire?" asked Prydon.

"What?"

Prydon smiled. "I told you I have never left your side."

A sudden embarrassing thought entered Darius's mind. He recalled all the insults he had screamed into the air when he had first left the mire and was reading the horrible book on dragons.

Prydon seemed to know what he was thinking and laughed. "I believe you have learned that I can indeed be trusted and have no desire to devour you or any other human. But in the mire...I saw when you slipped. I was just about to come down and help when I saw the white flash. Was it also she who saved you then?"

The possibility gave Darius reason to pause, and he said, "I don't see how...I mean..."

Prydon nodded. "So tell me about this dream that is now urging you to face Klavon before the valley?"

Darius told Prydon every detail he could remember about the dream. Well almost—he felt uncomfortable divulging the tension Sira seemed so apt to create, especially regarding his lips.

"I mean, it had to be a dream, right?" said Darius. "And he would be caught off guard."

"Since she is from Klavon's village and since Alara

had just asked for our help, it would make sense that your mind might put those two together to create the thought of Sira asking for the same help when it came to Klavon." Prydon stirred the fire with one of the spikes in his tail. "However, if it was really Sira, it could be a plot to bring you to Klavon when you are most vulnerable."

"But how could she?" asked Darius. "How could she have been there?"

"Sorcerers often have others in their service who feed from their power," said Prydon.

Darius was beginning to feel that he lacked a considerable amount of knowledge about wizards and sorcerers, and that placed him at a horrible disadvantage.

"It is also possible," Prydon continued, "that Klavon staged that fight to test your strength before sending Sira to you."

"What?" exclaimed Darius.

"I told you the fight was too easy. I also told you the sorcerer was somehow familiar," said Prydon.

"Then you think it was Klavon after all," said Darius. "But Sira saved me…she was even there when the thieves attacked me. In my dream, she told me that she was just about to help when you showed up—"

"Which is exactly something she might say if she were really there—if it were not a dream," said Prydon, ending Darius's sentence.

Darius stared again at the flames. They had grown since Prydon stirred the fire, and the warmth covered his face. "It's not worth it," he said. "It's not worth the risk. I should face the valley first."

Prydon shook his head. "I agree."

"Do we tell Barsovy?" asked Darius. "About the dream?"

Prydon considered the question only for a moment. "No. There is no need. You are facing the valley as planned, and you must then face Klavon as planned. Whether or not it was Klavon testing you, and whether or not it was a dream, is irrelevant to your training and the valley."

Darius lay there that night under a blanket of stars, a peaceful moment before the storm he knew was to come. He thought of Sira and wondered if she was truly in league with Klavon. But why save him—in the mire—in the stalks—at the thieves? It didn't make sense—it would have been a perfect time for Klavon to kill him—but he had learned to be cautious. A shooting start blazed across the sky, and an owl screeched in the far distance. He breathed in the fresh air…and fell asleep.

Chapter Twenty-six

The Lie

Sira felt the sting as the back of Klavon's hand slammed against her cheek, and a small drop of blood escaped the edge of her mouth.

Fraenir stood perched nearby, and she could see the pleasure in his expression. She lifted her head and stood taller, looking away from Fraenir and directly at Klavon.

"This is the second time you have failed me. Your incompetence is wearing on my nerves!" said Klavon.

Fraenir stepped forward and said, "Perhaps I should—"

"No!" commanded Klavon. "Your concern lies with Prydon."

"You are aware that the first failure to which you refer," said Sira, "was not my failure but yours. Have you forgotten the serum did not wor—"

"How dare you!" Klavon shouted. He raised his hand again, but then stopped, breathing heavily and holding it above her.

"I did not fail you, and while I took the risk of you being angry, I could not bring myself to convince the boy to come straight to you."

Sira lied. She had tried, but the boy was more difficult to persuade than even she had considered. And then there was Prydon. She knew it would be difficult to affect the influence of a dragon. And it proved not only difficult but impossible. But this was something Klavon would not understand—to admit Prydon was formidable.

Now she had to devise a plan that would retain Klavon's favor yet maintain her lie.

"Sir," she said, "I know your strength, and I know your pride. Would you truly feel successful if you convinced Darius to join you before he had faced his final trial? You are powerful, and that is beneath you."

"How dare you decide what is or isn't beneath me," Klavon said slowly, but he lowered his hand and turned his back to her—something he often did.

Sira knew he was, in a way, tempting her—testing her. Turning his back provided her the opportunity to attack when he was most vulnerable, but she was no fool.

"I'm sorry," said Sira. "I couldn't bear the thought of the whispers behind your back. I could hear the accusations of weakness."

Klavon hesitated, and Sira could see him turn his ear toward her. He was listening as she fed his ego.

"But you are powerful. I know your desire to have this done and bring *her* here, but it must be done so that your leadership, strength, and power are not questioned."

Klavon turned his head slightly more so she could see the profile of his face. She restrained from openly smiling—she had him.

"I simply couldn't stand that. I'm truly sorry," she

said one last time. "I will return to the boy and do as you require."

"Wait," said Klavon, and he turned back to face her. "I would kill anyone who would question my power, but…"

Sira refrained from smiling, but she quietly breathed relief—she had succeeded. Careful not to change his mind, she bowed and waited for further instruction.

Klavon stood in his lab, holding two vials of potions that he was now blending into one. Sira was seated on a stool on the opposite side of the table. The girl was correct. It was beneath him to stoop to…cheating. Yes, there was no other word for it.

So the boy would face the valley. Then Darius would come to him, join him, and serve him, and it would all happen with no question of Klavon's power. His realm would be loyal, not because of any weak rule but because of his power.

Yet, it wouldn't hurt to aid the curse and possibly influence the outcome of the boy's results in the valley. It wasn't really cheating, after all. In all actuality, it was simply adding to his test, defining his strength or lack of.

"You will not disobey this time, or I will kill you," he said, holding the vial of the combined potions out to Sira. "It need only touch his lips to work."

Chapter Twenty-seven

The Valley of Wizards

They would arrive at the training fields the next day, and Darius was anxious and nervous to face this final challenge. Prydon had insisted on one last night's rest before facing the valley, so they had made camp and eaten a full meal.

"Goodnight, Prydon," Darius said as he lay back on his bedroll

"Goodnight," replied Prydon, and the dragon curled up around the fire across from Darius.

Darius could feel the heat radiate from Prydon's scales back toward him, and with a full stomach, he fell asleep quicker than he'd expected. And when he drifted deeper into his sleep, he was visited by her.

Alara was standing in front of him in a pale nightdress. Her hair cascaded over her shoulders and across her chest, and she walked slowly up to him.

"Thank you, Darius," she said, and she leaned toward him, placing one hand on his shoulder and the other behind his head.

Then she kissed him passionately. He closed his eyes, and when the kiss ended with a gentle peck on his lips, he smiled. When he opened his eyes to look at her, he jumped back.

Standing in front of him was Sira. Her white hair floated about her, and her pale skin seemed to glow.

"Goodbye, Darius," she said. "We will see each other soon."

Darius woke up suddenly and looked around. A thin white wisp floated above the fire and into the sky. He shook his head and stared at the flames.

Smoke, he though. *It must have been smoke.*

Darius ran the back of his finger across his lips, his brows furrowed as he frowned. Then he lay back on his bed and stared into the sky for quite time before he fell back asleep.

"I send you to face your past and you come back with a broken rib! And stitches!" yelled Barsovy. "And you let him fight another wizard? Before facing the valley? Do you realize just how dangerous that could have been?"

Prydon grinned. "He performed quite well."

"Did you now? Did you?" Barsovy said with a scolding tongue. He glared at Darius, burning him with a stare that made even his ribs go numb.

"Sorry?" A mixture of remorse and fear gripped Darius's throat, and his answer came out as a squeak.

"Oh, well, since you're sorry." Barsovy's sarcasm produced a chuckle from Prydon, but Barsovy ignored him and instead turned his glare to the ground, pacing the familiar circle.

This was a ritual Darius witnessed many times in his training. Barsovy slipped into a focused state of concentration, and Darius knew that nothing would distract him—not without retribution, a consequence Darius had no desire to witness. Besides, a solution was soon at hand, and Darius couldn't help breathe a sigh of relief as the pain, not only from the broken rib but also from the tight bandages that swore not to let it move, was quite annoying.

"Nope." Barsovy halted and stared at Darius as if he'd read his thoughts. "I have no solution. You will simply have to face the valley in your present state. Unless, of course, you'd like to wait until that heals on its own."

Darius froze. "But…"

"But what?" asked Barsovy.

"Well, I was hoping you could use some kind of medical…magic or something," said Darius.

Barsovy laughed incredulously. "Medical magic? That takes years of study and is not learned in this place. As a matter of fact, most wizards have others in their service dedicated solely to that art. But not here."

"But—" Darius tried to say.

"But nothing! Why do you think we have the protective spells as you train? No, I have no time to mend broken wizards to be! Nor do I want a constant companion to follow me around tending to weaklings!"

Darius rubbed his ribs.

"So you'll just have to deal with it," added Barsovy. "Nope. No time to heal for you, young man. I say you'll do fine, and that is the end of it. Now, follow me."

Prydon shrugged, and Darius was left with no choice but to accept his painful situation. He rubbed the bandage around his chest.

Barsovy turned and stood still, facing a wall of trees. With eyes closed and after a few awkward moments, a thick cluster of trees began to shake violently. The roots pulled up from the ground, and dirt showered down as they stepped away from each other, revealing the start of a hidden path.

Barsovy walked into the newly formed tunnel, and Darius followed. The trees continued to uproot themselves, creating a path as they progressed, and when Darius looked behind, the dislodged trees returned to their beds of dirt and closed in once more. The ground covering their roots returned to an undisturbed state, and had he not observed it, he would never have known a path had once weaved in their place. The walk was long, and when their path came to an end, they were greeted by a small clearing and the steep side of a mountain. As they moved closer, Darius noticed a small crevice opened in its side.

"Here. Enter when you see fit." Barsovy pointed and then walked underneath a canopy of trees and sat. He crossed his legs and closed his eyes as if he were no longer of this world.

Darius stood with Prydon by his side. "This is it," said Darius as he rocked on his heels. He felt like a child leaving for his first day of school, only worse. He was going to face judgment.

"You'll be fine," said Prydon.

Darius bit the side of his lip and looked at the small

opening. "So what exactly am I supposed to do in there?"

Prydon lowered his muzzle near Darius's face. "In there, you will do as all wizards before you have done."

"That's not very helpful."

Prydon smiled. "Your heart will guide you."

The dragon gently nudged Darius toward the opening, and when he stepped into the crevice, everything went dark. A soft purple hue glowed like moonlight even though Darius knew the sun was still high in the sky. As he followed a cramped path, his heart pounded inside his chest like a waterfall beating the river below. He breathed slowly and blew his breath between tightened lips. Although it was not cold, his breath condensed, forming a fog in front of his face. His hands trembled as he braced himself on the damp walls, and he ducked beneath jetting rocks.

The path sloped downward amongst loose rocks, and he planted each step carefully; a broken leg to match his rib would surely do him no good, not to mention the anger it would provoke in Barsovy. And Darius didn't relish the thought of crawling back out of the crevice, dragging his leg behind him. No. His goal was ahead and would not be impeded by carelessness.

It became darker, and the rocks that obstructed his path were now entwined with massive, thick roots; roots from trees Darius could not see. The roots, however, provided some hold, and his movement was quickened with their assistance.

When the path opened into a valley, Darius stopped and gaped at what was before him. This was nothing like the valley in which he had trained—and nothing like he would have expected.

The Valley of Wizards was dark, the sunlight banished behind a dreary veil of clouds. The trees were large with gnarled limbs interwoven to form canopies that blocked out any light the clouds might have let escape. It was almost as if the valley were a massive cave, the sky being nothing more than a vague illusion.

Darius walked slowly forward, following a well worn path and wondering when he would reach the wizards of old. Wisps of purple light darted past like ribbons blowing in a strong wind, and Darius thought he could hear whispers brush against his ears.

The trees opened, and their entangled limbs liberated themselves. The ground began to shake and Darius almost lost his footing. Like the trees he had encountered following Barsovy, the trees here uprooted themselves and pulled back. Instead of a small path being formed, however, these massive trees formed a tight ring around a vast clearing and planted their roots once again.

The purple wisps accumulated around Darius, and he turned about, not sure what to make of them. All of the sudden, the ribbons flew straight up into the sky and vanished. Darius stood silently, alone in the opening, and the darkness hung over him. A thick fog rolled in like a wave of oppression, and Darius's throat tightened as the sky darkened even more. Soon he could see nothing.

A stab of panic forced his breathing, and he wondered if he'd somehow taken a wrong turn and stumbled into some warped version of hell. The fog pushed down on him, and he fell to one knee. He looked down at the invisible ground, his hands beneath him hidden by the haze. He pressed against the rocks to make sure he wasn't floating and would at any moment crash to a distant ground and, perhaps, his death. He wasn't, and for a moment he felt foolish for checking.

Darius tried to stand, but the weight of the darkness held him down, and panic grew inside. Moments dragged on and insanity threatened, but just when he thought he might lose his mind, a wave of light, a small hazy ribbon, floated from above and penetrated his body. He looked up. The darkness continued to surround him, but some unseen energy told him to stand. He hesitated, but the unease melted away and was replaced with indomitable determination. Darius stood tall, and his breathing steadied. It was time.

A bolt of lightning shot from the sky, and in its path stood a crystal shard, at least seven feet tall. Darius shielded his eyes as the lightning continued to strike all around him, shaking the ground beneath his feet. After what seemed an eternity it ceased. The entire area was covered with crystals, each one pulsing identically with a white blue light.

The fog diminished until there was only a thin layer on the ground, swirling around his feet. He approached one of the crystals and looked deep inside. Darius gasped as he gazed at a young boy, with perfect clarity, standing inside the shard. And that boy was him!

He stepped back and bumped into another. Turning, he again stared at himself. As he staggered about the field of prismatic towers, each crystal housed another replica.

Darius sat in the center of the objects, resolved to know their purpose, and closed his eyes. Thoughts filled his mind; thoughts of home, thoughts of his mother, his father, Prydon, Alara, thoughts of Klavon and Sira, thoughts of Barsovy, his training, the mark on his hand.

The mark on his hand began to pulse, the red tendrils throbbing beneath his skin. He stood and walked to a crystal. Staring at his face, the eyes moved and returned his gaze. But they weren't his eyes. They were different, not remotely like the eyes that greeted him when he looked into the river at home in Brandor, and Darius did not like what he saw. He raised his sword and struck the crystal. It shattered, and a dark red light darted into the sky with a scream.

Surprised by his own actions, Darius turned to another shard. This time, the self gazed with eyes he could not see. Again, Darius struck the shard, and another red light shot to the sky, a red deeper and darker than the first.

He paused. So was this it? In judging the character of the Dariuses within the crystals, was he revealing his own? Darius walked from crystal to crystal, gazing into each face, his own face, each one representing a certain path—a possible character either light or dark, strong or weak, compassionate or selfish. The wizards of old were testing the depths of his character, his ability to discern the right way—and more importantly to choose it.

Darius stared into the crystals. Some of the faces were hideous, vicious and cruel—at least that was his perception—and Darius immediately made waste of them. Others were more difficult to read, and he struggled with the subtleties of their expressions. With those less obvious, he would place his hands on the crystal, close his eyes, and attempt to determine the depth of the one within. He would develop an image in his mind, but always, there was a mist surrounding it, never allowing him to clearly distinguish a true path. As if to make it even more difficult, Darius wasn't sure if the image was pure fabrication or guidance from some more powerful source—maybe even the curse.

Darius struggled but knew he had no choice. It would have to be enough for him to make a decision, and shard after shard, wisps of light shot into the air with a shriek. When red and amber wisps screamed forth, Darius knew he made the right decision. Sometimes, when he made his choice, the tendrils in his hand would burn like fire as if destruction of the shard in some small way caused destruction to the curse. It was at these times that Darius would fall to his knees, grasping his wrist and catching his breath, but always with a small sense of victory.

Other times, the less subtle shades of red, bordering on pink or even white, were not so encouraging, and the tendrils would remain calm. Still, Darius was determined. He would not allow himself to be filled with doubt, for doubt would surely cloud his judgment.

In time, only two shards were left. He studied the two with all intensity, and each returned his gaze. Both sets of eyes showed leadership and strength, but there had to be more—some subtle nuance he was missing. Darius stood between the two, leaning from one to the other, pressing his hands against the shards and trying to read them, trying to visualize the essence of each, trying to comprehend the character within and know which one represented the true, pure way.

With each he saw images, scattered and random, but again he wondered if it was his own fabricated illusion or a deceitful picture presented by the curse. Finally he made his choice, believing the one to be left untouched was of the purest character. He raised his sword against the other and the crystal shattered to the ground. When he did, however, the familiar wisp of color did not whirl into the air. Instead, as shards of crystal fell to the ground, a mist stood where the crystal had fallen. And as the mist faded, Darius stood facing himself, in all form solid.

"What have you done?" the now solid Darius yelled. "You have chosen incorrectly!"

With a shocked impulse, Darius raised his sword and struck at the other Darius. "No! You are not the one!"

"You fool!" screamed the other, deflecting Darius's blow. "You are flawed! That mark has clouded your judgment!"

Darius's heart pumped hot blood through his veins, and he glanced at his hand. The crimson tendrils were boiling beneath the surface of this skin. "No! This can't be! I was right!"

Darius raised his sword again, and the fight continued, but with every blow Darius struck, the other Darius volleyed and returned the same. Minutes passed, and Darius pulled out his staff. It was no more effective. In fact, every spell simply dispersed into a puff of smoke.

The other Darius laughed as one in utter disbelief. "So what do you plan on doing? Fight me all day? You cannot defeat me. I am you, and you are I. Neither of us can possibly defeat the other as we are one and the same. Surely you must see that now."

Darius was tired and his wounds, although healing, ached. He stopped and leaned against the last crystal. The other Darius showed exhaustion as well and did nothing but stand.

"You know I am right," he said. "I can fight you forever if you'd like, but where would that put us?"

Darius stared at him.

"The wizards of old have shown you mercy." The other Darius's eyes softened. "They know that mark, and they have granted you a second chance."

Darius scoured the face of his opponent, trying to read what was beneath. "A second chance?"

"Yes," acknowledged the other Darius. "Now, choose the right one! And be thankful that I had the strength to fight!"

Darius looked into the remaining crystal. The eyes were pure, clear as day, tender and caring.

The other Darius approached him, breathing down his neck and speaking deliberately in his ear. "He is weak. You have witnessed my strength. I am your true design. Why else would the wizards of old have allowed me to stay when you struck my crystal?"

Darius turned his head and locked eyes with the one who stood so close behind him. In those eyes, he sensed raw strength, true power. The other Darius, an odd smile on his lips, bowed submissively.

Darius turned back to the one in the crystal and

stared deeply into his eyes. In those eyes he could envision people, guided and protected by the one housed in the crystal prison. In those eyes he could envision favor and love for those over whom he stood.

Darius returned his staff and drew his sword.

The other Darius nodded his head and smiled. "Yes," he said. "I am pleased."

Darius raised his sword. "I am too," he said calmly as the sword fell hard and struck not the crystal shard but the other Darius.

Shock housed the face of the solid reflection as he held the sword sticking through his stomach. "No!" And with a flash of red lightning, he was gone.

Darius turned back to the last crystal shard. The Darius inside smiled and bowed, and for a moment he thought he saw his father's face staring back at him. But all too quickly the image vanished and was replaced with an opaque swirling of color, much like that in the stones of his staff and sword. He stared at it, and the cloudiness dissipated until all that was left was clear white light. Relief washed over him and he felt a weight lift from his heart and mind…but the mark in his hand began to pulse, and Darius buckled as the pain increased. He looked up at the shard once again and…a faint shade of red flashed deep inside the crystal.

Darius's heart stopped, and he threw his hands against the shard. "No!" He stared deeply into the depths of the light, hoping it was only his imagination…It was there, faint and intermittent, but the red flash was no illusion.

As if to finalize the decision, two bolts of light shot

from the shard and, with the shriek of a dragon, crashed against the crystals in Darius's weapons. The color pulsed within the stones, mirroring that which was within the shard, and Darius fell to his knees. Tears filled his eyes and he lay against the crystal tower.

It was some time before he gained the strength—physically, emotionally—to make his way out of the valley. There was nothing more he could do. He had been judged. The mark on his hand had done its deed.

Chapter Twenty-eight

Success

Sira had struggled to create the dream. Darius had, in the training fields, pushed her from his mind forever. But with the weakened state of his body, she floated into his mind. Sira was, however, shocked that the only way to initiate and seal the kiss was do so under the guise of Alara. Stupid boy! What did he see in her, anyway? She had no power, no strength, and she was…plain—ordinary of the most boring kind.

Of course, Sira ended the dream with herself so that Darius would know it was really her to whom he was truly attracted.

Now she floated above the valley, waiting for the boy to emerge, and when he did, she saw it.

Klavon had no use for the Valley of Wizards or for the opinions of wizards long dead. However, the flash of red did intrigue him. Never would he have truly suspected that his curse could have influenced the outcome, even with the additional potion Sira had delivered. Yet…the curse had taken its hold well…quite well indeed.

"You have done well," he said. "Go, prepare for when he arrives. You know what to do."

Sira backed out of his room as she always did, and he walked to the window and looked out over the mire toward where Miora was.

"It won't be long, my sweet, and you will be mine."

Chapter Twenty-nine

Leaving the Valley

"You say you were fighting yourself?" asked Barsovy.

"Yes, sir," answered Darius in an anesthetized tone. He didn't look up at his trainer. His head was slumped against his folded arms, his knees propping the weight. His whole body felt numb.

Prydon growled. "Barsovy, has there ever been a case where—"

"Never! Never has anything like this ever happened!" snapped Barsovy. "They enter the valley, they make their choices to provide insight to the Wizards of Old—granted each in a different way but never in battle—and then they exit."

Darius could hear Barsovy pacing his familiar circle, but this time he didn't care. From his perspective, all was hopeless. He had failed. As if reading his thoughts, Prydon nuzzled him gently, knocking his arms from beneath his head. Darius looked up, and Prydon smiled tenderly.

In a soft voice, Prydon said, "You have not failed, my friend."

Barsovy stopped. "He is correct, Darius. You have not failed. I believe that curse sabotaged your trial, or at least it tried to. I believe that curse placed that particular shard intentionally, with the sole purpose of producing your other self in an attempt to influence your decisions. And if that is the case—and I am usually correct—you made the correct choice."

"But he said the wizards recognized I was marked and were giving me a second chance. How do we know that's not the case? Has anyone else ever entered the valley marked by a curse?" Darius stood up quickly and held out his sword and staff. "And these? This red flash?"

"That red flash," continued Barsovy, "could simply be a reflection of the curse that plagues you, but we will not know until you complete your task."

"Prydon, you once told me that Segrath crafts the sword and staff only once a young wizard has passed through the trials of Mount Tyria, one who has faced himself and the possibility of who he can become. I never did that. Segrath had no idea who I was or would be before crafting this sword and staff. What if there is no connection? What if these aren't truly meant for me?"

"You are allowing doubt to cloud your judgment," answered Prydon. "You were presented with no options once Klavon brought that curse upon you. Segrath knew this."

Barsovy added. "I know Segrath, and I know her power. She is never in error in creation of a wizard's tools. Despite your situation, she knows your heart. She knows the heart of every wizard even before they complete the trials."

"Then what good are the trials in the first place?" snapped Darius.

Barsovy slapped Darius hard across the face, not in reprimand but in crude awakening. "You are crossing boundaries of which you should respect! Even though Segrath sees within the wizard, the wizard himself does not. The trials give *you* that. Yes, you were disadvantaged in not having that discovery of yourself, but you have learned much in your time here, and I believe you know who you are. More importantly, I believe you know who you must become. And to do that, young man, you must face Klavon and destroy this curse once and for all!"

The sting remained strong in Darius's cheek. "All right," said Darius, laying his sword and staff across a nearby rock. "Let's say I defeat Klavon. What's to say that this curse won't linger in some way, haunting me forever?"

"There is no way to know for sure, but there is one thing that is certain," replied Barsovy.

"Nothing is certain," said Darius, his voice trailing.

Barsovy placed a gentle hand on Darius's shoulder. "Son, this is certain. If you do not face Klavon, then that curse will remain with you forever, consuming you within the very bowels of the evil it now projects."

Darius had never been called "son" by anyone, and he regretted speaking so harshly to his teacher, his mentor, his friend.

Barsovy paused and looked straight into Darius's eyes. He spoke with all sincerity. "And what of the people of Brandor? Are they to be abandoned, left to die at the hands of Klavon...or worse, left to serve him? No. You have no choice. Your path is decided."

Barsovy squeezed Darius's shoulder, his lips tight in a strong, determined expression, and Darius knew that Barsovy was trying to give him strength. Darius stared at his hand. The red tendrils were laughing at him, victoriously dancing about his wrist. He wanted to fight it, wanted to be strong...for Barsovy, for Prydon, for himself. It was the first time in a long time that he had felt such self-doubt, and he was not pleased with the sensation it manifested within his body. He was even less pleased that he could not pull from the strength that Barsovy so earnestly offered.

"Remember when I told you that even the strongest, in time, can be corrupted?" asked Prydon.

Darius looked up at Prydon, his brows curled together. "Yes. You think I have weakened?"

"Not necessarily, but if you listen to what you are saying—and what you are feeling—you cannot ignore that this mark has had an impact on you. And now that you denied it its victory in the valley, I am quite certain the curse will fight even harder than before. We must make haste in getting you to Klavon. You must be rid of this...and soon." Prydon glanced at the sky and then back at Darius. "We leave now. Are you ready?"

Darius's jaw dropped. "Am I ready?"

Barsovy nodded. "It is a valid question. One that only you can answer."

Darius stared blankly at his hand and leaned against the rock on which lay his sword and staff. The stones were clear, but the pulse of red that throbbed within continued to stab sharply at his eyes. Taking his staff in hand, he closed his eyes and gently leaned his forehead against the stone. He breathed slowly, inhaling the power from the staff, allowing it to consume his body.

Visions of the past month played clearly in his mind—training, his father's death, Alara's village, the valley. And then he saw it…without a doubt…his father's face smiling back at him in that last shard. Clarity came to him like a clear lake whose fog had been banished by the brilliant sun. His father had fought and died to protect his village, Miora, and him, and Darius would do the same. Barsovy was correct. His path was decided.

Darius opened his eyes, stood, and sheathed his sword. With a surge of determined anger, he answered, "Yes. I am ready. No more doubt. I will not allow Klavon to take me, nor will Klavon be allowed to destroy another village as he did my father's."

Barsovy grinned. "That is exactly what I wanted to hear. You, Darius, are master of your choices. Not some wretched curse. And now it is time. Farewell, young one."

Prydon kneeled, and Darius climbed on his back. Barsovy bowed, and with a rush of wind, he and Prydon took to the sky.

The wave of the barrier brushed across Darius's body, the protection of the valley soon far behind him. He wondered if he would ever lay eyes on his master or this valley again. He glanced at his gloved hand, grasping to his dear friend, and also wondered if he would ever be free of this curse, completely, totally, without a hint of crimson to remind him of its evil hold. His future was uncertain, but his goal was not. Defeat Klavon and save Brandor. Beyond that, all he could do was hope.

Darkness had already shadowed the sky when they landed inside Klavon's territory, but it was nothing compared to the darkness that loomed as Darius came closer and closer to the event that framed this entire journey. That day when he left Brandor now seemed a vague memory, almost a dream.

The first time he had entered Klavon's realm, he'd almost been pummeled to death by dead stalks, a barrier to keep others out or, perhaps, to keep victims in. Had it not been for the aid of the mysterious, young woman, Sira, he might never have made it through. And his master plan to sneak into Klavon's lair, steal the book, and escape unnoticed was halted by a band of robbers. Had it not been for Prydon and his diligent watch, Darius would not only have lost his belongings, he would surely have lost his life. And again, there was Sira.

Darius frowned at his idiocy, his dependency on others to clean up after his reckless choices and pull him out danger. He would no more have been able to defeat a mouse much less Klavon. How much he'd changed. Darius was now a wizard, through and through, and the naïve boy who left Brandor was only a memory.

As Darius slipped off of Prydon's back, he struggled to discern the shapes about them, scouring the area for any indication that they had been discovered as they entered through the barrier. The light of the moon cast long shadows on the ground, and the wind that gently brushed through the trees brought them to life. The shadows danced in and out of hiding, any of which could be a traitor laying in wait, and Darius with Prydon's help thoroughly combed the area.

Once their task was complete, Darius asked, "Do you think he knows?"

"I doubt it." Prydon began gathering straw to form a soft bed. "This is the most desolate part of his kingdom, away from prying eyes. We are several days out from his castle, and it would require too much energy of him to monitor his entire realm."

"Isn't that what the barrier is for? To warn him?"

"Yes, but even Klavon does not have time to concern himself with every flying creature to pass. At least not so far out. And his arrogance causes him to believe he is invulnerable, and that is to our advantage."

Darius nodded and looked around. It was quite beautiful, actually, the moon illuminating a horizon of mountains in the distance. "So we are two—maybe three—days out? Flying? Just how big is his territory?"

"Not flying. If I were to fly in," stated Prydon, "then Klavon would be alerted to our presence, and your advantage would be lost. From here we walk."

"Walk?" Darius groaned as he helped Prydon gather straw.

"Patience, Darius. I know you are anxious, but you must have patience."

The next morning, Darius awoke with a piece of straw pressed into his cheek. He peeled it away and sat up. The morning air was cool and crisp, and the smell of freshly cooked meat provided a pleasing fragrance.

Prydon held out a nicely scorched piece of fowl. "I've already eaten. This is for you."

No fire warmed their campsite. That might have aroused suspicion and notice. Darius could only guess that fire from Prydon's breath cooked the meat, but he took it graciously.

"Thanks."

Not much conversation floated between the two as they began their hike. Several days would give Darius plenty of time to contemplate his attack, but it also meant several more days for Klavon to destroy Brandor…and for the curse to further entrench itself deeper into his soul. He shook the thought from his mind, trying to create his own barrier against its poison.

Three days later, Darius and Prydon stood hidden in a cluster of trees. A tall mountain stood ominously before them, the outline of a structure dark against a stormy sky—Klavon's castle.

Chapter Thirty

The Arrival

Sira sat in the damp forest. Where was he? How long would it take for him to arrive in Klavon's realm. Surely the dragon would fly him here. Surely Darius had not become victim to a field of stalks, again!

She grinned. She almost missed the old Darius, klutz, clumsy, and awkward. But the Darius she had seen in the village, fighting the minions and Klavon showed her a more mature, young man. And she ran her fingers along her lips, remembering the kiss she had given him a few days before—the kiss that Darius hadn't realized was…real.

She looked hard into the sky on the horizon. But Prydon was smart—they would not fly to the castle. Still, it had become tiresome waiting day-after-day for the boy to arrive. Not even her cat was present to keep her company, assigned with another task.

Sira had just settled in for another day of painful surveillance when she heard it.

Chapter Thirty-one

The Hidden Journey

Darius was rested, as ready as he'd ever be to face Klavon. Prydon had made sure of that, insisting that they rest adequately each night. He had also eaten well. Prydon was quite competent in his selection and preparation of food. Both contributed to Darius's strength after his time in the Valley of Wizards.

His emotional state was also stronger. Prydon's companionship and support over the past days helped Darius come to terms with what transpired in the valley, and with that acceptance came a resigned confidence.

"So, how do we approach?" asked Darius.

The question was one they discussed many times as they traveled, but a definite answer eluded them. The thought of flight was mentioned, but again, the element of surprise would be lost. The only option they devised was for Darius to hike the hillside alone. Prydon would attract too much attention. Once the battle began, Prydon would join him, taking on the astaroth, Fraenir.

But they still had no idea how to maximize their element of surprise. When Darius reached the castle, he would need to enter undetected. But how?

"I know a secret path into the castle," whispered a voice from behind them.

Darius started, and Prydon glared at a young woman who stood only feet away.

Sira grinned. "You see, I have been sneaking in there for years."

"Sira," stated Prydon.

Sira's mouth fell open in a surprised grin. "You know of me? I'm surprised. Did he tell you that I saved his life?"

"I wouldn't go so far as to say that, but—"

"Oh, really?" Sira turned to Prydon and folded her arms. "He was trying to get through a trap set by Klavon, and I saved him. He would have been pounded into the ground if I hadn't shown up."

"I saw it," said Prydon.

"You saw it? So you know I saved his life. And I would have saved him again when the thieves attacked but you showed up." She loosened her arms and looked at Darius. "So why'd you leave?"

Prydon stared at her, his eyes narrowing. "What business do you have here?"

"No business. Just thought I'd help…again. I know he's here to fight Klavon, and I want to help."

"Help?" asked Darius. "Why?"

"Same reason as before." Sira sat on a rock and crossed her legs. "Look. Klavon is no favorite of mine. I've been trying to find a way to help my people for ages. When you showed up, I figured…I help you…you help me…and then you left. Oh, and may I add that you don't seem such the bumbling idiot as before."

"I'm not," said Darius flatly.

"Then let me help you help me. It's that simple."

"And why would you know a secret path into the castle?" asked Prydon suspiciously.

"My family needs food. Have you seen the weather here? Yes, we get rain, but the sun rarely shows its face. Things don't grow well in the dark."

Darius, in sincere confusion, asked. "Why would Klavon, if he's so powerful, have a secret path into his castle?"

"You really don't get sorcerers, do you? They're all so suspicious. He built several hidden paths in the mountains so, should he ever be attacked—and by attacked I mean by many wizards at once—he could make his escape. You know, the whole wizard thing about live to fight another day and all." Sira casually pushed a few strands of hair from her face.

"Really?" asked Darius, his hopes raised by the prospect of a hidden path.

Prydon interrupted and asked, "May I speak with you, in private?"

"That's fine," said Sira. "I'll just be over here." She hopped off the rock and walked several yards away to a thick log and sat once again.

When Sira was adequately out of earshot, Prydon spoke. "I don't trust her, Darius."

"Why? She's only helped."

"Or she's trying to trick you," said Prydon. "She may have actually come to you in Alara's village, as we discussed before."

"That doesn't make sense," said Darius.

"Why not?"

"Because she hasn't mentioned it at all, which she would have. 'Yay, you showed up to help me after all!' or something like that. Besides, what alternative do I have?" asked Darius.

"If she is working with Klavon, then this could be a trap," said Prydon, shaking his head.

"Well, if she was working with Klavon, then that means he already knows we are here and would have already attacked, right?" asked Darius.

Prydon appeared less than convinced. "Perhaps."

"Look. We've already spoken about the potential for detection as I climb this mountain, not to mention how difficult it would be as I attempt to approach the castle once I get up there. This way, I'm certain not to be discovered ahead of time."

"And if it is a trap?" asked Prydon.

Darius stared up at the castle above. "I really don't see any other choice. I have to trust her."

"Are you sure your judgment isn't being clouded by her beauty?" asked Prydon.

Darius's eyes widened at the blunt statement. "Uh...no...of course not."

Prydon raised a brow.

"I mean she's pretty and all, but...don't you think I've learned anything in this time? This is too important to let something as ridiculous as beauty interfere."

Prydon remained silent.

"I just can't see it as a trap. Why would she have helped me before? Klavon could have easily disposed of me when I first came here. You, more than anyone, are aware of that. If she were in league with him, why would she have saved me?"

"Klavon is not always easily understood. I have no answer for that, but if you are determined, I do recommend caution."

"Wait," said Darius, and then he spoke out to Sira. "Sira, do you even know my name?"

"Well, of course I do," she said. "It's...it's...You know. Maybe I don't...weird, huh? So what is it?"

Darius turned back to Prydon. "In my dream, she knew my name. She had heard you say it during the battle."

"Has it not occurred to you that she could be lying to you?" asked Prydon.

Darius shook his head. "Perhaps, but as I said, I don't have a choice, and I'll be careful. You just be ready when the battle begins."

Prydon glanced at the girl. She sat, twirling her white hair with her fingers and staring off into the distance.

"When it begins?" Prydon asked. "No. I'll come with you."

"All right, Sira. We're ready to go."

"Great. This way—um..."

Darius paused, not sure of why she was hesitating. Then it struck him. "Oh, Darius," he said, seeing no reason to keep his name from her any longer.

"Nice name," she said and walked away.

Darius and Prydon followed Sira a short distance

until they reached a small cave in the side of the mountain. It was bordered by bushes and a thick outcropping of rock and vines—it would have been impossible to see if they had not known it was there.

"Think you could help out here?" Sira picked up two small torches and held them out to Prydon.

"You always carry around torches?" asked Darius.

Sira raised an eyebrow, and her lips tilted as she rolled her eyes. "I told you," she said, motioning a small pile of torches stashed off to one side of the opening, "I sneak up there from time to time, and—unlike others I have met—I am always prepared." She looked back at Prydon.

Prydon obliged, and with a short burst of flames, the torches lit.

"Thanks," she said and disappeared behind the small opening.

Darius could see the glow from inside and followed. Prydon stayed close behind, and as they progressed, it became suddenly apparent that Prydon was at a disadvantage for space.

When the path became even smaller, Sira stopped. "I'm afraid your friend will have to wait here."

Darius looked at Prydon. "Same as before. I'll signal you."

"I don't like this, Darius," said Prydon.

Darius looked at the tight path. "Me neither, but it's the best option we have."

Prydon lowered his head until it was very close to Darius's face. "I encourage you to reconsider."

"I'll watch out for him," added Sira. "I promise.

He'll be fine."

Prydon shot an icy glare at Sira, and Darius smiled softly.

"Prydon, I'll be fine. I'm not so foolish as I was before. Trust me."

"I do trust *you*." Prydon stressed his reference to Darius as he continued to glare at Sira.

"Well, that's not very kind of you," she snapped. "I'm only trying to help. And even though I have my own selfish intentions here, it's in his best interest, too."

"I'll be fine." Darius touched Prydon's face and smiled again.

Prydon turned his eyes to Darius. "Be wary. Be alert. I will wait as we have already discussed."

Darius nodded and smiled. With a last glance backwards, he vanished from his friend's site.

The path wound about this way and that. When they reached a fork, Sira headed toward the right. Darius picked up a rock and discreetly scratched a small arrow into the cave. He didn't know why, but it seemed the thing to do. Each time they came to a fork, he did the same.

"Why?" he thought to himself, but he brushed it off to nerves and Prydon's words of caution.

When light shown at the end of their path, Darius emerged behind the castle in a small clearing, sheltered from view by massive trees.

"We're here," said Sira.

A rustling sound in some nearby bushes caused Darius to draw his sword.

"Don't worry about that," snickered Sira. "It's just

my...pet."

A massive creature jumped from the bushes—a cat! It lunged, knocking Darius's sword from his hands. Before Darius could get to his feet, a silken net was thrown over him, and all his energy was sapped.

Sira laughed. "You are way too trusting, you know. Prydon is much wiser than you. Good thing he couldn't fit in our tunnel. Of course, we planned it that way all along." The beast, a catlike creature, sauntered up and purred as it rubbed against her.

Darius's initial shock dissipated. "What are you doing? And why?"

"Isn't it apparent?" she smiled. "You really aren't that bright are you. But my master does require your presence."

"No!" Darius yelled, but the net pulsed as he attempted to move. It was as if the net drained him, leaving him with no energy, no strength, and soon no will. His mind began to fill with a foggy haze, and he fainted.

When he awoke, he was strapped to a table, turned up on end so he was in a standing position. The cold around him was accented by the room of heavy stone. A rat scurried along the edge of one wall and vanished into a small crack at the base. Water dripped along another wall and pooled in a sunken ledge before overrunning into a grate in the floor.

Darius's weapons were gone—no surprise there. His muscles ached. There was no way to determine how long he'd been bound, but he was sure Prydon would be suspect at this point. He tried to speak a few words to release his bindings, but his lips seemed to be as bound as his hands. He slowed his breathing and closed his eyes. Thinking the words should do it.

He concentrated; the leather straps did not budge.

"Don't bother, my son. No magic can be used in this room." The sorcerer appeared from a dark corner and walked to a small table. He poured a glass of what appeared to be water. "Yes, your assumption is correct. I am Klavon." Klavon leaned casually against the table and took a sip from the glass. "So here's the deal. I want to talk to you. That's all, talk. So I'm going to give you a serum that will release your vocal cords. But," he emphasized, "you must behave yourself. Is that understood?"

Darius clenched his teeth and scowled at Klavon.

"You don't trust me? Now why would that be? Fine. I'll show you that the serum is not toxic. I have no desire to kill you." Klavon picked up a vial of blue liquid from the table and took a sip, opening his mouth so that Darius could see the substance on his tongue. "See. Nothing. So, do we have a deal? You will behave?"

Darius had no intention of behaving nor did he trust Klavon. He answered by tightening his lips.

"Really, now. You wouldn't want me to force it upon you, would you? And I can assume you will not behave. So what to do?" Klavon paced back and forth in front of Darius, all the while starring at him with one brow raised and a humorous twist on his lips. "You leave me no choice. Yes, I will probably regret this, but we must talk."

Klavon approached Darius and grabbed his jaw, squeezing the back with pressure Darius could not fight.

Darius and the Dragon's Stone

His lips parted only enough for Klavon to force the contents of the vial into his mouth. Darius spat, blowing a blue slime across Klavon's face, and Klavon responded with a backhand across Darius's cheek.

Darius grinned as Klavon backed away, wiping the mixture from his skin with the cuff of his robe. His eyes blazed with a fire that reminded Darius of the crimson rain that fell when the book was lost, but Darius remained defiant, and as his vocal cords loosened, he laughed out loud.

"You son of a.... No! I will not say such things of your mother." Klavon stormed out of the room, leaving Darius hanging with only the company of the rat.

Laughter had worked; he cleared his throat and tried to speak. His voice returned, sure enough, but he had no idea how long it would take the blue liquid to kill him.

The door squeaked open, and Sira entered.

"You really are an idiot, you know," she said, tossing her white hair over her shoulder.

Her pet was at her side, and she stroked its head.

"So how long until I die?" Darius asked, spitting the words at her much as he had the contents of the vial at Klavon.

"Die? You're not going to die. As much as you'd like to believe, my master has no desire to kill you," she said.

"Really? Then what does he want?" Darius asked.

"He wants only to talk to you."

Darius rolled his eyes. "So he destroys Brandor only with the intention of talking to me? Couldn't he have chosen a less destructive way to accomplish that?"

"Now, Darius, you do epitomize idiocy. Honestly, I can't see what he sees in you. Nevertheless, would you have willingly come to talk to him?"

Darius returned to clenching his jaws.

"I thought not. Now, be a good boy and let my master speak to you. All right?"

Darius tried to freeze her with an icy stare. It didn't work.

"That's a good boy." Sira walked over and patted Darius on his head.

He snapped at her hand, and her pet lunged and growled, his bare teeth a little too close to Darius's midsection, and Darius tried to flatten himself against the wood behind his back.

Sira laughed. "Maybe it's the spunk. But he will have to do something about your stupidity. One so senseless will not survive in his realm—favor or not."

Darius closed his mouth. Speaking to her was of no use. It never was, and he wondered why he'd ever trusted her. Funny. She didn't seem as beautiful.

The door shut behind Sira, and Darius was once again left alone.

It was hours before Klavon returned. His expression again housed that initial arrogance Darius observed when they'd first met, but before Darius would allow Klavon to become comfortable with his advantage, he spoke.

"Your face looked better with a shade of blue. So what do you want?" Darius asked.

Klavon ignored Darius's attempt and poured

himself another glass of what Darius no long assumed was water. "Remember the battle you experienced, against a young sorcerer?"

Darius's eye shot wide. So he and Prydon had been correct. He quickly regained control of his expressions, but Klavon grinned. He knew that Darius understood.

"My boy, that was a test. I wanted to give you the chance to show me your abilities, to first determine your worth to me. And I must say you performed quite well."

"So one of your servants attacked that village just to lure me there."

Klavon laughed. "Not one of my servants. That was me—a younger and somewhat altered me, but me nonetheless. And your intentions have always been to come here. No, it was no lure. It was, as I said, a test."

"But I defeated him," said Darius.

"No. He…I left willingly," stated Klavon.

"Willingly? No, you couldn't defeat me! So now you are going to finish what you couldn't do there? I guess you want to murder me just like you did my father!" Darius could feel heat in the tips of his ears.

"Your father?" responded Klavon coldly, his face remaining controlled. "I did not murder your father."

"I saw it! You can not lie to me!" Flashes of his father death filled his mind, and the expression on Klavon's face when he impaled Thyre was as clear as if a thick fog had lifted from his eyes.

"Well, I must admit that I am responsible for your father's death, but it was in self-defense. It was he or I. A sad reality really, but reality nonetheless."

"Self-defense? You call an all out invasion of his village self-defense?"

"Let's not get caught up in semantics." Klavon waved his hand as if brushing away the topic of discussion. "Now down to my reason for detaining you. I want you to join me here, you and your mother."

Darius stared at Klavon, and for a moment he was completely speechless. "Are you insane?" He shook his head, and as Klavon's words finally sunk in, he added. "You are completely crazy, you know." Darius was almost on the brink of bursting into uncontrollable laughter at the idea.

"No. I am quite serious. You see, your mother and I—"

Darius screamed, "Never, and I mean never, include my mother in any conjunction with you!"

Klavon smiled. "You can deny the truth if you wish, but it does not change the fact that your mother and I have a history together, a very…intimate history."

Darius wrenched at his bindings. Klavon continued to ramble as he thrashed about. His wrists hurt, and a small trickle of blood ran down his hand, bringing life to the crimson that was already there.

"…take you as my son and your mother as my wife."

Darius wished his hearing was lost, muffled, even drowned by the piercing shriek of the fiery beast that gave him the curse that brought him here. Staring at the ground, Darius hissed. "I will never stay here with you, and my mother would rather die!"

Klavon laughed, but all Darius could hear was an echo of evil in his head. Then silence fell. Klavon was gone.

Darius woke to Sira tending his wrist. "You really should take better care of yourself."

"Go away!" Darius yelled.

"It's only a scratch. You'll live." Sira sat down on the table, her pet curled up on the floor beneath her.

"Does that thing ever leave your side?" asked Darius.

"Never," she said matter-of-factly, twirling her hair senselessly between her fingers. "Don't you remember? I mentioned him when I talked with you at that village…the one Klavon attacked?" Sira stopped twisting her hair—it fell perfectly straight next to her slender face—and sat still. "So why didn't you take my advice? Why did you return to your precious valley?"

Darius said nothing, silently chiding himself for being so foolish. How could he not have known it was her? How could he have thought it was only a dream?

"It won't help you, you know," she said. "In fact, given that hint of red, I'd say it was a mistake. But I guess that's better for Klavon anyway."

"Why are you here?" asked Darius. His breathing was forced, and he knew Sira could see his annoyance and that she took extreme pleasure in it.

Sira made no reply, but a satisfied smile settled on her lips.

"Are you here to gloat? You do seem to enjoy that quite a bit. You know, some may say that's a flaw, a weakness, reveling in the misfortunes of others." Darius's gaze locked on her face, hoping to see some hint that he had, even in some small way, annoyed her as well.

"Nope," she replied. To his frustration, his comments appeared to have no affect on her.

As uncomfortable as it was, Darius maintained his stare, but she said nothing. "So why are you here?"

Sira shrugged. "To clean up that blood before it stains our floor."

Darius frowned. "Why do you lie like that?"

"Fine," she said, with a tone that could only be interpreted as a false sense of surrender. "I admit that this floor couldn't be in much worse shape, but you must admit that adding blood to the filth would only serve to worsen the condition. Wouldn't you agree?"

Darius closed his eyes. Talking to Sira was giving him a headache. After several minutes, he opened his eyes. Sira was still there.

"What do you want?" he screamed.

"Nothing more," she laughed, and she hopped off the table and opened the door. Before she closed it behind her, she added, "Always nice to see you angry."

The door shut before Darius could retort. That was fine with him. He had nothing he wanted to say to her anyway.

In a short time, Klavon returned.

"Well, there is no shortage of visits around here, even if the company is somewhat limited." Darius tilted his head, challenging Klavon as best he could, given his current situation.

"Witty. I like that. But now I shall await your answer." Klavon leaned against the table.

"Answer to what?" asked Darius.

"To whether or not you will allow me to take you in as my son," said Klavon. "Did you hear nothing of what I said earlier?"

"You were joking, right?" Darius asked. When he received nothing more than a raised brow from Klavon, he added. "I'm my father's son! What would ever make you think I could possibly be with you?"

Klavon paused. "Your crystal. It has a hint of crimson, does it not?"

"It's this stupid curse of yours, a curse I will in time overcome." Darius ground his teeth.

"That curse, as you call it, is merely an affirmation of your bond with me. But none of this matters. You will soon discover that your place is indeed here. And your mother—"

"Never! My mother has nothing to do with any of this!"

"Your mother has everything to do with this! She was never intended for your father. She and I should have been together."

"I highly doubt that!" snapped Darius.

Klavon ignored him. "But I will forgive her. I have even decided to take her son as my own."

"I highly doubt that, too," said Darius.

"Doubt what you will," said Klavon, "but you will not be able to deny the truth when you are gently encouraged. You and your mother will be here with me, and willingly so."

Klavon opened the door and stepped out, but before the door shut behind him, Darius laughed. "Not in my lifetime."

The door shut with a click, and Darius glared at the closed door.

Chapter Thirty-two

Brandor

Darius woke to the smell of freshly fried bacon and eggs.

"Darius! Get up or you'll be late. Mr. Athus is kind, but you must not take advantage of him that way."

Darius sat up in the soft bed. Tears filled his eyes as the feminine voice caressed his ears. They could not have been more stern, but to Darius they were as gentle as a spring breeze.

"Mom?"

"Get up!" Miora's voice rang with finality.

Darius looked around. In his mind he could see flashes of strange images—strange but familiar—yet the images felt distant, like an old book he'd read that somehow managed to linger in his thoughts. Still….

He pinched himself. It hurt. A flash of red appeared in his mind, the image vivid and clear, and the book was stolen. The fiery beast grabbed his arm and he almost buckled with the searing pain.

As suddenly as it had come, it faded, and he was

once again sitting in his bed. Darius's eyes shot to his hand. No tendrils, no bloody red vines adorning his wrist. The images in his mind returned to the distance in which they had originally presided, vague and obscure yet haunting him nonetheless.

Darius instinctively spoke words that would summon light to his dimly lit room. Nothing happened. He shook his head and rubbed his temples. The distant images were at last fading. He got up and dressed, checking his clothes and drawers in the nearby chest for anything—a staff, sword, books on spells—just to be certain. Nothing was there.

He walked apprehensively toward the kitchen he knew so well, wondering if…why didn't he remember his name? But the face…the face was the one thing that was clear in his mind. And he wondered if this man would be sitting beside her, his mother, laughing at his triumph. Triumph? Wait. There was an offer…but he'd refused. What was going on?

He closed his eyes and stepped through the door. Opening them, he saw his mother, as welcome a sight as any he could remember, sitting alone at the table.

Darius's mother looked up and gestured to the chair across from her. "Eat."

Her smile was sincere, and before Darius could even sit, he lunged toward her, kneeling on the floor and hugging her.

"Darius? What's going on? Have you gone mad?" Laughter filled her words.

"Have I been gone long?" Still holding her tightly

with his face buried in her chest, Darius's voice choked back tears.

"Gone? Darius, what are you talking about? You went to work yesterday as you do all days, but then you came home." She held his shoulders and pushed him up. Staring at him, she asked, "Darius, are you all right?"

Darius gazed into her eyes. They were hers. Her face was true. A tear escaped his eyes and rolled down his cheek.

"Darius, you're scaring me." Miora's soft face wrinkled, and her breathing quickened.

"No, Mom. It's fine. I...I guess I had a bad dream." He attempted to smile sincerely. "I guess it's all the books Mr. Athus has been giving me."

Miora's smile returned, and she cupped Darius's cheek with her hand. "Are you sure? That spider..."

"What spider?" asked Darius.

"Don't you remember? A few weeks ago, you were bitten...when you were at the well. We never did find out what it was, really, but we're pretty sure it was some spider. It was horrible. The fever...the dreams. You were in bed for over a week." Tears glistened in Miora's eyes. "I thought we were going to lose you. If it hadn't been for the concoction, I'm quite certain we would have."

"Concoction?" asked Darius.

"Mr. Athus. He brewed it from the wizard's stores. Are you feverish again?" Miora placed her palms over Darius's face and neck. "Let me see your hand."

Miora grabbed his hand...the same one Darius had envisioned had been grabbed by the beast.

"I was bitten?" asked Darius, not expecting an answer but as if trying to work out a puzzle.

"I don't see anything. Do I need to tell Mr. Athus you need rest? You know, it hasn't been too long you've tried to work again. Perhaps it's just too soon."

"No, mom," said Darius. "I'm fine."

He hated to lie to her, but what else could he do? He wasn't fine—well, not completely—even if there were no red marks, no spells, no nameless man.

Miora was perceptive, as always, and concern etched in the crease of her brow. "Hmmm...eat before you head to the tower. And if you begin to feel the slightest bit warm, you come straight home. I mean it—straight home!"

Darius hugged his mother once again and sat opposite her. Even with the odd disquiet, he couldn't ignore the amazing feast that lay before him. He grabbed a plate and piled it with the delicious food—bacon, eggs, biscuits with homemade jam—and he ate until he could eat no more.

"Take your dishes to the sink for me?" his mother asked as she carried a heavy load of laundry outside.

Darius placed his dishes in the sink, as he had been asked, and moved to the doorway. He looked at his mother as she hung the wet clothes. "It was simply a fever brought on by a bite. That would explain everything. And Brandor was safe. We're safe," he thought, but a deep frown joined his eyebrows. He stepped outside into the warm sun.

"I love you, mom," he said as he hugged her yet again.

"I love you, too. And you're certain? You're all

right?"

"I'm fine. I'm just…" Darius looked into his mother's eyes and tried to laugh. "Really, I'm fine."

"All right, then. But take it easy," said his mother.

Darius smiled and headed up the hill toward the village he knew so well.

Everything was as it was—was as it should be. Nothing was missing. He paused at the bridge over the small stream to watch two small fish fight over the last remnants of what Darius thought was a bug. The voice behind should not have come as a surprise, but he bristled nonetheless.

"Morning, Darius," came the gruff voice.

Darius stood still, clenching the railing to the bridge. He closes his eyes and shook his head. Something was different—he was different.

"Darius? Do you hear me, boy?"

The words cut into him, and he turned. "What? What do you want with me?" he snarled. Not this time; he would not tolerate her today.

Mrs. Keedle's eyes shot open as if the very thought of closing them would cause immense pain. "How dare you speak to me like that! Why, after all this town has done—after all I have done—for you and your mother. You ungrateful little beggar. I shall have words with Mr. Athus indeed!" She stood, dropping her knitting on the porch floor, and slammed the door as she disappeared into her insignificant house.

And why did he care if she vanished? Darius raised a brow and yelled at the door, "I'm sure my mother will have your stinking clothes ready soon!"

Darius grinned as he turned and walked toward the tower. His mind was enlivened at the thrill of his accomplishment. Never before had he spoken in that fashion to her—nor anyone else for that matter—in the village. It felt strangely good.

A sharp bump in the shoulder brought his face up from ground level.

"Hey! Watch where you are going!" Garp stood eye level with Darius, his face worn and wrinkled, not from hard work but from years of anger and accusation.

"I believe you are the one who ran into me," said Darius, standing tall to challenge his opponent.

"Me? You're the one with your head in the clouds, boy—a silly grin creasing your face so." Garp's face wrinkled even more, a feat Darius had not thought possible.

"My grin, as you say, is sincere as I have had an enjoyable morning." Darius grinned even wider. "You, however, will never experience an enjoyable moment in your life as you are a sour, bitter, old man!"

"You! You!" Garp's face turned deep purple and his lips quivered in anger as the words tangled he tongue. The artery in his neck bulged like a swelling river about to burst its dam.

Darius laughed and walked past him, leaving him to his rant and enjoying it immensely. When he arrived at the tower, he stopped at the outbuilding and gathered his cleaning supplies as he'd always done. Then he opened the door and entered the familiar tower.

"Darius, my boy." The voice was sincere, and

Darius scoured his master with his eyes.

How good it was to see him again, yet despite his pleasing face and even though he'd enjoyed a few moments of vengeance against those who had always treated him so unkindly, his joy was clouded once again.

The image that had been so real earlier that day—the image of the book stolen and his hand burning—came flooding back now that he stood so close to where the book was kept. "Mr. Athus, I had a dream, or at least I think it was a dream. It was so real."

"We all have dreams," said Mr. Athus.

"No. This was different. The book had been stolen and—"

"I have just come from the tower. The book is fine." Mr. Athus laughed. "It must be those books I've been giving you, seeping into your sleep."

"But—"

"Or remnants of your illness," Mr. Athus said, interrupting Darius's words.

Mr. Athus placed his hand on Darius's shoulder. It felt real; everything felt real. All his senses appeared more alive than ever before, and his confrontations with Mrs. Keedle and Garp had invigorated him. But the euphoria was fading, and the dream was haunting his thoughts.

"Don't give it another thought. The book is safe, I can assure you." Mr. Athus stepped toward the stairs leading up the tower. "Now, we have important business to attend to today. Put those cleaning supplies away and follow me."

Darius set down the pail and mop. He wanted to say

more, but never had Mr. Athus been so excited. Besides, what good would it do? Darius had no proof, and why should he? He'd already tried to conjure a spell, unsuccessfully. Of course, nothing happened. He followed Mr. Athus up the stairs toward the top of the tower, deciding to write off all these strange thoughts and feelings to the fever he had endured.

At the landing, Mr. Athus opened the door to the wizard's chamber, now his own quarters. Darius glanced inside as Mr. Athus entered his room. Darius hesitated, intending to wait outside the door, but the thought of the book only a few steps away…his feet continued to climb the stairs until he reached the top. The elegant book sat on its pedestal as always. Darius's shoulders sank. He almost wished it wasn't there. Yet, as quickly as he thought it, it was as if a firm slap struck his face, and he realized what he was thinking. How could he wish it gone? How could he wish the events in his dream were real? Guilt clenched his throat, and he swallowed hard to force it away.

"Darius, not up there, boy. Here. I need you to help me collect some things." The voice echoed up to the book.

Darius returned to the landing and stopped outside the door.

"Well, come on," said Mr. Athus.

"I…I've never been in there." Darius stood frozen at the door, not sure what to do next.

"What are you talking about? You've been in here many times." Mr. Athus motioned for Darius to enter.

Darius frowned, his eyes blinking in confusion, but slowly entered. The room was large, the full expanse of the tower. A small cot lay in the corner, but the remainder of the room overflowed with all manners of curiosities that could only be the effects of a wizard. A small window cast flecked light across a table filled with vials, tubes, jars, and bags of strange liquids and objects. Herbs hung dried from the ceiling. The fire in a stone fireplace blazed beneath a brewing cauldron; it did not smell like food.

Mr. Athus picked up a book and blew the dust from its jacket. "Here. This is it."

Darius read the spine, *Concoctions for the Commoner*.

"What is that?" he asked.

"This will tell me which of these vials we will need," said Mr. Athus, "just as it told me which I would use when you were ill."

"I don't understand. Is someone sick?"

"In a manner of speaking. There is a sickness of bad behavior running rampant in our peaceful village and unacceptable to our wizard." Mr. Athus began fingering through the book. "And I have been instructed to take action."

"Action?" asked Darius.

"Yes. Our wizard wishes it," Mr. Athus said. "Ah! Here it is."

"Your wizard? Is he back?" asked Darius.

"Not yet, but soon." Mr. Athus laid the book on the table so that the page would be clearly visible. "This is the time he wants us to cleanse our town; make right some wrongs. Now, I know we have never had to deal out retribution, and it will be difficult for you to watch, but it must be done." Mr. Athus turned his back on Darius and began his work, mixing potions and corking the small vials without the slightest concern.

He remembered someone telling him that some wizards had others in their employ who focused solely on medicinal concoctions. Maybe Mr. Athus was that for Brandor's wizard. Then Darius shook his head. Who had told him that?

"Yes, sir," Darius whispered.

When Mr. Athus finished gathering the vials he wanted, he turned to Darius. "Now, as my assistant, I am counting on you to administer the solution."

Darius hardly noticed. A fog had filled his mind—he was still trying to remember what he had learned and, more importantly, when and where he had learned it. "What? Oh, sorry. What, sir?"

Mr. Athus's brows raised and his eyes became wide. "Well, well, well. You are distracted today, aren't you. But that will not do. As I was saying—and I need you to pay close attention—as my assistant, I am counting on you to administer the solution." Mr. Athus repeated is previous instructions, speaking his words slowly and very determined. "Darius, this is very important—very important indeed."

Darius tried to focus on his current assignment as Mr. Athus required. "Me? Why?"

"They hold great strength. It is almost certain I would falter," said Mr. Athus.

Darius couldn't respond. He had no idea what was going on, what was going to happen. What did he mean retribution? Suddenly he looked at the vials in Mr. Athus's hands. It was as if he'd seen them for the very first time, strange liquid swirling about as if it refused to blend completely. He had no idea what they held, and he wasn't sure he wanted to find out. "But…"

Mr. Athus smiled and place a hand on Darius's shoulder. "Son, I am old. You are young and strong, and I need your help."

"Son." What a strange sound, that word, echoing in Darius's ears. He blankly nodded and followed Mr. Athus down the stairs of the tower and out the door. They traveled toward the edge of town where a grand house stood tall. Three boys were sitting at a table covered by the shade of a thick tree, eating ice cream. When Mr. Athus approached, the boys' father came outside.

"What do you want, bringing that misfit boy into my yard?" said the man.

"I am here to bring justice to your sons. The wizard will be returning soon, and he asked that I take care of certain problems."

"Justice? What justice? They have done nothing that would warrant such action."

Mr. Athus pulled a vial from his cloak and let a few drops of the clear blue liquid fall to the ground. A massive cloud filled the air. As it cleared, a perfect picture appeared.

As Darius watched, he was in shock. The three boys were sneaking into a neighbor's garden, stealing some watermelons. They snickered and ran from the yard, carrying their load, but as if to insult further, they smashed the fruit onto the ground. They ran back and took other fruit and vegetables, each time smashing them to the ground or stomping them with their feet if the item was not inclined to burst easily. When they were done, the translucent cloud vanished.

"What is this?" demanded the father.

"This is what they have done. This is what they must be punished for." Mr. Athus pulled another vial from his cloak and handed it to Darius. "A drop on each tongue, and the wizard's wishes will be done."

Darius looked from Mr. Athus to the boys, who were now trying to hide behind their large father. "But, sir—"

"Darius, remember. I need your help here."

Darius apprehensively took the vial.

"You're not going to touch my sons, even if you do speak for our wizard in his absence, and I definitely won't let you use this brat to do the wizard's work!"

Mr. Athus grinned. "I thought you would say that." He pulled another vial from his cloak and poured four drops to the ground. Each spread like wild weeds, and vines shot out, swirling about the father and the three boys until they could not move.

"Now, Darius, a drop on each tongue."

Darius slowly stepped forward, and the father made to say something. A vine shot up and around his mouth, so the words came out as a garbled growl. The boys were terrified, each with their mouths clamped shut. Darius approached the first, but he refused to open his mouth.

"I wouldn't do that if I were you," said Mr. Athus.

"I do have another vial, but it might prove a bit painful."

The boy whimpered and opened his mouth. Darius hesitated, but his wrist began to itch where he had been bitten—a bite he couldn't see—and he almost dropped the vial as he instinctively scratched at it.

"Careful," said Mr. Athus.

The irritation subsided, and something seemed to compel Darius to continue. Slowly, he poured a drop on the boy's tongue; nothing happened. He did the same with the other boys, and in a minute the results were obvious. Each child was throwing up profusely.

Mr. Athus turned and walked away. Darius followed, looking back at the boys and father, still bound by the vines. "But, sir. The vines."

Mr. Athus snapped his finger, and the vines vanished. By then they were stepping back onto the road, and Darius looked back again. The mother appeared from their house, wiping the boys' mouths as they cried, with tears in her eyes.

"Was that really necessary, sir?" asked Darius. "I mean, they're just boys being mischievous. Not the best actions, I admit, but they're still just boys. Wouldn't it have been more productive to have them…I don't know…work in the garden until it was back to normal?"

"It was as the wizard wished. And there was no real harm done. Maybe next time, they will think again before they steal something," said Mr. Athus.

Darius couldn't help but feel the punishment they had endured was harsh and likely not effective—he could see himself as a young boy doing it again just for spite—

but he said no more.

The next stop was Garp's home, and Darius couldn't imagine what he could have done. He was grumpy, true, but bitterness had a way of bringing that out in a person.

"Garp, you have been charged with killing your neighbor's dog." Mr. Athus continued with the same oration about the wizard, but that seemed of little interest to Garp.

"That dog comes into my yard every day, defecating in my garden and then trying to bite me as I chase it away! I was merely defending myself." Garp's stood with his chin held high and his lower jaw protruding, daring Mr. Athus to prove otherwise.

"Really? Then perhaps this will interest you." Mr. Athus pulled out the vial, let the drops hit the ground, and displayed the crime.

Darius watched as a little dog walked past Garp's fence. With a piece of meat, Garp enticed the animal into his yard. While the dog finished its small feast, Garp came down hard with an ax, and the animal's head rolled in the grass.

"That…that…that dog comes in my yard every day, I tell you!" screeched Garp.

"Darius?" Mr. Athus said calmly, ignoring Garp.

Darius walked slowly to Garp. He hated this old man, but he was reluctant to drop the mixture on his tongue. He thought about the innocent dog and decided vomiting was a small price to pay for its life, more appropriate than it had been with the young boys. Still, something tugged at his throat and he swallowed hard, nervously waiting to do as he was told.

"You can't let this...this interloper touch me," snarled Garp. Darius could hear fear in his voice—a shakiness amidst the venom—although Garp was attempting to maintain his continual disregard for Darius.

"Oh, but he can," answered Mr. Athus. "It is his duty."

Garp made to move away. Mr. Athus let drops fall from the vial that administered the vines, entangling Garp's legs and weaving up his body until he was unable to move, much less escape. With pinched lips and eyes that formed hateful slits, Garp refused to open his mouth. Mr. Athus threatened the other vial, as he had done with the boys.

"This is..." Garp fumbled with words. "This is..."

Mr. Athus held up the unknown vial, and Garp held still. Darius stepped up and allowed a single drop to fall on Garp's tongue. *Why did I just do that?*, thought Darius.

Garp's breathing was forced, and Darius stepped back. The vines released as Mr. Athus snapped his finger, but Garp just stood there. Garp's breathing quickened even more, but now it was with a sense of triumph. A huge grin covered his face as he patted his face, chest, and thighs as if to prove that nothing was happening.

"See!" Garp squealed with excitement. "The wizard doesn't want me punished!"

Garp barely finished his words when he was thrown to the ground by some invisible hand. He began to roll around in pain, and as Darius watched, whip marks appeared across his back. Garp screamed for help, but there was nothing Darius could do.

"Mr. Athus!" Darius pleaded.

"It is as the wizard wishes," said Mr. Athus.

Darius watched as the old man attempted escape from his unseen enemy, but it was of no use. No matter which way Garp tossed and turned, the whip found his back. When it was done, Garp's shirt was in tatters, and blood trickled down the wounds.

Darius ran to his side and reached out, trying to help him stand. "Garp...I never..."

Garp glared up at Darius and refused his hand. The old man stood slowly, fighting to regain his footing, first with one leg and then the other. His lips, his entire body, were trembling, and his gaze froze on Darius.

Garp looked at him through pain filled eyes. "Go away," he growled. "You have done enough here!"

Darius hesitated. Garp's jaw tensed, and Darius slowly backed away. Mr. Athus was already heading down the road, and Darius turned, stumbled for a moment, and then jogged to catch up.

"Mr. Athus," said Darius, pleading.

Mr. Athus smiled and patted Darius's shoulder. "I know. It is difficult, but it is as our wizard wishes. These things are being dealt with to rid this village of some horrible wrongdoings."

Darius struggled with what was happening. This wasn't Mr. Athus. This wasn't the Brandor he remembered. Still, he was powerless, even felt bound to continue. The bite began to pulse....

The next two stops resulted in a forced dousing in

water that almost resulted in drowning and lightning that somehow caused a burn but didn't kill.

"Why?" asked Darius. As they left, the last victim's burns were being tended by her husband. "I can't believe these people deserve such...such violence."

"The punishment fits the crime, Darius," answered Mr. Athus. "Our wizard knows the truth of their actions and the intent in their hearts. They are being cleansed and appropriately so, I might add. They should be thankful, given a new start."

Darius was finding it very difficult to find the correlation. He had learned that villages that were blessed with a compassionate wizard lived in safety and care. Only those who were unfortunate to be taken by a sorcerer would be subject to such devices, and he was not pleased at all with his part in this. But where had he heard this...was this a dream as well? If not, would that mean that Brandor's wizard was actually a sorcerer? There was something very wrong with this entire situation, and Darius struggled as he tried to make sense if it all. His thoughts were so deep that he was startled when Mr. Athus again spoke.

"One last stop." Mr. Athus approached a group of young men, a little older than Darius, as they sat beneath a large tree enjoying the shade. "You boys know why I am here?"

"Who you callin' boys, old man?" snarled one of the four.

"Well, in all reality, I guess you would be considered men, but from your actions?" Mr. Athus stroked his chin and exaggerated a thoughtful gaze. "Well, actually, you might be right. Boys would never do such a thing."

One of the four stood up, and the other three followed suit, standing behind him like a pack of wolves ready to pounce. "And what did we supposedly do? More importantly, what are you going to do about it, old man?"

Mr. Athus pulled out the vial and looked at Darius. "This, you will definitely want to see."

Darius frowned and looked at the cloud as it cleared and began playing its story. His mother appeared, pinning wet laundry to a clothesline. The boys approached and ripped her work to the ground. Darius could not hear the words, but his mother was clearly angry, yelling at the group.

They surrounded her until Darius could only catch glimpses of her face, her angry face. One of them grabbed her shoulders and laughed as he tossed her to another. He could see her fist pound at their shoulders as she was tossed around. Finally, Miora collapsed on the ground in the middle of the group, but her face was strong.

Darius's jaw tensed as he watched the cruel scene. He glanced from the image to the group. They were laughing. He looked back at his mother. One of the young men stepped forward and yanked her from the ground, pressing his lips firmly against hers. When he was done, he tossed her to another. The ritual was repeated until all four had befouled her lips, and she fell in a heap on the ground. Her shoulders were sagging, and Darius could see a single tear run down her dirt smudged face. The boys in the image laughed and said something. Her head remained bent; she refused to look up at them. Then they left.

It was more than Darius could stand. "How dare you?" he yelled.

"Easy now, Darius," said Mr. Athus calmly.

"Your mother, even though she is a pitiful outsider, is beautiful nonetheless," said the leader of the group. "It is a waste for her not to have a man. She needed a man; we gave her four."

Darius lunged at the group. They pounced on him, punching his face repeatedly until a twist of vines caught hold and pulled them away. Darius stood, his lip bleeding.

One of the boys sneered. "What did we do wrong? We only kissed her! Since when is it a crime to kiss a woman?"

Darius lunged again, but before he could punch the young man in the mouth, Mr. Athus grabbed his arm.

"Do not worry, son. This vial is for them."

Darius opened it quickly, ready to administer whatever the vial would give. But before he let the first drop hit the man's tongue, he looked at the liquid inside. It swirled in the same defiant way as the others, but somehow, it was different. He turned back to Mr. Athus.

"What will it do to him?" Darius asked.

"Darius, what does it matter? He forced himself on your mother!"

"I know. He's a jerk who deserved to have his butt kicked, and I would be more than happy to oblige, but what will this liquid do?"

Mr. Athus frowned. "I don't know."

"You have to. All day long, the punishments have been getting worse and worse. So what's left?" he asked.

His words showed no respect for Mr. Athus, and although he was surprised by this, he was not bothered by it.

The spot on his wrist began to burn, and Darius looked at the contents of the vial. It looked different than the other he'd been using, its color deep red...crimson. Darius blinked. A rush of images filled his mind, images of Prydon, Barsovy, Alara and her village, training, the valley...and Klavon! That was the name that had escaped him earlier that day.

Darius stood up and corked the vial. "I will not continue in this. This is wrong, horribly wrong."

Mr. Athus exploded. "How dare you question the wizard!" He grabbed Darius's hand and stared deeply into his face. "You will do this."

He was much stronger than he appeared and certainly much stronger than he had implied. In fact, he dragged Darius over to the young man and forced him to pour a drop on the young man's tongue. Then he released Darius's hand, and Darius stepped backwards, horrified as he looked from Mr. Athus to the young man who was now choking on the liquid.

The man tried to reach out to Darius, but the vines prevented it. "Help.... Please," came his raspy voice.

Within moments, the man convulsed so drastically that Mr. Athus had no need to snap his fingers; the vines were shredded. Then with one last convulsive screech, the man died, bent and broken on the ground.

"See! The wizard says they deserve death! Now do it!" Mr. Athus pointed to the vial still in Darius's hands. "Finish the job!"

Darius stood there, staring at the dead man. The other three were begging for their lives the way cowards often do when they realize their current match is not nearly so weak as their previous victim.

"See! They are cowards, plain and simple." Mr. Athus's voice softened, almost a whisper against Darius's ear. "Now do it."

Darius turned and spoke slowly and with a power that only a trained wizard could muster. "No." He threw the vial to the ground. It shattered, and the liquid seeped into the ground, quickly turning the green grass putrid brown.

"You fool!" yelled Mr. Athus. "What have you done?"

But the voice changed, and Darius became dizzy, falling to the ground. He stared up in the sky as the words continued to echo. The clouds were spinning as were the trees, birds, leaves, air. He blinked hard several times until everything was replaced with a dark haze.

When his sight returned, Klavon was still yelling at him. "You fool! You were so close!"

The tendrils in Darius's hands were throbbing like they had never done before. He felt they might burst his skin, they burned so badly. He tried to sit up, but the dizziness pulled his head back down to the wooden table. He blinked and raised his head to look down at his wrists, tightly bound as they had been before. He laid his head back down on the table and smiled as Klavon stormed out of the room.

Darius was back.

Chapter Thirty-three

The Battle

Darius lay there on the wooden table, bound at the feet and wrists. His small triumph over Klavon was short lived as he was quite shaken by the very real dream he had endured. His eyes filled with tears as he realized what happened. Klavon used his past, used the people of Brandor who had ostracized him for so many years, to caress him into choosing evil. And had Klavon's plan worked? While he knew he had held strong in the end, Darius's heart ached as the tendrils on his hand pulsed and burned like poisonous snakes injecting their venom deep into his soul. He couldn't help but wonder if it was too late—if he'd succumb to the sweet temptations of revenge.

The door squeaked, and Sira sauntered in followed by her pet. "You really are making this unreasonably difficult, you know."

Darius turned his face away. He couldn't wipe the tears that lay pooled around his eyes. He blinked, and they fell down the side of his face and nose, a drop clinging to the tip like a beacon in the night.

"Go away!" he hissed.

He could hear her slithering steps as she came

closer. "Aw. You've been crying. Here, let me wipe those off for you."

"Don't you touch me!" Darius snapped. The words stuck in his throat, and he yanked at the binds, wanting to put his hands around her slender, greasy neck.

"Well," Sira said, feigning astonished hurt. "Now that's gratitude for you. Fine then. Look like a baby. Why should I care?" Sira proceeded to pick up a syringe and fill it with a bluish liquid. "This shouldn't hurt…much." She leaned to inject the contents into Darius's arm.

"Hey! What are you doing?" Darius tugged at his bindings, but the movement only caused the needle to jab painfully into his upper arm, and he winced.

"Careful. You'll make me break it, but nothing to worry about. We aren't going to make you dream again. That obviously didn't work." Sira blotted the blood from where she removed the needle. "This is just to help you wake up. Klavon wishes to have words with you."

"I have nothing to say to him!"

Sira placed a finger on her chin, looking off into the distance in exaggerated confusion. "Really?" She dropped her hand to her sides, palms up, as if begging for understanding. "Your own mother, and you couldn't kill the guys who attacked her? Now, that's cold."

"They didn't attack my mother! None of it was real!"

"Yes, but you didn't know that at the time, did you? What a pity. Well, at least Klavon loves her."

"Klavon doesn't know the meaning of love!"

Sira lowered her face until her nose brushed closely

to Darius's, and he could feel her warm breath on his cheek. "Ah, but that is where you are wrong. Klavon loves your mother, and thus he loves you. Why else would you still be alive?" She stroked his hair and traced the contour of his face with her eyes. "I must admit, you do have a certain attraction about you."

"Get away from me!"

Sira leaned in even closer and kissed him soundly on the lips. "See, it might not be so bad here after all."

"Get your vile mouth away from me." The vein in Darius's neck pulsed, and he spat in her face.

Sira's eyes became like fire as she wiped the spit from her cheek. It was the first time he'd ever seen her rattled, and he quite liked it. He was about to gloat, but before he could say anything, the door to the dungeon crashed open. Concoctions on a nearby shelf toppled and exploded with a puff of smoke. Sira jumped and whipped around.

In the doorway stood Alara, holding a club, and Loklan, holding his staff in one hand and sword in the other. Sira's face twisted, and she yelled for her pet to attack. Loklan slammed his staff to the ground, sending a wave of force toward the cat. The pulse threw the animal toward the wall, but the agile beast pushed against the stones with its paws and flipped upright. It landed without a sound, snarling, in front of Sira.

"You fools!" she hissed. Darius could almost see a split tongue form the words.

Sira continued hissing words Darius did not understand, and she threw a vial in the center of the room, shattering it on the stone floor. A haze of noxious gas grew from the broken glass. Loklan countered, but it seemed only to worsen the situation as the green gas more rapidly permeated the room.

Visibility became impossible, and Darius lay there coughing as the cloud enveloped him. Someone touched his hands, and through the thickness he could make out Alara's welcome face.

"Here," she said. "Now let's get out of here."

"But how are you here?" asked Darius, fearful he might be dreaming again.

"Prydon, now we have to go!" said Loklan.

Darius's binds fell from his wrists and ankles, and two sets of hands began pulling him through the room. In seconds they were out, all three coughing from the gas that had managed its way into their lungs.

Sira laughed, the sound echoing behind them as she appeared, unaffected, out of the cloud and into the vacant hall.

"You think he would choose you over me?" she said directly to Alara.

On those words, Sira's beast lunged at Alara, frothy spit dripping from its protruding fangs. Alara's club made solid contact, and she sent the beast flying. This time it stumbled.

"Why not? Intelligence did," replied Alara.

Darius ran to Alara's side, but Loklan yelled. "Go! We'll take care of this!"

"But..."

"Go!" demanded Alara. "Before Klavon catches

wind of this!"

Loklan was already fighting Sira, and Alara kissed Darius square on his lips before she, too, moved in to attack. With a slight hesitation, Darius turned and ran up the stairs. For a moment, he wondered at the two friends who had somehow shown up to help him, but there was no time for ineffective thoughts. Darius needed to find his sword and staff and then face Klavon.

As he thought of Klavon, the tendrils in his hand pulsed, and Darius glanced at the red veins. There was no turning back. These stairs would lead Darius to face his past, the past that killed his father and left his mother destitute. And somehow in the process, Darius knew he must put those feelings aside to save Brandor, the town that had shown no kindness—all of this without sacrificing his soul.

Darius slowed as he reached the top of the stairs. He cautiously leaned out into the opening. Before him, extending what seemed to be the entire length of the castle, ran an immense corridor. Torches floated above staggered doors, and an elegant carpet ran down the center of the wide hallway. Statues of winged creatures lined the walls as if to grab anyone who dare pass.

Strangely, there were no guards. Darius slipped down the hall, keeping a watchful eye on the statues should they prove to have life beyond their stone faces. No, they remained frozen in rock, and Darius rolled his eyes. Klavon's confidence was nauseating, the man arrogantly believing that no one would dream of attacking him inside his territory, much less his own castle. Klavon was wrong.

Darius and the Dragon's Stone

He came upon a room and leaned his ear against the wood. He listened; no sound could be heard. He slowly opened the door and slid inside. No one was about, and Darius set to the task of searching the room for his sword and staff. Nothing. He continued on, room after room. When he reached the last room he stopped, frozen in his steps.

Beside the door rose a steep set of polished stairs. Darius stared at them. He had noticed it while he was outside, a tall, sturdy spire reaching up into the sky, shadowing dominance over the villagers below. No doubt the Great Book would be hidden there...and Klavon, gazing out over his domain like a peacock strutting around for all to see.

Darius pulled his gaze and turned to the last door. Surely his sword and staff would have to be here. He swallowed hard, not sure what to do if it wasn't. He opened the door, and with a burst of finality, he stepped in. In plain sight on a rough wooden table sat his treasures. A breath of relief blew over him, and he picked up his tools. The crimson flash was still visible, but there was no turning back—no other option. He donned his sword and staff like a true wizard and then slid back out into the corridor.

Turning back to the stairs, Darius's nose wrinkled. The stench of Klavon's arrogance seemed to slither down the stairs, filling the entire castle. Darius's lips pursed in determination, and he bounded up the steps two at a time.

The passage ended at a smooth wooden door. The face of a lion carved neatly into the wood stared down at him. No, not a lion. It gloated and growled in the likeness of Sira's cat-beast. Darius resisted the urge to spit in its face. Instead, he turned the latch. With a click, he pushed the door; it was not locked. Darius quietly entered, but it was of no benefit. In front of him stood the one he had come to face. Raising his staff he prepared for a wizard's battle; he prepared to defeat the one who killed his father and was destroying Brandor.

Klavon turned slowly. "It took you long enough. Perhaps I gave you too much credit."

Outside the window, Darius could see Prydon, heave in battle with Fraenir.

Darius's voice was smooth and strong. "If you give me the book now, there will be no need for me to destroy you, even though you deserve it. I might even call Prydon to allow your precious Fraenir to live as well."

The eyes of his foe seared upon him, burning through his very flesh. "I think not."

"So be it." Darius struck first, but the old sorcerer simply laughed, easily deflecting the blow.

"Do you really believe you can kill me?" Klavon raised his staff, and a blaze of red fire crashed down upon Darius.

Darius was prepared. All those nights he'd spent facing the shadow, learning from its stance, its movement, paid off. He knew what was coming and jumped aside, avoiding the fiery stream.

Klavon laughed, a cold and sinister laugh, echoing through the tall empty tower as he eluded Darius's response. The two navigated around the circular room, exchanging blows.

Darius and the Dragon's Stone

"You will not defeat me, simply because you do not possess the ability, and I will not defeat you, because of...well, shall we say your mother?"

The lustful grin on Klavon's face brought a rush of burning blood through Darius's body. "You disgusting man!" Darius struck; Klavon parried.

"Disgusting? No. But this battle you insist on waging will only result in what the dream serum failed to do. You will become what your father feared. That is why he died. So you would not learn of your powers and become what he most envied; a strong and great wizard such as myself."

"I will never become like you!" Darius circled the room with Klavon matching his moves, and the volley of strikes continued.

"Your father didn't think so. Your mother and I were destined. Even if I hadn't defeated him, she would have come to me, and brought with her the son I would raise as my own. Your father knew this."

"You're wrong! My mother loved my father!" Darius struck again, hatred overtaking him.

"Do I see a hint of red in your crystal? Are those tendrils burning up your arm? The temptation is strong, is it not? That is because it is where you are supposed to be, and you know it."

"I am not tempted by anything here! I am here only to retrieve the book!" said Darius, striking yet again.

"Ah, but you are tempted. Your desire for revenge will lead you exactly where your father feared. To me. And how is your mother?" Klavon sneered as he sent a spell which Darius avoided as he rolled out of the way.

"My mother is of no concern to you!" Darius moved in closer, and they met with swords.

Several strikes advanced the fight, but neither gained ground. Darius and Klavon both lunged, and the blades slid upward until their swords were crossed, and their faces stood only inches from each other.

Klavon said, "I looked for her all those years...and to think I almost gave up."

As the blades slid apart, there was a pause in the fight as they parted. Outside, Darius could see Fraenir dive at Prydon, slicing his back, but Darius's attention was set quickly back on Klavon.

"Fortune smiled when I built this fortress," Klavon said, circling the outside edge of the room with Darius moving opposite him. "I could see the tall tower across the marshy lands. Then it came to me. The one place to which she would not possibly escape, she did. Brandor had taken her in. She must have given something very valuable, very valuable indeed, to convince them to let you stay. Gold? No, she would have had nothing of that sort to offer. Perhaps...well, she is beautiful."

Darius fumed. "My mother would never do such things!"

"Of course not," replied Klavon. "Nonetheless, it must have been something of great value. In any case, the book was most interesting. The book fulfilled my desire. I knew that if you were there, you would be the only one they could send. You would be the only one unaffected by the fate of the pages." Klavon raised his staff, and a red hot fire shot directly at Darius. "But you won't be unaffected by this!"

Darius dodged the blaze, but it curved and landed directly on the tendrils wrapped around his wrist. For a moment, Darius felt weakened. The tendrils began to burn, so strongly, in fact, that at any moment, he was certain the heat would melt his veins and boil his skin. He fell to his knees, grabbing his throbbing wrist.

Klavon laughed and began circling him as he said, "I've been toying with you. Did you really believe you could defeat me? No, you will succumb, and your mother will be mine at last."

As Darius leaned forward, propping himself on the floor, his thoughts turned to Prydon, Barsovy, his training, the Valley of Wizards. And as Klavon stood patiently waiting for Darius to fall, to lose his soul in the poison of the curse he so long fought against, Darius heard soft whispers. He heard the voices of his mother and father, voices from before he was even born. The purity, the sincerity, the love—self sacrificing love. In that instant, revenge was of no use to him, and the tendrils ceased to burn. His parents' gentle voices showered upon him in a soft blue mist, and Darius's mind was cleared. No more confusion. No more anger. He stood slowly and faced Klavon.

"Yes, that's it, my son," said Klavon, misreading Darius's intentions. "I am pleased that I did not have to kill you."

Darius laughed, and Klavon's face became twisted as he realized his mistake.

"You fool! You will become as my own or you will die!" yelled Klavon.

The sorcerer raised his staff and began a rage of attacks Darius had never experienced before. But the calm within his heart allowed his training to ring clear. He easily deflected the spells, and Klavon's face contorted even further.

"Not today, Klavon. You have failed," said Darius. "And you are weak. You did not defeat my father. He sacrificed himself to save me, and..." Klavon continued to volley spells intent on killing Darius, but Darius returned with his own series of strikes—strikes that even Barsovy could not have predicted. "I will not..." another strike, "be tempted..." strike, "by your lies!"

Klavon darted out the door and ran down the stairs, throwing obstacles behind him. Darius followed, jumping over fallen sconces and dodging pillars of fire. They landed in the courtyard where above Prydon and Fraenir were heavy in battle.

"Fraenir!" called Klavon.

Darius grinned at Klavon's fear and expected to see Fraenir come to Klavon's aid. Instead, he looked up to see the beast grabbing Prydon's wing, his jaws tearing at Prydon's flesh.

"No!" Darius yelled.

In that moment, Darius felt a slice against his arm, Klavon having taken advantage of the distraction.

Darius glanced at the cut. He raised his stare and stood strong in front of Klavon. Klavon raised his staff again, but before anything was cast, the sorcerer was thrown back as a streak of pure light spewed from the tip of Darius's staff. So clear was the blast that Klavon did not see it. As the bolt struck him, Klavon screeched. A blood-red cloud surrounded him and flashed as he writhed in pain. He was lifted from the ground, and with a burst of scarlet light…he was gone. All that remained was a broken staff and shards of crimson stone, crimson that quickly faded to black as the stone fragments disintegrated into dust.

    Darius blinked. His could hardly believe it as he looked at the ground. Klavon was gone.

Chapter Thirty-four

Prydon

"Get back inside!" yelled Prydon.

Darius looked up to see the two in battle. He could hardly believe that Prydon was losing! As they flew about each other, flames and claws created a cascade of color and pain. Fraenir tore at Prydon's leg, the sound of breaking bones echoing in the clearing. Darius tried to use his staff to stop Fraenir, but they were too high up, and their fight raged on.

Prydon was struggling to stay in the air, and as Fraenir swept his claws across Prydon's other wing, Darius saw it. A dragon's stone was glowing in Fraenir's chest…the reason for Fraenir's success.

"How?" gasped Darius.

Prydon fell the ground, the bones in his wings shattered. Fraenir landed nearby and roared a sinister victory.

Darius darted between them. "Don't touch him! Just stay away!"

"Darius, no," gasped Prydon, struggling to breath out the words.

Fraenir leaned down so his face was right in front of

Darius and the Dragon's Stone

Darius. "I have a debt to collect, the payment Prydon's life."

Darius jumped back and ran directly in front of Prydon. Fraenir laughed and quickly closed the small gap that had been between them, his jaws wide as if to devour Darius in one bite. But as Fraenir took the last step to reach his target, Darius lunged forward and raised his staff. A bolt of fire shot into Fraenir's chest, directly over the stone. The beast faltered, his eyes filled with surprise, but he lunged toward Prydon.

"You think you can protect him?" Fraenir growled, curling his head around to look down at Darius.

Fraenir place his front leg directly on Prydon's chest and began crushing it. Prydon screamed in pain, and Darius was shocked as he saw blood run from his best friend's mouth.

"Stop!" Darius yelled, and he ran to Fraenir.

Fraenir opened his mouth to consume Darius, but before he could even lower his head, Darius stabbed his sword deep into Fraenir's chest, shattering the dragon's stone.

Fraenir fell back. He opened his jaws and seemed to struggle to breath. Darius's pulled out the sword, and Fraenir fell to the ground. Within seconds, the creature's body caught fire and was reduced to a pile of red ash, the fragments of stone lying lifeless at the edge of the heap.

Darius ran to Prydon's side, throwing his weapons aside as he dropped to the ground next to his friend. Sobbing, he began rubbing the blood away from Prydon's mouth. "You're going to be alright."

Prydon coughed. "No, but at least I die in peace."

"Don't say that!" cried Darius. "I have to save you!"

Prydon's breathing was labored as he struggled to speak. "You must save Brandor...the book."

"Forget the book," said Darius.

He searched with his hands trying to discover what he should do. He leaned his head against Prydon's side, searching his memory, but there were no words of healing, no words of resurrection. His eyes scoured his friend, and pain shot down his throat like a hot coal.

Blood-stained scratches wove harsh patterns over Prydon's body, and deep gashes dug into the flesh on his side and neck. One of his wings unnaturally twisted over his back, while the other was a mangled mess of broken bones, the flesh torn away.

"I have to help you, Prydon."

Prydon's eyelids fell heavy as he strained to keep them open. "I believe it is too late for that." He coughed. "You have done well. Your father would be proud—" Another cough choked his words, and more blood spewed from his mouth, "—as am I." The dragon managed one last smile as the light left his eyes.

From Prydon's chest floated an iridescent fog. It swirled about Darius as if embracing him warmly before it shot through the air. Darius knew what that meant—Prydon's essence was returning to Mount Tyria.

"No!" shouted Darius. He screamed at the top of his lungs, crying violently.

Throwing his arms around his friend, he leaned his

Darius and the Dragon's Stone

face against Prydon's, willing that his life's energy would somehow enter the dragon and bring him back to life—he would gladly give his life for his friend. Sobbing, he did not hear Alara and Loklan as they kneeled behind him.

"Darius?" Loklan said quietly, resting his hand on Darius's shoulder.

Alara leaned closer and rested her head against Darius's back, and he felt her arms gently embrace him as she cried softly and said, "I'm sorry."

Out of nowhere, a raging wind began to howl, and the sky darkened even more as an enormous shadow fell upon them. Darius couldn't help but turn and look up, and for a moment, he froze.

He leapt to his feet, grabbing his sword in hand and holding it out as the dragon, nearly twice Prydon's size, landed right in front of him.

But as the dragon approached, her eyes glowed as fire, and black waves rippled through her green scales. Darius felt powerless. The stone in his sword began to shake so violently that the sword was ripped from his hands and fell to the ground.

He looked over to see Loklan immediately drop to his knee and bow. Alara seemed confused, however, and clung to Darius's arm.

"Segrath," said Loklan. "I…"

"Loklan," she said. "You and this young woman must leave."

Segrath raised a clawed hand, and before Darius's friends could respond, they vanished. Darius, alone, faced a creature that was larger than anything he had ever seen.

Segrath walked up to Prydon. "It was not your time," she said, then turning to Darius, "You killed Fraenir, shattered the dragon's stone embedded in his chest?"

"Y...yes," said Darius.

"Do you know who I am?" she asked.

"No," said Darius.

"I am Segrath," she said. "I am the one you should have faced before you were given your sword and staff."

Darius knew the story; Prydon had told him.

Segrath looked at the shattered stone still lying on the ground. "That stone was not his to have," she continued as if no further discussion was needed regarding Darius's weapons. "As such, Prydon was killed not by Fraenir but by the strength derived from the essence that is a dragon."

Her words made no sense to Darius. "I guess so," he said dumbly.

"That defies the laws that create the stones."

Darius was even more confused, and Segrath tilted her head and stared into his eyes as if considering him. It made him feel very uncomfortable, and he shifted his weight.

"Prydon's death is not to be," she said, "and as you are the one who destroyed the dragon's stone that caused his death..."

Before Darius knew what was happening, Segrath grabbed him easily with one hand and held him over the broken fragments of the dragon's stone that remained next to Fraenir's ashes. With her other hand, she pushed Prydon's lifeless body farther onto its side.

Darius flinched as he heard the bones crack and saw

the gaping wounds, still fresh from battle, and the deep scar directly over Prydon's heart. Segrath placed her hand on the scar.

The broken stone beneath him began to rise and circle around him, shimmering to life and spiraling faster and faster. Suddenly, the shards exploded and rained down on him.

The pain was like nothing he had ever endured, and he screamed in agony. White light from the shards snaked along the surface of his body until he thought his skin might begin to melt.

He almost passed out from the pain when he heard Segrath screech. But as her shrieks became louder and more intense, the agony Darius felt began to diminish.

When the pain became more bearable, Darius could see that the streaks of light were leaving his body and entering Segrath's.

He watched as the light grew, and the black streaks that had previously adorned her scales now shown a brilliant white, so bright Darius had to shield his eyes.

Segrath's bellows continued, and the ripples of light on her body seemed to explode from her hand directly into Prydon's heart.

She fell to the ground, dropping Darius next to Fraenir's ashes. He sat for a moment, wondering what had just happened.

"Go to him," Segrath said, and she pulled herself up to tower above him. "Go to Prydon and place your hand on his heart."

Darius was confused, but he did as she said. He

stood next to his friend, and touched Prydon's heart. In moments, an iridescent cloud circled both of them before disappearing directly into Prydon's chest. That instant, Prydon inhaled as if he'd only been holding his breath.

"Prydon?" cried Darius.

He jumped back and watched as the wounds caused by the battle began to heal. The bones seemed to set themselves, and the scales multiplied to cover the gaping holes. Prydon's breathing became more regular, and he opened his eyes. For a moment, he just lay there, taking in long breaths.

Then he sat up quite suddenly and looked up at Segrath. "Why?" was all Prydon said.

"When you came to retrieve the sword and staff for this young man, Fraenir was also there. He stole one of the stones while we were distracted," she said. "Had it not been for this young man destroying that stone, I would not have been able to affect your return."

"Thank you, Darius," said Prydon.

"You have earned those tools," she said to Darius, pushing up from the ground and flying away.

Darius began to cry and hugged Prydon.

"Darius, the curse is gone," said Prydon.

For the first time, Darius looked at his wrist. The crimson tendrils were gone, along with Klavon and Fraenir. He hesitated before resting his eyes on the stones that adorned his staff and sword. Clear as could possibly be, the hint of red was gone.

"You have one final task," said Prydon.

"The book!" Darius had almost forgotten.

"Go. In the tower..." said Prydon.

Darius headed straight for the high chamber, Klavon's sanctuary and the most likely place he would keep the book. When he ran through the door, Prydon was hovering just outside the window.

Darius's his eyes darted about the room. "I don't see it!"

"There," said Prydon.

Hanging from a rod against one wall was a black tapestry covered with symbols embroidered in crimson thread. He yanked it to the side to reveal an arched hallway, no more than five feet long that led to a secret room. A surge of fear flushed across his face—not the kind of fear one experiences when in the presence of an enemy. This was the fear of being too late.

He closed his eyes and breathed deeply before entering the room. As he opened the small door and stepped inside, his worst nightmare unfolded before his eyes. With each shred of paper strewn about the room, he could see the people of Brandor, as ghosts, vanishing from the village like wisps of smoke flung in an open breeze. The book had been reduced to an empty cover, its pages shattered as the lives they once held. He fell to his knees, his face falling into his cupped hands.

Darius became dulled, unaware of time as if time itself were merely an illusion. He heard Prydon call from outside and walked back to the window.

"It's shredded...gone," he said. "I've failed."

Prydon's eyes softened. "Perhaps there is still a way. Retrieve it, every piece of it, and we'll take it back to

Brandor. Perhaps the wizard there can help."

Darius, the weight of finality pushing upon him, gathered every last scrap of the book and wrapped it in a soft cloth. Then he gently placed it in a leather bag. Gloom followed him as he returned downstairs.

"Let us be gone. All is not lost," said Prydon, leaning down so Darius could climb on.

The voice of his friend showed encouragement, but hope could not have been farther away, and Darius's heart sank. Brandor was gone, now only shredded paper in a dusty, old bag.

Chapter Thirty-five

Home

"You're alive," yelled Alara, throwing her arms around Darius as he slid off the dragon's back. "And Prydon." She looked up at the dragon, tears in her eyes.

"What happened?" asked Loklan. "How?"

"Segrath...brought him back," said Darius.

"That's..." Loklan stood, his mouth open.

"I know," said Darius. "It was quite phenomenal."

Prydon smiled. "Apparently, it was not my time. Although Klavon and Fraenir were not so fortunate."

Suddenly, Darius thought of Sira. "What happened to her...to Sira?"

"Well, we're not sure," answered Alara. "We killed the beast, but she kind of—"

"Kind of evaporated," answered Loklan. "I don't think it was anything I did, but I don't think she's coming back either."

"It's highly unlikely," said Prydon. "Her kind only have power when attached to a sorcerer. With Klavon gone, she is nothing. I suspect she vanished when Darius killed him."

"Good," said Alara. "So where are we, anyway?

Loklan and I just showed up here, but we don't know where *here* is?"

Darius stopped and looked around for the first time since they landed. The scene seized the breath from his lungs, and his heart dropped. Where there had been a quaint village surrounded by massive trees groomed to perfection, now stood barren land, spotted with sparse, misshapen trunks. There was no order, no reasonable layout. The few houses that still existed were scattered, and the villagers were nowhere to be seen.

"Brandor," Darius said.

"But the book?" asked Loklan.

"It has yet to be repaired," said Prydon.

"If it can be repaired," added Darius.

He turned toward the village. No one spoke. The devastation itself seemed to speak for everyone. The magnitude of destruction—no, destruction was not the right word—the magnitude of utter loss weighed upon them like a heavy anvil.

He continued to walk slowly up what remained of the road, no longer beautifully bordered by trees, and came to the stream. There was no bridge, and as he stepped through the water, he looked down, remembering the fish he would watch as he passed.

A door slammed, and Mrs. Keedle came out of the house nearby.

"You! You!" she screamed.

Garp appeared behind her. "How dare you show your face here? And with a dragon!" Garp backed away as if the porch could protect him from such a massive beast.

Darius and the Dragon's Stone

"I dare because I have the book." Darius recalled the way he reacted to them during the dream induced by Klavon, how he had spoken so disrespectfully. Even if they deserved no respect, Darius reigned in his anger. "And this is Prydon, a friend."

"Really," Garp sneered sarcastically. "A friend of yours, perhaps. I suppose he's here to exact revenge on all of us. But a lot of good that will do. Everyone is gone!"

"You're not, and where's my mother?" Darius could feel the heat surge at the tops of his ears.

"She's gone, too," said Mrs. Keedle.

"That's not possible," said Darius.

"No, you idiot," said Garp. "She left when she realized that Mr. Athus was gone. Good thing, too. He was the only one stopping me from kicking her out myself!"

Prydon growled, and a rumble formed in his chest as if fire was building and would escape at any moment. Garp backed behind a pillar on the porch, and Prydon laughed.

"You disgusting, rude man," snarled Alara.

"All of you. You don't belong here." Mrs. Keedle squeaked. "This is our town, at least what's left of it."

Prydon stepped closer.

Mrs. Keedle screamed. "Are you now threatening us with a dragon after all you have already done?"

"All he has done," said Prydon, "is attempt to save Brandor, and I believe he has succeeded."

"Succeeded?" replied Garp. "Does this look like success to you? No one is left!"

"You are," said Loklan. "She is. That's a start, isn't

it? And he's saved the book, so there is no way you will suffer the same fate as the others. You have that."

"I will determine the success," boomed a voice from behind.

Darius turned to see an older man, dressed as a wizard, walking toward him. His mother was by his side. Garp made a sound as if to speak, but the older man held up his hand, silencing him.

Darius ran to his mother and hugged her. "I was so worried about you."

"You? Worried about me?" Miora cupped his face. "It is I who have been worried about you." She stepped back. "Darius, this is Aidan, an old friend of your father and the wizard of Brandor."

The man approached and took Darius's hand in a firm handshake. "I am sure you have many questions, so let me try to explain."

"Brandor's wizard?" Darius's voice faded, and then his eyes shot open as thoughts filled his mind. "A wizard! Sir!" Darius pulled out the bag containing the book. "Can you fix it?"

"No, I can not." The older man was holding up his hand and shaking his head.

The response came quicker than Darius would have liked. "But—"

"It is all my fault, you see," Aidan said. "I left Brandor hoping to detract attention from the village, knowing your mother would have to seek refuge here. I put up the shield to offer what protection I could. The book was to preserve Brandor in my absence and to let me know if anything catastrophic happened."

"Well, I'd say the loss of the book was pretty catastrophic. Why didn't you go after the book when you knew it was gone?" asked Alara. "Why didn't you fight Klavon?"

"Klavon was powerful, and without the help of a dragon, I could not hope to defeat him," said Aidan. "All I could do was hope that you were truly your father's son...and you are. You see, I spoke with Barsovy—"

"You did what?" asked Darius.

"Darius, both of us believed this was your battle, your providence, and I had not the tools to defeat Klavon." Aidan walked to Darius, and placed both hands on Darius's shoulders, facing him straight on. "Even though I could not attempt to fight Klavon, I see now that Barsovy was correct. This was all as it was meant to be. You were meant to learn of your past, you were meant to train, you were meant to battle Klavon, and you were meant to retrieve the book and save Brandor."

"But I have failed," said Darius, holding the leather bag full of shredded papers in his hand.

"No, you have not." The wizard stepped back and began drawing a circle on the ground.

"You said that you couldn't fix it," said Darius, ignoring Aidan's actions. "Most of the village is gone. What else is that if not failure?"

"It is true that I can't fix it," said Aidan. He gestured to the circle. "But you can."

Darius stared at the ring in the dirt, and Aidan smiled as he again gestured to the rough drawing on the ground. Darius stepped forward and into the circle, but he shook his head. Surely he misunderstood...surely the old wizard was mistaken.

Aidan stood tall. "You alone have the power. Only the one who defeated Klavon can undo this. Only you can fix the book."

Darius looked at Loklan, Alara, and then Prydon.

Prydon bowed his head, and his brows furrowed with intense seriousness above his eyes. "The mark is gone. You are as pure as any wizard. Do this."

Darius stared at his hand once more. This time, he concentrated on every possible spec of flesh. The mark had completely vanished. He took the wrapped cloth from the bag and dumped the shredded pieces on the ground. A mysterious, clear wall surrounded him. There was no breeze, and the pieces lay still. Darius closed his eyes, and spoke words under his breath. It was not so much what he said but his will to restore that transformed Brandor.

With eyes closed, he did not see the buildings return, the people brought back, but he could sense it. His voice became stronger, and with each breath, with each phrase, he could hear more sounds of townsmen and women floating around him. The ground shook as trees sprung forth to become as they were, and birds returned to their nests. Every flower, every blade of grass returned— the bridge overlooking the fish, the tower, the well. When he opened his eyes, the book lay on the ground, complete. Brandor was whole again.

Darius picked up the book and handed it to Aidan. The old wizard took the book in one hand and touched the surface with the other. As if cementing the history, the book seemed to absorb directly in to Aidan's chest.

Mr. Athus came running. After kissing the wizard's hand, he turned to Darius. "I knew you could do it!"

Darius smiled. "I owe it all to you...and Prydon...and Alara and Loklan."

"You owe it to no one but yourself," said Prydon.

Darius looked around. The townspeople gathered, in awe of their wizard's return, but also in repentant respect for Darius. Even Mrs. Keedle and Garp appeared less angry, less hostile.

"And what can we do to repay you?" asked Aidan.

Darius walked to his mother. "What did you give them that allowed us to stay? All those years ago."

Miora's eyes swelled with tears. "My wedding band."

D.L. Torrent

D. L. Torrent grew up a variety of states. She was always a writer, but her creativity truly began when she found herself raising three children in the rural, remote, yet wildly beautiful Texas hill country. Homeschooling her kids and the seclusion of this quiet ranch community contributed to her natural inclination toward escapism.

In her interaction with the outside world, she found youth to be much more engaging. This naturally led her to focus on adolescent and young adult fantasy fiction. An adventurer in her own mind, she often finds her protagonists facing untold dangers and overcoming severe obstacles. Her writing invites the reader deep into a wonderful world of fantasy, allowing them to experience a magical realm that only they can own.

Besides her own novels, she has co-written, with Sharon Cramer and Michelle McCammond, three screenplays based on books by Sharon Cramer.

Debra's education includes Bachelor's degree in Computer Science, Bachelor's degree in Mathematics, a Master's in Education, but she is most proud of her PHD in the school of hard knocks.

She now resides happily next to a beautiful river in Spokane Valley, Washington. Her husband keeps the coffee on and enjoys his sports—on the other side of the house—while she writes. Her cat, essentially useless, does keep the keyboard warm and sometimes adds unexpected dialogue, should she step away from her computer.

Made in the USA
Middletown, DE
06 November 2023